# WYNDHAM LEWIS

## The Wild Body

'A Soldier of Humour' and Other Stories

with an introduction by Paul O'Keeffe

PENGUIN BOOKS

PENGUIN BOOKS

Published by the Penguin Group
Penguin Books Ltd, 80 Strand, London WC2R 0RL, England
Penguin Putnam Inc., 375 Hudson Street, New York, New York 10014, USA
Penguin Books Australia Ltd, 250 Camberwell Road, Camberwell, Victoria 3124, Australia
Penguin Books Canada Ltd, 10 Alcorn Avenue, Toronto, Ontario, Canada M4V 3B2
Penguin Books India (P) Ltd, 11 Community Centre, Panchsheel Park, New Delhi – 110 017, India
Penguin Books (NZ) Ltd, Cnr Rosedale and Airborne Roads, Albany, Auckland, New Zealand
Penguin Books (South Africa) (Pty) Ltd, 24 Sturdee Avenue, Rosebank 2196, South Africa

Penguin Books Ltd, Registered Offices: 80 Strand, London WC2R 0RL, England

www.penguin.com

First published by Chatto and Windus 1927
Published in Penguin Books 2004

3

Set in 9.75/12.5pt Minion by Palimpsest Book Production Limited, Polmont, Stirlingshire
Printed in England by Clays Ltd, St Ives plc

ISBN 978-0-14-118763-1

www.greenpenguin.co.uk

MIX
Paper | Supporting
responsible forestry
FSC® C018179
www.fsc.org

Penguin Books is committed to a sustainable future
for our business, our readers and our planet.
The book in your hands is made from paper
certified by the Forest Stewardship Council.

# Contents

# Introduction

*1*

Ford Madox Hueffer (later Ford Madox Ford), editor of the *English Review*, recalled his first encounter with the twenty-six-year-old Percy Wyndham Lewis, at the bend of a dark staircase. Lewis was dressed like a stage conspirator in a black coat, black cape and wide-brimmed black hat. A manuscript was drawn from an inside pocket and pressed into the editor's hands, its author departing, down into the shadows, without a word. Hueffer told another version in which a less taciturn, but identically dressed young man cornered him in his bathtub and insisted upon reading the manuscript aloud while the corpulent editor made his ablutions. Whichever version is to be believed, 'The "Pole"', Lewis's first published work, appeared in the *English Review* of May 1909. Revised, as 'Beau Séjour', almost two decades later, it became the second in the collection of stories he entitled *The Wild Body*.

Before he became famous on the brink of the Great War as leader of the Vorticist movement, chief proponent of its harsh abstractions and, as editor of the eccentrically typeset *Blast*, its chief propagandist; before he dropped one Christian name, 'Percy', and made of himself the formidable satirist and truculent 'Enemy' of the Bloomsbury Group, Wyndham Lewis was primarily known – to a small readership and a smaller circle of acquaintance – as a writer. While still an art student at the Slade School at the turn of the twentieth century, they called him 'the Poet'; and, following his expulsion from that academy of painting and drawing, as he wandered through Spain and Brittany in 1907 and 1908, it was with a writer's eye, as much as a painter's, that he looked about him.

The germ of what would become the fifth story of *The Wild Body*, 'The Death of the Ankou', was jotted down after an encounter with picturesque poverty in the Breton town of Gestel:

[S]itting on a bench near the church we found two remarkable figures, a young man raggedly clothed, with a strange reckless face, and an old man bent over and leaning on a heavy stick. The latter was largely built, his legs half naked, and a dark metallic colour; and his feet thrust into the straw of his enormous sabots, one ankle swollen and wounded . . . With a heavy grey mat of hair, he was dark-skin'd and . . . the flesh was pucker'd round his eyes into innumerable deep wrinkles, as though some torrid sun were constantly in his eyes . . . He looked at us steadily when we spoke to him and answer'd our questions slowly. My companion[1] ask'd him if he would be painted; he made no difficulty. When asked where was his home . . . he replied simply, with that deep and tragic voice . . . 'On the stones' ('sur les pierres',): it was there that he sat the greater part of the day, on the cobbles, to receive alms.[2]

The formal representation Lewis produced of this piteous spectacle is lost but the written sketch – distinct from but complementary to that captured in paint – was preserved. 'The "short story"', he declared, 'was the crystallization *of what I had to keep out of my consciousness while painting*. Otherwise the painting would have been a bad painting.'[3] No painting – good or bad – by Lewis's hand survives from this time but the harsh landscape and barbaric peasantry he encountered in Brittany provided him enough 'raw rich visual food'[4] to nourish a truly muscular prose style, together with a savage humour, later productive of the most dazzling and virulent satirical writing of the last century. The ragged west coast of Brittany – the 'Atlantic air . . . the squealing of the pipes, the crashing of the ocean – induced a creative torpor', he recalled:

Mine was . . . a drowsy sun-baked ferment, watching with delight the great comic effigies which erupted beneath my rather saturnine but astonished gaze: Brotcotnaz, Bestre, and the rest.[5]

Only one of the 'effigies' paraded through the pages of *The Wild Body* can be conclusively identified with a real person and place. The eponymous protagonist of the third story, Bestre, is a Breton of Spanish extraction. The character was based upon an innkeeper by the name of Peron,[6] with whom Lewis lodged at Doëlan. Peron's establishment was known locally, and mysteriously, as 'Peste', French for plague or menace. It may have been something unwholesome about the ambience of the inn, by the slipway on the east side of the harbour, or simply the proprietor's forbidding demeanour, that gave it this sinister appellation, but it was from the sound of the word 'Peste' that Lewis derived the name of his monstrous creation, 'Bestre'.[7]

The first version of the story, 'Some Innkeepers and Bestre',[8] like 'The "Pole"', appeared in the *English Review*, as did 'Les Saltimbanques', the account of a wretched family of travelling circus performers, later revised as 'The Cornac and his Wife'. When Lewis's association with the *English Review* came to an end, *The Tramp: an Open Air Magazine*, edited by Douglas Goldring, provided an appropriately named forum for 'Le Père François (A Full-Length Portrait of a Tramp)'. This was revised, for *The Wild Body*, as 'Franciscan Adventures', while 'Brobdingnag', in another periodical, *The New Age*, became 'Brotcotnaz'.

The core of *The Wild Body* is the six stories set in Brittany and one, 'A Soldier of Humour', set in Spain. This, the first story of the collection, was the last to be published in its original form, over two issues of the *Little Review*, December 1917 and January 1918. It was, however, written about 1910 and even at that stage intended as the lead story of a projected collection. 'What do you think of "A Soldier of Humour" as a title for a book of stories and articles . . . ?' he asked his mentor and friend Thomas Sturge Moore in early 1911.[9]

The story differs from the other six in that the narrator is not merely an observer, but a participant in the drama. As well as being the object of M. Valmore's campaign of persecution, he is, ultimately, chief engineer of that rectangular, pseudo-American

Frenchman's humiliation. As if to fit him for this more responsible role of carrying the narrative, the first person discloses an identity: in the *Little Review* it was 'Mr Pine', but in the final version of the story he bears the more distinctive surname Ker-Orr.

My father is a family doctor on the Clyde. The Ker-Orrs have been doctors usually. I have not seen him for some time: my mother, who is separated from him, lives with a noted hungarian physician. She gives me money that she gets from the physician, and it is she that I recognize as my principal parent. It is owing to this conjunction of circumstances that I am able to move about so much . . . (p. 6)

The pedigree relates to Lewis's in only one respect: his mother also was his 'principal parent', having been deserted by her husband when the boy was ten years old. She never remarried and the money that enabled her only son 'to move about so much' in Brittany and Spain came from her failing laundry business and sporadic maintenance payments from his feckless father.[10]

### 2

As publication of the 'book of stories and articles', mentioned in 1911, was deferred, first by war and then by a proliferation of other critical, fictional and philosophical works competing for his time in the 1920s, so the gulf widened between the Percy Wyndham Lewis who had confronted the editor of the *English Review* on the stairs (or in his bath) and the formidable polymath that was Wyndham Lewis at the age of forty-five. His 1914 drama, *The Enemy of the Stars*, would undergo revision in 1932 as if to take account of the difference, as would his 1918 novel, *Tarr*, in 1928. By the same token, the earlier short stories required extensive reworking. As he wrote in his foreword to the Chatto & Windus edition:

the material, when I took it up again . . . , seemed to me to deserve the hand of a better artist than I was when I made those few hasty notes of very early travel.[11](p. 1)

Revised, the stories became unified thematically into 'a new story', he explained. The previously anonymous narrator is now Ker-Orr, although in only two of the seven is he actually referred to by that name.

In the savage world of *The Wild Body* the weapons used are seldom conventional or straightforward. The Slav émigrés of 'Beau Séjour' have, it is true, occasional recourse to firearms, but their outbursts of violence, in the tradition of Chekhov, end in farce. In 'The Cornac and his Wife', while the entertainer's hatred is directed at those he entertains, the violence he inflicts is upon himself. Because his little daughter has been forbidden to perform by the Commissioner of Police, the mournful acrobat defiantly endangers life and limb, as if to spite:

He seemed courting misfortune. 'Any mortal injury sustained by me, M. le Commissaire, during the performance, will be at your door! The Public must be satisfied. I am the servant of the Public. You have decreed that it shall be me (all my intestines displaced by thirty years of contortions) that shall satisfy them. Very well! I know my duty, if you don't know yours. Good! It shall be done as you have ordered, M. le Commissaire!' (p. 99)

Brotcotnaz in the story of that name inflicts routine violence upon his bibulous wife, until she is run over by a cart, sustaining far more serious injuries than even he is capable of giving her. As if discovering himself cuckolded, he sinks into a depression, his marital role usurped, his manhood impugned. However, Julie is in a sense 'empowered' by her accidental mutilation, achieving a bitter ascendancy over her husband as the story ends:

After the removal of her arm, and possibly a foot . . . she would be more difficult to get on with than formerly. The bottle of eau-de-vie would remain no doubt in full view, to hand, on the counter, and Brotcotnaz would be unable to lay a finger on her: in all likelihood she meant that arm to come off. (pp. 147–8)

Bestre intimidates with a look. His 'chosen weapon' in the psychological warfare he conducts against those unwary enough to fall foul of him is the eye. And if Bestre's eye is the weapon, its ammunition comes from behind and below that organ: 'drawn from all the most skunk-like provender, the most ugly mucins, fungoid glands, of his physique' (p. 83) – in short, from the 'Wild Body' itself. In a fantastic orgy of unsavoury metaphor, Lewis made of his protagonist the very incarnation of that concept. Here is Bestre in conversation:

His very large eyeballs, the small saffron ocellation in their centre, the tiny spot through which light entered the obese wilderness of his body; his bronzed bovine arms, swollen handles for a variety of indolent little ingenuities; his inflated digestive case, lent their expressiveness to say these things; with every tart and biting condiment that eye-fluid, flaunting of fatness (the well-filled), the insult of the comic, implications of indecency, could provide. Every variety of bottom-tapping resounded from his dumb bulk. His tongue stuck out, his lips eructated with the incredible indecorum that appears to be the monopoly of liquids, his brown arms were for the moment genitals, snakes in one massive twist beneath his mamillary slabs, gently riding on a pancreatic swell, each hair on his oil-bearing skin contributing its message of porcine affront. (p. 77)

Along with the seven stories that form the core of the collection Lewis offered his readers not one essay explaining the ideas behind them, but two. 'Inferior Religions', written and published in its original version in 1917,[12] suggests that the lives, actions and obsessions of Bestre, Brotocotnaz and the rest, in common with those of other primitive peoples, are dictated by fetish and ritual:

. . . Julie's bruises are the markings upon an idol; . . . Brotcotnaz circles round [her] with gestures a million times repeated. Zoborov camps against and encircles Mademoiselle Péronnette and her lover Carl. Bestre is the eternal watchdog, with an elaborate civilized ritual. Similarly the Cornac is engaged in a death struggle with his 'Public.' All religion has the mechanism of the celestial bodies, has a dance. (p. 150)

The second essay, written in 1927 and promising in its very title a conclusive explanation of the collection, refers back to the philosophy of William James and Henri Bergson, while at the same time anticipating the existentialism of Albert Camus. What Lewis gained from his youthful wanderings was a notion of the Absurd, but it was not for another two decades, in 'The Meaning of the Wild Body', that he formulated it into a philosophical viewpoint.[13] Absurdity is rooted in a realization of the fundamental incomprehensibility of that which is other than ourselves. It is a concept that would be borne strongly in upon the thoughtful individual when, in a foreign country, he observed the behaviour of his fellow men from a position of alienation. Inability to understand the language might contribute to this sense of alienation and, although Lewis was fluent in French, he confessed to an unfamiliarity with Breton. Looked at from the perspective of an outsider, his fellow men cease to be fellows, becoming instead fleshy automata. 'Men, too, secrete the inhuman,' Albert Camus was to declare, fifteen years after publication of *The Wild Body*:

At certain moments of lucidity, the mechanical aspect of their gestures, their meaningless pantomime make silly everything that surrounds them. A man is talking on the telephone behind a glass partition; you cannot hear him but you see his incomprehensible dumb-show: you wonder why he is alive. The discomfort in the face of man's own inhumanity, this incalculable tumble before the image of what we are . . . is also the absurd.[14]

Furthermore, the sense of alienation must, logically, be extended to our view of ourselves:

Likewise the stranger who at certain seconds comes to meet us in a mirror, the familiar and yet alarming brother we encounter in our own photographs is also the absurd.[15]

And, *avant la lettre*, Lewis observed that we are all strangers to the physical apparatus which transports us around. Hence, Ker-Orr:

This forked, strange-scented, blond-skinned gut-bag, with its two bright rolling marbles with which it sees, bull's-eyes full of mockery and madness, is my stalking-horse. I hang somewhere in its midst operating it with detachment. (pp. 6–7)

The dichotomy of mind and body also formed the basis of Henri Bergson's theory of the comic. According to Bergson, laughter is provoked by an awareness of the essentially noble mind being let down by the ridiculous, lumpen body, as when a public speaker sneezes at the most serious and moving point of his discourse. At such a moment a person appears as a thing. Lewis inverted the formula:

The root of the Comic is to be sought in the sensations resulting from the observations of a *thing* behaving like a person. But from that point of view all men are necessarily comic: for they are all *things*, or physical bodies, behaving as *persons*. (p. 158)

So pessimistic an evaluation of humanity made this the ideal vehicle for satire. Lewis's monumental novel, *The Apes Of God*, teeming with grotesque puppetry representative of the pseudo-painters and poetasters of Bloomsbury and Chelsea, was published only three years later.

### 3

Separated from the other seven stories and the two essays, as if appendices, are 'Sigismund' and 'You Broke My Dream, or An Experiment with Time'. Of later composition than most of the other material, 'Sigismund' was first published in 1920,[16] the opening third of 'You Broke My Dream . . .' in 1922.[17]

It does not require too energetic a stretch to link 'Sigismund' thematically with the rest of the collection. Although its English upper-class setting is far removed from Breton peasantry, its protagonist is just as much ruled by a type of 'inferior religion' or fetish. Sigismund's consuming obsession is pedigree, doting with pride upon his bulldog Pym, and vainly attempting to trace the lineage of his gigantic aristocratic 'trophy wife' in her unlined, but disconcertingly hairy palm. The Honourable Deborah Libyon-Bosselwood herself can be seen as a transitional stage of the Wild

Body's evolution between the Breton savages of the early stories and the sophisticated, but no less absurd, clockwork exquisites in *The Apes of God*. Different in both style and vintage from its forebears in the collection, 'Sigismund' can be appreciated as an undeniably comic story in its own right. Some passages, as when the hapless hero drives a pin into the thigh of one of his wife's relatives, so as to record for posterity what he imagines to be the fabled, piratical war-cry of the Libyon-Bosselwoods, even bring P. G. Wodehouse to mind.

The final story is a curiously hybrid production. The first few pages, up to and including the words: '. . . they sit side by side, like offended toys, at the foot of the stairs' (p. 184), had been written as the first episode of a serial, 'Will Eccles', and published in the first number of Lewis's periodical, *The Tyro*. The magazine itself only ran to one more number but the serial must have promised even less potential for continuity because no further episodes were written. Then, in the spring of 1927, while putting together his collection of stories and essays for Chatto & Windus, and not wishing the book to appear underweight, Lewis took up the five-year-old literary *non sequitur*, altered the protagonist's surname from 'Eccles' to 'Blood', inserted three new paragraphs and expanded four more. The original piece was extended by another two thousand or so words, consisting of conversation between the two A.B.C. waitresses 'at the foot of the stairs', and between one of them, Gladys, and Will Blood. This new material transformed the fragment into a satire on a book that had been published only a couple of months before: *An Experiment with Time*,[18] by J. W. Dunne. In this work of popular psychology the author recounts his vivid dreams of incidents – volcanic eruptions, aeroplane crashes and train wrecks – which he subsequently read about in newspaper reports. He would place a notebook and pencil under his pillow so as to record his dreams immediately upon waking; 'nine-tenths . . . are completely forgotten within five seconds,' he points out, 'and the few which survive rarely outlast the operation of shaving'.[19] The purpose of the experiment was to distinguish between pre-cognition and *imagined* pre-cognition – déjà-vu or 'what doctors call "Identifying Paramnesia"' – that is, gaining a false recollection of having dreamed about the event while reading the newspaper report. It was intended to show:

That dreams – dreams in general, all dreams, everybody's dreams – were composed of *images of past experience and images of future experience blended together in approximately equal proportions.*[20]

Briefly recounted, Lewis's parody has Will Blood waking up, noting down what he can remember of his dream and repairing to an A.B.C. tea shop for his breakfast. While in conversation with one of the waitresses, she chances to repeat what he recognizes as a key element of his dream, and the story ends with a postcard from the ecstatic William Blood to 'R. Dunne Esq.', reporting the success of the experiment:

Time is vindicated! . . . It is certain that in our dreams the future is available for the least of us. Time *is* the reality . . . Past, Present and Future is a territory over which what we call *I* crawls, and in its dreams it goes backwards and forwards at will . . . Hip! Hip! (p. 189)

A simple story and a makeweight, but it is to be applauded for its topicality in responding to a work only months older than itself. The compositional timespan of the collection had commenced in 1909 and was complete, none too soon, in the year of its belated publication, 1927.

## Notes

1. The painter Henry Lamb.
2. Quoted in Paul Edwards, 'Wyndham Lewis's Narrative of Origins: "The Death of the Ankou"', *Modern Language Review*, January 1997.
3. Wyndham Lewis et al., *Beginnings* (London, Edinburgh, Paris, Toronto, New York: Thos. Nelson & Sons Ltd., 1935), p. 101. 'The Death of the Ankou', however, was the only story in the 1927 collection that had not made a published appearance in an earlier form. Only the prose fragment remains to anchor its conception to Gestel in 1907.

**4.** *Rude Assignment*, ed. Toby Foshay (Santa Barbara, CA: Black Sparrow Press, 1984), p. 125.

**5.** Ibid.

**6.** The name was feminized and converted into French for the landlady of 'Beau Séjour': Mademoiselle Péronnette.

**7.** A letter from Lytton Strachey to Ottoline Morrell, dated 22 October 1912, told of finding the story 'Some Innkeepers and Bestre' in a back issue of the *English Review* and recognizing the landlord he himself had stayed with the previous summer. The story was 'cleverly done', Strachey observed, 'fiendish observation, and very original ideas. Yet the whole thing was most disagreeable.' Topographical details of the port of Doëlan are from Keith Clement's *Henry Lamb: The Artist and His Friends* (Bristol: Redcliff Press, 1985), p. 93.

**8.** There would be a second version in 1922, when it underwent minor revisions in Lewis's short-lived periodical *The Tyro*, before the definitive, third, version was published in 1927.

**9.** When the collection was published sixteen years later, its subtitle was *A Soldier of Humour and other stories.*

**10.** Charles Edward Lewis did not allow his wife's refusal to countenance divorce to stand in the way of his subsequently contracting at least one, and possible two, bigamous 'marriages'.

**11.** The 'Author's Foreword' here reprinted should not be taken as entirely accurate. 'Sigismund' was first published in 1920, not 1922, while 'Beau Séjour' was not a 'new story' but, as has already been stated, a heavily revised version of 'The "Pole"'.

**12.** In the September issue of *The Little Review.*

**13.** Bernard Lafourcade has pointed out that in 'The Meaning of the Wild Body' the word 'absurd' occurs no less than nine times in seven pages, 'excluding the synonyms with which the text abounds'. ('The Taming of the Wild Body' in *Wyndham Lewis: A Revaluation*, ed. Jeffrey Meyers (London: Athlone Press, 1980).

**14.** *The Myth of Sisyphus*, trans. Justin O'Brien (London: Penguin Books, 1975), pp. 20–21.

**15.** Ibid., p. 21.

**16.** *Art and Letters*, Winter issue, 1920.

**17.** *The Tyro*, first issue, 1922.

**18.** *An Experiment with Time*, published in 1927 by A. & C. Black. It ran to another edition in 1929, and Faber republished it in 1934, with a further edition in 1954. There was a French translation, *Le Temps et le Rêve*, re-published in 1948.

**19.** Ibid., p. 56.

**20.** Ibid., p. 54.

# Foreword

This collection is composed either (1) of stories now entirely rewritten within the last few months, or (2) of new stories written upon a theme already sketched and in an earlier form already published, or (3) of stories written within the last few months and now published for the first time. Titles have in most cases been changed.

The last two stories (*Sigismund*, which appeared in *Art and Letters*, 1922, and *You Broke My Dream*) are of more recent date. The others now form a series all belonging to an imaginary story-teller, whom I have named Ker-Orr. They represent my entire literary output prior to the war, with the exception of *The Enemy of the Stars*, a play which appeared in the 1914 *Blast*, and a group of war-stories.

What I have done in this book is to take the original matter rather as a theme for a new story. My reason for doing this was that the material, when I took it up again with a view to republishing, seemed to me to deserve the hand of a better artist than I was when I made those few hasty notes of very early travel.

The first story of the series, *The Soldier of Humour*, appeared in its original form in *The Little Review* (an american publication) of 1917–18. In it the showman, Ker-Orr, is, we are to suppose, at a later stage of his comic technique than in the accounts of his adventures in Brittany. *Beau Séjour* is the first hotel at which he stops. (This, except for the note at the end, is a new story.) *Inferior Religions*, which also was first printed in *The Little Review* during the war, and the notes attached to it, which are new material, will serve as a commentary on the system of feeling developed in these tales, and as an explanation, if that is needed, of the title I have chosen for the collection, *The Wild Body*.

Wyndham Lewis
*July* 6, 1927

# A Soldier of Humour

## Part I

Spain is an overflow of sombreness. 'Africa commences at the Pyrenees.' Spain is a checkboard of Black and Goth, on which primitive gallic chivalry played its most brilliant games. At the gates of Spain the landscape gradually becomes historic with Roland. His fame dies as difficultly as the flourish of the cor de chasse. It lives like a superfine antelope in the gorges of the Pyrenees, becoming more and more ethereal and gentle. Charlemagne moves Knights and Queens beneath that tree; there is something eternal and rembrandtesque about his proceedings. A stormy and threatening tide of history meets you at the frontier.

Several summers ago I was cast by fate for a fierce and prolonged little comedy – an essentially spanish comedy. It appropriately began at Bayonne, where Spain, not Africa, begins.

I am a large blond clown, ever so vaguely reminiscent (in person) of William Blake, and some great american boxer whose name I forget. I have large strong teeth which I gnash and flash when I laugh. But usually a look of settled and aggressive naïveté rests on my face. I know much more about myself than people generally do. For instance I am aware that I am a barbarian. By rights I should be paddling about in a coracle. My body is large, white and savage. But all the fierceness has become transformed into *laughter*. It still looks like a visi-gothic fighting-machine, but it is in reality a *laughing* machine. As I have remarked, when I laugh I gnash my teeth, which is another brutal survival and a thing laughter has taken over from war. Everywhere where formerly I would fly at throats, I now howl with laughter. That is me.

So I have never forgotten that I am really a barbarian. I have clung coldly to this consciousness. I realize, similarly, the uncivilized nature of my laughter. It does not easily climb into the neat japanese box, which is the cosa salada of the Spaniard, or become french esprit. It sprawls into everything. It has become my life. The result is that I am *never* serious about anything. I simply cannot help converting everything into burlesque patterns. And I admit that I am disposed to forget that people are real – that they are, that is, not subjective patterns belonging specifically to me, in the course of this joke-life, which indeed has for its very principle a denial of the accepted actual.

My father is a family doctor on the Clyde. The Ker-Orrs have been doctors usually. I have not seen him for some time: my mother, who is separated from him, lives with a noted hungarian physician. She gives me money that she gets from the physician, and it is she that I recognize as my principal parent. It is owing to this conjunction of circumstances that I am able to move about so much, and to feed the beast of humour that is within me with such a variety of dishes.

My mother is short and dark: it is from my father that I have my stature, and this strange northern appearance.

*Vom Vater hab' ich die Statur . . .*

It must be from my mother that I get the *Lust zu fabulieren*. I experience no embarrassment in following the promptings of my fine physique. My sense of humour in its mature phase has arisen in this very acute consciousness of what is *me*. In playing that off against another hostile *me*, that does not like the smell of mine, probably finds my large teeth, height and so forth abominable, I am in a sense working off my alarm at myself. So I move on a more primitive level than most men, I expose my essential *me* quite coolly, and all men shy a little. This forked, strange-scented, blond-skinned gut-bag, with its two bright rolling marbles with which it sees, bull's-eyes full of mockery and madness, is my stalking-horse. I hang somewhere in its midst operating it with detachment.

I snatch this great body out of their reach when they grow dangerously enraged at the sight of it, and laugh at them. And what I would insist upon is that at the bottom of the chemistry of my sense of humour is some philosopher's stone. A primitive unity is there, to which, with my laughter, I am appealing. Freud explains everything by *sex*: I explain everything by *laughter*. So in these accounts of my adventures there is no sex interest at all: only over and over again what is perhaps the natural enemy of sex: so I must apologize. 'Sex' makes me yawn my head off; but my eye sparkles at once if I catch sight of some stylistic anomaly that will provide me with a new pattern for my grotesque realism. The sex-specialist or the sex-snob hates what I like, and calls his occupation the only *real* one. No compromise, I fear, is possible between him and me, and people will continue to call 'real' what interests them most. I boldly pit my major interest against the sex-appeal, which will restrict me to a masculine audience, but I shall not complain whatever happens.

I am quite sure that many of the soldiers and adventurers of the Middle Ages were really *Soldiers of Humour*, unrecognized and unclassified. I know that many a duel has been fought in this solemn cause. A man of this temper and category will, perhaps, carefully cherish a wide circle of accessible enemies, that his sword may not rust. Any other quarrel may be patched up. But what can be described as a *quarrel of humour* divides men for ever. That is my english creed.

I could fill pages with descriptions of myself and my ways. But such abstractions from the life lived are apt to be misleading, because most men do not easily detach the principle from the living thing in that manner, and so when handed the abstraction alone do not know what to do with it, or they apply it wrongly. I exist with an equal ease in the abstract world of principle and in the concrete world of fact. As I can express myself equally well in either, I will stick to the latter here, as then I am more likely to be understood.

So I will show you myself in action, manœuvring in the heart of the reality. But before proceeding, this qualification of the above account of myself is necessary: owing to protracted foreign travel at an early age, following my mother's change of husbands, I have known french very well since boyhood. Most other Western languages I am fairly familiar with. This has a considerable bearing on the reception accorded to me by the general run of people in the countries where these scenes are laid.

There is some local genius or god of adventure haunting the soil of Spain, of an especially active and resourceful type. I have seen people that have personified him. In Spain it is safer to seek adventures than to avoid them. That is at least the sensation you will have if you are sensitive to this national principle, which is impregnated with *burla*, or burlesque excitants. It certainly requires *horseplay*, and it is even safer not to attempt to evade it. Should you refrain from charging the windmills, they are capable of charging you, you come to understand: in short, you will in the end wonder less at Don Quixote's behaviour. But the deity of this volcanic soil has become civilized. My analysis of myself would serve equally well for him in this respect. Your life is no longer one of the materials he asks for to supply you with constant entertainment, as the conjurer asks for the gentleman's silk hat. Not your life, – but a rib or two, your comfort, or a five-pound note, are all he politely begs or rudely snatches. With these he juggles and conjures from morning till night, keeping you perpetually amused and on the qui vive.

It might have been a friend, but as it happened it was the most implacable enemy I have ever had that Providence provided me with, as her agent and representative for this journey. The comedy I took part in was a spanish one, then, at once piquant and elemental. But a Frenchman filled the principal rôle. When I add that this Frenchman was convinced the greater part of the time that he was taking part in a tragedy, and was perpetually on the point of transplanting my adventure bodily into that other category, and that although his actions drew their vehemence from the virgin source of a racial hatred, yet it was not as a Frenchman or a Spaniard that he acted, then you will conceive what extremely complex and unmanageable forces were about to be set in motion for my edification.

What I have said about my barbarism and my laughter is a key to the militant figure chosen at the head of this account. In those modifications of the primitive such another extravagant warrior as Don Quixote is produced, existing in a vortex of strenuous and burlesque encounters. Mystical and humorous, astonished at everything at bottom (the settled naïveté I have noted) he inclines to worship and deride, to pursue like a riotous moth the comic and unconscious luminary he discovers; to make war on it and to cherish it like a lover, at once.

## *Part II*

It was about eleven o'clock at night when I reached Bayonne. I had started from Paris the evening before. In the market square adjoining the station the traveller is immediately solicited by a row of rather obscene little hotels, crudely painted. Each frail structure shines and sparkles with a hard, livid and disreputable electricity, every floor illuminated. The blazonry of cheap ice-cream wells, under a striped umbrella, is what they suggest: and as I stepped into this place all that was not a small, sparkling, competitive universe, inviting the stranger to pass into it, was spangled with the vivid spanish stars. 'Fonda del Universo,' 'Fonda del Mundo': Universal Inn and World Inn, two of these places were called, I noticed. I was tired and not particular as to which universe I entered. They all looked the same. To keep up a show of discrimination I chose the second, not the first. I advanced along a narrow passage-way and found myself suddenly in the heart of the Fonda del Mundo. On the left lay the dining-room in which sat two travellers. I was standing in the kitchen: this was a large courtyard, the rest of the hotel and several houses at the back were built round it. It had a glass roof on a level with the house proper, which was of two storeys only.

A half-dozen stoves with sinks, each managed by a separate crew of grim, oily workers, formed a semicircle. Hands were as cheap, and every bit as dirty, as dirt; you felt that the lowest scullery-maid could afford a servant to do the roughest of her work, and that girl in turn another. The abundance of cheap beings was of the same meridional order as the wine and food. Instead of buying a wheel-barrow, would not you attach a man to your business; instead of hiring a removing van, engage a gang of carriers? In every way that man could replace the implement that here would be done. An air of leisurely but continual activity pervaded this precinct. Cooking on the grand scale was going forward. Later on I learnt that this was a preparation for the market on the following day. But to enter at eleven in the evening this large and apparently empty building, as far as customers went, and find a methodically busy population in its midst, cooking a nameless feast, was impressive. A broad stair-case was the only avenue in this building to the sleeping apartments; a shining cut-glass door beneath it seemed the direction I ought to take when I should have made up my mind to advance. This door, the stairs, the bread given you at the table d'hôte, all had the same unsubstantial pretentiously new appearance.

So I stood unnoticed in an indifferent enigmatical universe, to which yet I had no clue, my rug on my arm. I certainly had reached immediately the most intimate centre of it, without ceremony. Perhaps there were other entrances, which I had not observed? I was turning back when the hostess appeared through the glass door – a very stout woman in a garment like a dressing-gown. She had that air of sinking into herself as if into a hot, enervating bath, with the sleepy, leaden intensity of expression belonging to many Spaniards. Her face was so still and impassible, that the ready and apt answers coming to your questions were startling, her *si señors* and *como nons*. However, I knew this kind of patronne; and the air of dull resentment would mean nothing except that I was indifferent to her. I was one of those troublesome people she only had to see twice – when they arrived, and when they came to pay at the end of their stay.

She turned to the busy scene at our right and poured out a few guttural remarks (it was a spanish staff), all having some bearing on my fate, some connected with my supper, the others with my sleeping accommodation or luggage. They fell on the crowd of leisurely workers without ruffling the surface. Gradually they reached their destination, however. First, I noticed a significant stir and a dull flare rose in the murky atmosphere, a stove lid had been slid back; great copper pans were disturbed, their covers wrenched up: some morsel was to be fished out for me, swimming in oil. Elsewhere a slim, handsome young witch left her cauldron and passed me, going into the dining-room. I followed her, and the hostess went back through the cut-glass door. It was behind that that she lived.

The dining-room was compact with hard light. Nothing in its glare could escape detection, so it symbolized *honesty* on the one hand, and *newness* on the other. There was nothing at all you could not *see*, and scrutinize, only too well. Everything within sight was totally unconscious of its cheapness or of any limitation at all. Inspect me! Inspect me! – exclaimed the coarse white linen upon the table, the Condy's fluid in the decanter, the paper-bread, the hideous mouldings on the wall. – I am the goods!

I took my seat at the long table. Of the two diners, only one was left. I poured myself out a glass of the wine *rosée* of Nowhere, set it to my lips, drank and shuddered. Two spoonfuls of a nameless soup, and the edge of my appetite was, it seemed, for ever blunted. Bacallao, or cod, that nightmare of the Spaniard of the Atlantic seaboard, followed. Its white and tasteless leather remained on my plate, with the markings of my white teeth all over it, like a cast of a dentist. I was really hungry and the stew that came next found its way inside me in glutinous draughts. The preserved fruit in syrup was eaten too. Heladas came next, no doubt frozen up from stinking water. Then I fell back in my chair, my coffee in front of me, and stared round at the other occupant of the dining-room. He stared blankly back at me. When I had turned my head away, as though the words had been mechanically released in response to my wish, he exclaimed:

'Il fait beau ce soir!'

I took no notice: but after a few moments I turned in his direction again. He was staring at me without anything more than a little surprise. Immediately his lips opened again, and he exclaimed dogmatically, loudly (was I deaf, he had no doubt thought):

'Il fait beau ce soir!'

'Not at all. It's by no means a fine night. It's cold, and what's more it's going to rain.'

I cannot say why I contradicted him in this fashion. Perhaps the insolent and mystical gage of drollery his appearance generally flung down was the cause. I had no reason for supposing that the weather at Bayonne was anything but fine and settled.

I had made my rejoinder as though I were a Frenchman, and I concluded my neighbour would take me for that.

He accepted my response quite stolidly. This initial rudeness of mine would probably have had no effect whatever on him, had not a revelation made shortly afterwards at once changed our relative positions, and caused him to regard me with changed eyes. He then went back, remembered this first incivility of mine, and took it, retrospectively, in a different spirit to that shown contemporaneously. He now merely enquired:

'You have come far?'

'From Paris,' I answered, my eyes fixed on a piece of cheese which the high voltage of the electricity revealed in all its instability. I reflected how bad the food was here compared to its spanish counterpart, and wondered if I should have time to go into the town before my train left. I then looked at my neighbour, and wondered what sort of stomach he could have. He showed every sign of the extremest hardiness. He lay back in his chair, his hat on the back of his head, finishing a bottle of wine with bravado. His waistcoat was open, and this was the only thing about him that did not denote the most facile of victories. This, equivalent to rolling up the sleeves, might be accepted as showing that he respected his enemy.

His straw hat served rather as a heavy coffee-coloured nimbus – such as some browningesque florentine painter, the worse for drink, might have placed behind the head of his saint. Above his veined and redly sunburnt forehead gushed a ragged volute of dry black hair. His face had the vexed wolfish look of the grimy commercial Midi. It was full of character, certainly, but it had been niggled at and worked all over, at once minutely and loosely, by a hundred little blows and chisellings of fretful passion. His beard did not sprout with any shape or symmetry. Yet in an odd and baffling way there was a breadth, a look of possible largeness somewhere. You were forced at length to attribute it to just that *blankness* of expression I have mentioned. This sort of blank intensity spoke of a possibility of real passion, of the sublime. (It was this sublime quality that I was about to waken, and was going to have an excellent opportunity of studying.)

He was dressed with sombre floridity. In his dark purple-slate suit with thin crimson lines, in his dark red hat-band, in his rosebuff tie, swarming with cerulean fire-flies, in his stormily flowered waistcoat, you felt that his taste for the violent and sumptuous had everywhere struggled to assert itself, and everywhere been overcome. But by what? That was the important secret of this man's entire machine, a secret unfolded by his subsequent conduct. Had I been of a superior penetration the cut of his clothes in their awkward amplitude, with their unorthodox shoulders and bellying hams, might have given me the key. He was not a commercial traveller. I was sure of that. For me, he issued from a void. I rejected in turn his claim, on the strength of his appearance, to be a small vineyard owner, a man in the automobile business and a *rentier*. He was part of the mystery of this hotel; his loneliness, his aplomb, his hardy appetite.

In the meantime his small sunken eyes were fixed on me imperturbably, with the blankness of two metal discs.

'I was in Paris last week,' he suddenly announced. 'I don't like

Paris. Why should I?' I thought he was working up for something now. He had had a good think. He took me for a Parisian, I supposed. 'They think they are up-to-date. Go and get a parcel sent you from abroad, then go and try and get it at the Station Depôt. Only see how many hours you will pass there trotting from one bureau clerk to another before they give it you! Then go to a café and ask for a drink! – Are you Parisian?' He asked this in the same tone, the blankness slightly deepening.

'No, I'm English,' I answered.

He looked at me steadfastly. This evidently at first seemed to him untrue. Then he suddenly appeared to accept it implicitly. His incredulity and belief appeared to be one block of the same material, or two sides of the same absolute coin. There was not room for a hair between these two states. They were not two, but one.

Several minutes of dead silence elapsed. His eyes had never winked. His changes had all occurred within one block of concrete undifferentiated blankness. At this period you became aware of a change: but when you looked at him he was completely uniform from moment to moment.

He now addressed me, to my surprise, in my own language. There was every evidence that it had crossed the Atlantic at least once since it had been in his possession; he had not inherited it, but acquired it with the sweat of his brow, it was clear.

'Oh! you're English? It's fine day!'

Now, we are going to begin all over again! And we are going to start, as before, with the weather. But I did not contradict him this time. My opinion of the weather had in no way changed. But for some reason I withdrew from my former perverse attitude.

'Yes,' I agreed.

Our eyes met, doubtfully. He had not forgotten my late incivility, and I remembered it at the same time. He was silent again. Evidently he was turning over dully in his mind the signification of this change on my part. My changes I expect presented themselves as occurring in as unruffled uniform a medium as his.

But there was a change now in him. I could both feel and see it. My weak withdrawal, I thought, had been unfortunate. Remembering my wounding obstinacy of five minutes before, a strong resentment took possession of him, swelling his person as it entered. I watched it enter him. It was as though the two sides of his sprawling portmanteau-body had tightened up, and his eyes drew in till he squinted.

Almost threateningly, then, he continued, – heavily, pointedly, steadily, as though to see if there were a spark of resistance anywhere left in me, that would spit up, under his trampling words.

'I guess eet 's darn fi' weather, and goin' to laast. A friend of mine, who ees skeeper, sailing for Bilbao this afternoon, said that mighty little sea was out zere, and all fine weather for his run. A skipper ought' know, I guess, ought'n he? Zey know sight more about zee weader than most. I guess zat's deir trade, – an't I right?'

Speaking the tongue of New York evidently injected him with a personal emotion that would not have been suspected, even, in the Frenchman. The strange blankness and impersonality had gone, or rather it had *woken up*, if one may so describe this phenomenon. He now looked at me with awakened eyes, coldly, judicially, fixedly. They were facetted eyes – the eyes of the forty-eight States of the Union. Considering he had crushed me enough, no doubt, he began talking about Paris, just as he had done in french. The one thing linguistically he had brought away from the United States intact was an american accent of almost alarming perfection. Whatever word or phrase he knew, in however muti-lated a form, had this stamp of colloquialism and air of being the real thing. He spoke english with a careless impudence at which I was not surprised; but the powerful consciousness of the authentic nature of his *accent* made him still more insolently heedless of the faults of his speech, it seemed, and rendered him immune from all care as to the correctness of the mere english. His was evidently to the full the american, or anglo-saxon american, state of mind: a colossal disdain for everything that does not possess in one way or another an american accent. My english, grammatically reg-ular though it was, lacking the american accent was but a poor vehicle for thought compared with his most blundering sentence.

Before going further I must make quite clear that I have no dislike of the american way of accenting english. American possesses an indolent vigour and dryness which is a most cunning arm when it snarls out its ironies. That accent is the language of Mark Twain, and is the tongue, at once naïve and cynical, of a thousand inimitable humourists. To my mind it is a better accent than the sentimental whimsicality of the Irish.

An illusion of superiority, at the expense of citizens of other states, the American shares with the Englishman. So the 'God's Own Country' attitude of some Americans is more anglo-saxon than their blood. I have met many outlandish Americans, from such un-american cities as Odessa, Trieste and Barcelona. America had done them little good, they tended to become dreamers, drunken with geographical immensities and opportunities they had never had. This man at once resembled and was different from them. The reason for this difference, I concluded, was explained when he informed me that he was a United States citizen. I believed him on the spot, unreservedly. Some air of security in him that only such a ratification can give convinced me.

He did not tell me at once. Between his commencing to speak in english and his announcing his citizenship, came an indetermined phase in our relations. During this phase he knew what he possessed, but he knew I was not yet aware of it. This caused him to make some allowance; since, undivulged, this fact was, for me at least, not yet a full fact. He was constrained, but the situation had not yet, he felt, fully matured.

In the same order as in our conversation in french, we progressed then, from the weather topic (a delicate subject with us) to Paris. Our acquaintance was by this time – scarcely ten minutes had elapsed – painfully ripe. I already felt instinctively that certain subjects of conversation were to be avoided. I knew already what shade of expression would cause suspicion, what hatred, and what snorting disdain. He, for his part, evidently with the intention of eschewing a subject fraught with dangers, did not once speak of

England. It was as though England were a subject that no one could expect him to keep his temper about. Should any one, as I did, come from England, he would naturally resent being reminded of it. The other, obviously, would be seeking to take an unfair advantage of him. In fact for the moment the assumption was – that was the only issue from this difficulty – that I was an American.

'Guess you' goin' to Spain?' he said. 'Waal, Americans are not like' very much in that country. That country, sir, is barb'rous; you *kant* believe how behind in everything that country is! All you have to do is to *look* smart there to make money. No need to worry there. No, by gosh! Just sit round and ye'll do bett' dan zee durn dagos!'

The american citizenship wiped out the repulsive fact of his southern birth, otherwise, being a Gascon, he would have been almost a dago himself.

'In Guadalquiveer – waal – kind of state-cap'tle, some manzanas, a bunch shacks, get me? – waal –'

I make these sentences of my neighbour's much more lucid than they in reality were. But he now plunged into this obscure and whirling idiom with a story to tell. The story was drowned; but I gathered it told of how, travelling in a motor car, he could find no petrol anywhere in a town of some importance. He was so interested in the telling of this story that I was thrown a little off my guard, and once or twice showed that I did not quite follow him. I did not understand his english, that is what unguardedly I showed. He finished his story rather abruptly. There was a deep silence. – It was after this silence that he divulged the fact of his american citizenship.

And now things began to wear at once an exceedingly gloomy and unpromising look.

With the revelation of this staggering fact I lost at one blow all the benefit of that convenient fiction in which we had temporarily indulged – namely, that I was american. It was now incumbent upon him to adopt an air of increased arrogance. The representative of the United States – there was no evading it, that was the dignity that the evulgation of his legal nationality imposed on him.

17

All compromise, all courteous resolve to ignore painful facts, was past. Things must stand out in their true colours, and men too.

As a result of this heightened attitude, he appeared to doubt the sincerity or exactitude of everything I said. His beard bristled round his drawling mouth, his thumbs sought his arm-pits, his varnished patterned shoes stood up erect and aggressive upon his heels. An insidious attempt on my part to induct the conversation back into french, unhappily detected, caused in him an alarming indignation. I was curious to see the change that would occur in my companion if I could trap him into using again his native speech. The sensation of the humbler tongue upon his lips would have, I was sure, an immediate effect. The perfidy of my intention only gradually dawned upon him. He seemed taken aback. For a few minutes he was silent as though stunned. The subtleties, the *ironies* to which the American is exposed!

'Oui, c'est vrai,' I went on, taking a frowning, business-like air, affecting a great absorption in the subject we were discussing, and to have overlooked the fact that I had changed to french 'les Espagnols ont du chic à se chausser. D'ailleurs, c'est tout ce qu'ils savent, en fait de toilette. C'est les Américains surtout qui savent s'habiller!'

His eyes at this became terrible. He had seen through the *manège*, had he not: and now *par surcroît de perfidie*, was I not *flattering* him – flattering Americans; and above all, praising their way of dressing! His cigar protruded from the right-hand corner of his mouth. He now with a gnashing and rolling movement conveyed it, in a series of revolutions, to the left-hand corner. He eyed me with a most unorthodox fierceness. In the language of his adopted land, but with an imported wildness in the dry figure that he must affect, he ground out, spitting with it the moist débris of the cigar:

'Yes, *sirr*, and that's more 'n zee durn English do!'

No doubt, in his perfect americanism – and at this ticklish moment, his impeccable accent threatened by an unscrupulous foe, who was attempting to stifle it temporarily – a definite analogy arose in his mind. The Redskin and his wiles, the hereditary and cunning foe of the american citizen, came vividly perhaps to his mind. Yes, wiles of that familiar sort were being used against him, Sioux-like, Blackfeet-like manoeuvres. He must meet them as the american citizen had always met them. He had at length overcome the Sioux and Cherokee. He turned on me a look as though I had been unmasked, and his accent became more raucous and formidable. The elemental that he contained and that often woke in him, I expect, manifested itself in his american accent, the capital vessel of his vitality.

After another significant pause he brusquely chose a new subject of conversation. It was a subject upon which, it was evident, he was persuaded that it would be quite impossible for us to agree. He took a long draught of the powerful fluid served to each diner. I disagreed with him at first out of politeness. But as he seemed resolved to work himself up slowly into a national passion, I changed round, and agreed with him. For a moment he glared at me. He felt at bay before this dreadful subtlety to which his americanism exposed him: then he warily changed his position in the argument, taking up the point of view he had begun by attacking.

We changed about alternately for a while. It was a most diverting game. At one time in taking my new stand, and asserting something, either I had changed too quickly, or he had not done so quite quickly enough. At all events, when he began speaking he found himself *agreeing* with me. This was a breathless moment. It was very close quarters indeed. I felt as one does at a show, standing on the same chair with an uncertain-tempered person. With an anxious swiftness I threw myself into the opposite opinion. The situation, for that time at least, was saved. A moment more, and we should have fallen on each other, or rather, he on me.

He buried his face again in the sinister potion in front of him, and consumed the last vestiges of the fearful food at his elbow. During these happenings we had not been interrupted. A dark figure, that of a Spaniard, I thought, had passed into the kitchen along the passage. From within the muffled uproar of the machinery of the kitchen reached us uninterruptedly.

He now with a snarling drawl engaged in a new discussion on another and still more delicate subject. I renewed my tactics, he his. Subject after subject was chosen. His volte-face, his change of attitude in the argument, became less and less leisurely. But my skill in reversing remained more than a match for his methods. At length, whatever I said he said the opposite, brutally and at once. At last, pushing his chair back violently with a frightful grating sound, and thrusting both his hands in his pockets – at this supreme moment the sort of blank look came back to his face again – he said slowly:

'Waal, zat may be so – you say so – waal! But what say you to England, hein? England! England! England!'

At last it had come! He repeated 'England' as though that word in itself were a question – an unanswerable question. 'England' was a form of question that a man could only ask when every device of normal courtesy had been exhausted. But it was a thing hanging over every Englishman, at any moment he might be silenced with it.

'England! ha! England! England!' he repeated, as though hypnotized by this word; as though pressing me harder and harder, and finally 'chawing me up' with the mere utterance of it.

'Why, mon vieux!' I said suddenly, getting up, 'how about the South of France, for that matter – the South of France! the South of France! The bloody Midi, your home-land, you poor bum!' I gnashed my teeth as I said this.

If I had said 'America,' he would have responded at once, no doubt. But 'the South of France!' A look of unspeakable vagueness came into his face. The South of France! This was at once without meaning, a stab in the back, an unfair blow, the sort of thing that was not said, some sort of paralysing nonsense, that robbed a man of the power of speech. I seemed to have drawn a chilly pall with glove-like tightness suddenly over the whole of his mind.

I fully expected to be forced to fight my way out of the salle à manger, and was wondering whether his pugilistic methods would be those of Chicago or Toulouse – whether he would skip round me, his fists working like piston rods, or whether he would plunge his head into the pit of my stomach, kick me on the chin and follow up with the 'coup de la fourchette,' which consists in doubling up one's fist, but allowing the index and little finger to protrude, so that they may enter the eyes on either side of the bridge of the nose.

But I had laid him out quite flat. The situation was totally outside his compass. And the word 'bum' lay like a load of dough upon his spirit. My last word had been *american*! As I made for the door, he sat first quite still. Then, slightly writhing on his chair, with a painful slowness, his face passed through a few degrees of the compass in an attempt to reach me in spite of the spell I had laid upon him. The fact of my leaving the room seemed to find him still more unprepared. My answer to his final apostrophe was a blow below the belt: I was following it up by vanishing from the ring altogether, as though the contest were over, while he lay paralysed in the centre of the picture. It had never occurred to him, apparently, that I might perhaps get up and leave the dining-room. – Sounds came from him, words too – hybrid syllables lost on the borderland between french and english, which appeared to signify protest, pure astonishment, alarmed question. But I had disappeared. I got safely into the kitchen. I sank into that deep hum of internal life, my eye glittering with the battle light of humour.

In the act of taking my candle from the hand of a chambermaid, I heard a nasal roar behind me. I mounted the stairs three steps at a time, the hotel boy at my heels, and the chambermaid breathlessly rushing up in his rear. Swiftly ushered into my room, I thrust outside the panting servants and locked and bolted the door.

Flinging myself on the bed, my blond poll rolling about in ecstasy upon the pillow, I howled like an exultant wolf. This penetrating howl of my kind – the humorous kind – shook the cardboard walls of the room, rattled the stucco frames; but the tumult beneath of the hotel staff must have prevented this sound from getting farther than the area of the bedrooms. My orgasm left me weak, and I lay conventionally mopping my brow, and affectedly gasping. Then, as usually happened with me, I began sentimentally pitying my victim. Poor little chap! My conduct had been unpardonable! I had brutalized this tender flower of the prairies of the West! Why had I dragged in the 'bloody Midi' after all? It was too bad altogether. I had certainly behaved very badly. I had a movement to go down immediately and apologize to him, a tear of laughter still hanging from a mournful lash.

My room was at the back. The window looked on to the kitchen; it was just over the stairs leading to the bedrooms. I now got up, for I imagined I heard some intemperate sound thrusting into the general mêlée of mechanical noise. From the naturally unsavoury and depressing porthole of my room, immediately above the main cauldrons, I was able, I found, to observe my opponent in the murky half-court, half-kitchen, beneath. There he was: by pointing my ear down I could catch sometimes what he was saying. But I found that the noise I had attributed to him had been my fancy only.

Inspected from this height he looked very different. I had not till then seen him on his feet. His yankee clothes, evidently cut beneath his direction by a gascon tailor, made him look as broad as he was long. His violently animated leanness imparted a precarious and toppling appearance to his architecture. He was performing a war-dance in this soft national armour just at present, beneath the sodden eyes of the proprietress. It had shuffling, vehement, jazz elements, aided by the gesticulation of the Gaul. This did not seem the same man I had been talking to before. He evidently, in this enchanted hotel, possessed a variety of personalities. It was *not* the same man. Somebody else had leapt into his clothes – which hardly fitted the newcomer – and was carrying on his quarrel. The original and more imposing man had disappeared. I had slain him. This little fellow had taken up his disorganized and overwrought life at that precise moment and place where I had left him knocked out in the dining-room, at identically the same pitch of passion, only with fresher nerves, and with the same racial sentiments as the man he had succeeded.

He was talking in spanish – much more correctly than he did in english. She listened with her leaden eyes crawling swiftly and sullenly over his person, with an air of angrily and lazily making an inventory. In his fiery attack on the depths of languor behind which her spirit lived, he would occasionally turn and appeal to one of the nearest of the servants, as though seeking corroboration of something. Of what crime was I being accused? I muttered rapid prayers to the effect that that sultry reserve of the proprietress might prove impregnable. Otherwise I might be cast bodily out of the Fonda del Mundo, and, in my present worn-out state, have to seek another and distant roof. I knew that I was the object of his discourse. What effectively could be said about me on so short an acquaintance? He would, though, certainly affirm that I was a designing ruffian of some sort; such a person as no respectable hotel would consent to harbour, or if it did, would do so at its peril. Probably he might be saying it was my intention to hold up the hotel later on, or he might have influence with the proprietress, be a regular customer and old friend. He might only be saying, 'I object to that person; I cannot express to you how I object to that person! I have never objected to any one to the same fearful degree. All my organs boil at the thought of him. I cannot explain to you how that island organism tears my members this way and that. Out with this abomination! Oh! out with it before I die at your feet from the fever of my *mauvais sang*!'

That personal appeal might prove effective. I went to bed with a feeling of extreme insecurity. I thought that, if nothing else happened, he might set fire to the hotel. But in spite of the dangers by which I was, manifestly, beset in this ill-starred establishment, I slept soundly enough. In the morning an overwhelming din shook me, and I rose with the stink of southern food in my nose.

Breakfast passed off without incident. I concluded that the Complete American was part of the night-time aspect of the Fonda del Mundo and had no part in its more normal day-life.

The square was full of peasants, the men wearing dark blouses and the béret basque. Several groups were sitting near me in the salle à manger. An intricate arrangement of chairs and tables, like an extensive man-trap, lay outside the hotel, extending a little distance into the square. From time to time one or more clumsy peasant would appear to become stuck or somehow involved in these iron contrivances. They would then, with becoming fatalism, sit down and call for a drink. Such was the impression conveyed, at least, by their embarrassed and reluctant movements in choosing a seat. I watched several parties come into this dangerous extension of the Fonda del Mundo. The proprietress would come out occasionally and stare moodily at them. She never looked at me.

A train would shortly leave for the frontier. I bade farewell to the patrona, and asked her if she could recommend me a hotel in Burgos or in Pontaisandra. When I mentioned Pontaisandra, she said at once, 'You are going to Pontaisandra?' With a sluggish ghost of a smile she turned to a loitering servant and then said, 'Yes, you can go to the Burgaleza at Pontaisandra. That is a good hotel.' They both showed a few ragged discoloured teeth, only appearing in moments of crafty burlesque. The night before I had told her that my destination was Pontaisandra, and she had looked at me stead-fastly and resentfully, as though I had said that my destination was Paradise, and that I intended to occupy the seat reserved for her. But that was the night before: and now Pontaisandra appeared to mean something different to her. The episode of the supper-room the night before I now regarded as an emanation of that place. The Fonda del Mundo was a mysterious hotel, though in the day its secrets seemed more obvious. I imagined it inhabited by solitary and hallucinated beings, like my friend the Perfect American – or such as I myself might have become. The large kitchen staff was occupied far into the night in preparing a strange and excessive table d'hôte. The explanation of this afforded in the morning by the sight of the crowding peasants did not efface that impression of midnight though it mitigated it. Perhaps the dreams caused by its lunches, the visions conjured up by its suppers, haunted the place. That was the spirit in which I remembered my over-night affair.

When eventually I started for the frontier, hoping by the inhal-ation of a picadura to dispose my tongue to the ordeal of framing passable castilian, I did not realize that the american adventure was the progenitor of other adventures; nor that the dreams of the Fonda del Mundo were to go with me into the heart of Spain.

## Part III

Burgos, I had intended, should be my first stopping place. But I decided afterwards that San Sebastian and Leon would be better.

This four days' journeying was an *entr'acte* filled with appropriate music; the lugubrious and splendid landscapes of Castile, the extremely self-conscious, pedantic and independent spirit of its inhabitants, met with en route. Fate was marking time, merely. With the second day's journey I changed trains and dined at Venta de Baños, the junction for the line that branches off in the direction of Palencia, Leon and the galician country.

While travelling, the spanish peasant has a marked preference for the next compartment to his own. No sooner has the train started, than, one after another, heads, arms, and shoulders appear above the wooden partition. There are times when you have all the members of the neighbouring compartment gazing with the melancholy stolidity of cattle into your own. In the case of some theatrical savage of the Sierras, who rears a dishevelled head before you in a pose of fierce abandon, and hangs there smoking like a chimney, you know that it may be some grandiose recoil of pride that prevents him from remaining in an undignified position huddled in a narrow carriage. In other cases it is probably a simple conviction that the occupants of other compartments are likely to be more interesting.

The whole way from Venta de Baños to Palencia the carriage was dense with people. Crowds of peasants poured into the train, loaded with their heavy vivid horse-rugs, gaudy bundles and baskets; which profusion of mere matter, combined with their exuberance, made the carriage appear positively to swarm with animal life. They would crowd in at one little station and out at another a short way along the line, where they were met by hordes of their relations awaiting them. They would rush or swing out of the door, charged with their property or recent purchases, and catch the nearest man or woman of their blood in their arms, with a turbulence that outdid our Northern people's most vehement occasions. The waiting group became twice as vital as average mankind upon the train's arrival, as though so much more blood had poured into their veins. Gradually we got beyond the sphere of this Fiesta, and in the small hours of the morning arrived at Leon.

Next day came the final stages of the journey to the Atlantic sea-board. We arrived within sight of the town that evening, just as the sun was setting. With its houses of green, rose, and white, in general effect a faded bouquet, its tints a scarcely coloured reminiscence, it looked like some oriental city represented in the nerveless tempera of an old wall. Its bay stretched between hills for many miles to the ocean, which lay beyond an island of scarcely visible rocks.

On the train drawing up in the central station, the shock troops furnished by every little ragamuffin café as well as stately hotel in the town were hurled against us. I had mislaid the address given me at Bayonne. I wished to find a hotel of medium luxury. The different hotel-attendants called hotly out their prices at me. I selected one who named a sum for board and lodging that only the frenzy of competition could have fathered, I thought. Also the name of this hotel was, it seemed to me, the one the patrona at Bayonne had mentioned. I had not then learnt to connect Burgaleza with Burgos: this was my first long visit to Spain. With this man I took a cab and was left seated in it at the door of the station, while he went after the heavy luggage. Now one by one, the hotel emissaries came up; their fury of a few minutes before contrasted oddly with their present listless calm. Putting themselves civilly at my disposition, they thrust forward matter-of-factly the card of their establishment, adding that they were sure that I would find out my mistake.

I now felt in a vague manner a tightening of the machinery of Fate – a certain uneasiness and strangeness, in the march and succession of facts and impressions, like a trembling of a decrepit motorbus about to start again. The interlude was over. After a long delay the hotel tout returned and we started. My misgivings were of a practical order. The price named was very low, too low perhaps. But I had found it a capital plan on former occasions to go to a cheap hotel and pay a few pesetas more a day for 'extras.' My palate was so conservative, that I found in any case that my main fare lay outside the spanish menu. Extras are very satisfactory. You always feel that a single individual has bent over the extra and carefully cooked it, and that it has not been bought in too wholesale a manner. I wished to live on extras – a privileged existence: and extras are much the same in one place as another. So I reassured myself.

The cabman and the hotel man were discussing some local event. But we penetrated farther and farther into a dismal and shabby quarter of the town. My misgivings began to revive. I asked the representative of the Burgaleza if he were sure that his house was a clean and comfortable house. He dismissed my doubtful glance with a gesture full of assurance. 'It's a splendid place! You wait and see; we shall be there directly,' he added.

We suddenly emerged into a broad and imposing street, on one side of which was a public garden, 'El Paseo,' I found out afterwards, the Town Promenade. Gazing idly at a palatial white building with a hotel omnibus drawn up before it, to my astonishment I found our driver also stopping at its door. A few minutes later, still scarcely able to credit my eyes, I got out and entered this palace, noticing 'Burgaleza' on the board of the omnibus as I passed. I followed the tout, having glimpses in passing of a superbly arrayed table with serviettes that were each a work of art, that one of the splendid guests entertained at this establishment (should I not be among them?) would soon haughtily pull to pieces to wipe his mouth on – tables groaning beneath gilded baskets tottering with a lavish variety of choice fruit. Then came a long hall, darkly panelled, at the end of which I could see several white-capped men shouting fiercely and clashing knives, women answering shrilly and juggling with crashing dishes; a kitchen – the most diabolically noisy and malodorous I had ever approached. We went straight on towards it. Were we going through it? At the very threshold we stopped, and opening the panel-like door in the wall, the porter disappeared with my portmanteau, appearing again without my portmanteau, and hurried away. At this moment my eye caught something else, a door ajar on the other side of the passage and a heavy, wooden, clothless table, with several squares of bread upon it, and a fork or two. In Spain there is a sort of bread for the rich, and a forbidding juiceless papery bread for the humble. The bread on that table was of the latter category, far more like paper than that I had had at Bayonne.

Suddenly the truth flashed upon me. With a theatrical gesture I dashed open again the panel and passed into the pitchy gloom within. I struck a match. It was a cupboard, quite windowless, with just enough room for a little bed; I was standing on my luggage. No doubt in the room across the passage I should be given some cod soup, permanganate of potash and artificial bread. Then, extremely tired after my journey, I should crawl into my kennel, the pandemonium of the kitchen at my ear for several hours.

In the central hall I found the smiling proprietor. He seemed to regard his boarders generally as a gentle joke, and those who slept in the cupboard near the kitchen a particularly good but rather low one. I informed him that I would pay the regular sum for a day's board and lodging, and said I must have another room. A valet accepted the responsibility of seeing that I was given a bedroom. The landlord walked slowly away, his iron-grey side-whiskers, with their traditional air of respectability, giving a disguised look to his rogue's face. I was transferred from one cupboard to another; or rather, I had exchanged a cupboard for a wardrobe – reduced to just half its size by a thick layer of skirts and cloaks, twenty deep, that protruded from all four walls. But still the little open space left in the centre ensured a square foot to wash and dress in, with a quite distinct square foot or two for sleep. And it was upstairs.

A quarter of an hour later, wandering along a dark passage on the way back to the hotel lounge, a door opened in a very violent and living way that made me start and look up, and a short rectangular figure, the size of a big square trunk, issued forth, just ahead of me. I recognized this figure fragmentarily – first, with a cold shudder, I recognized an excrescence of hair; then with a jump I recognized a hat held in its hand; then, with an instinctive shrinking, I realized that I had seen these flat traditional pseudo-american shoulders before. With a really comprehensive throb of universal emotion, I then recognized the whole man.

It was the implacable figure of my neighbour at dinner, of the Fonda del Mundo.

He moved along before me with wary rigidity, exhibiting none of the usual signs of recognition. He turned corners with difficulty, a rapid lurch precipitating him into the new path indicated when he reached the end of the wall. On the stairs he appeared to get stuck in much the way that a large american trunk would, borne by a sweating porter. At last he safely reached the hall. I was a yard or two behind him. He stopped to light a cigar, still taking up an unconscionable amount of space. I manœuvred round him, and gained one of the doors of the salle à manger. But as I came within his range of vision, I also became aware that my presence in the house was not a surprise to this sandwich-man of Western citizenship. His eye fastened upon me with ruthless bloodshot indignation, an eye-blast as it were crystallized from the episode at Bayonne. But he was so dead and inactive that he seemed a phantom of his former self: and in all my subsequent dealings with him, this feeling of having to deal with a ghost, although a particularly mischievous one, persisted. If before my anger at the trick that had been played on me had dictated a speedy change of lodging, now my anxiety to quit this roof had, naturally, an overwhelming incentive.

After dinner I went forth boldly in search of the wonderful american enemy. Surely I had been condemned, in some indirect way, by him, to the cupboard beside the kitchen. No dungeon could have been worse. Had I then known, as I learnt later, that he was the owner of this hotel, the mediæval analogy would have been still more complete. He now had me in his castle.

I found him seated, in sinister conjunction with the proprietor or manager, as I supposed he was, in the lobby of the hotel. He turned slightly away as I came up to him, with a sulky indifference due to self-restraint. Evidently the time for action was not ripe. There was no pretence of not recognizing me. As though our conversation in the Fonda del Mundo had taken place a half-hour before, we acknowledged in no way a consciousness of the lapse of time, only of the shifted scene.

'Well, colonel,' I said, adopting an allocution of the United States, 'taking the air?'

He went on smoking.

'This is a nice little town.'

'Vous vous plaisez ici, monsieur? C'est bien!' he replied in french, as though I were not worthy even to *hear* his american accent, and that, if any communication was to be held with me, french must serve.

'I shall make a stay of some weeks here,' I said, with indulgent defiance.

'Oui?'

'But not in this hotel.'

He got up with something of his Bayonne look about him.

'No, I shouldn't. You might not find it a very comfortable hotel,' he said vehemently in his mother-tongue.

He walked away hurriedly, as a powder magazine might walk away from a fuse, if it did not, for some reason, want to blow up just then.

That was our last encounter that day. The upstairs and less dreadful dungeon with its layer of clothes would have been an admirable place for a murder. Not a sound would have penetrated its woollen masses and the thick spanish walls enclosing it. But the next morning I was still alive. I set out after breakfast to look for new quarters. My practised eye had soon measured the inconsistencies of most of the Pensions of the town. But a place in the Calle Real suited me all right, and I decided to stop there for the time. There too the room was only a cupboard. But it was a human cupboard and not a clothes cupboard. It was one of the four tributaries of the dining-room. My bedroom door was just beside my place at table – I had simply to step out of bed in the right direction, and there was the morning coffee. The extracting of my baggage from the Burgaleza was easy enough, except that I was charged a heavy toll. I protested with the manager for some time, but he smiled and smiled. 'Those are our charges!' He shrugged his shoulders, dismissed the matter, and smiled absent-mindedly when I renewed my objections. As at Bayonne, there was no sign of the enemy in the morning. But I was not so sure this time that I had seen the last of him.

That evening I came amongst my new fellow-pensionnaires for the first time. This place had recommended itself to me, partly because the boarders would probably speak castilian, and so be practice for me. They were mostly not Gallegos, at least, who are the Bretons of Spain, and afford other Spaniards much amusement by their way of expressing themselves. My presence caused no stir whatever. Just as a stone dropped in a small pond which has long been untouched, and has an opaque coat of green decay, slips dully to the bottom, cutting a neat little hole on the surface, so I took my place at the bottom of the table. But as the pond will send up its personal odour at this intrusion, so these people revealed something of themselves in the first few minutes, in an illusive and immobile way. They must all have lived in that Pension together for an inconceivable length of time. My neighbour, however, promised to be a little El Dorado of spanish; a small mine of gossip, grammatical rules and willingness to impart these riches. I struck a deep shaft of friendship into him at once and began work without delay. Coming from Madrid, this ore was at least 30 carat, thoroughly thetaed and castilian stuff that he talked. What I gave him in exchange was insignificant. He knew several phrases in french and english, such as 'If you please,' and 'fine day'; I merely confirmed him in these. Every day he would hesitatingly say them over, and I would assent, 'quite right,' and 'very well pronounced.' He was a tall, bearded man, head of the orchestra of the principal Café in the town. Two large cuffs lay on either side of his plate during meals, the size of serviettes. Out of them his hands emerged without in any way disturbing them, and served him with his food as far as they could. But he had to remain with his mouth quite near his plate, for the cuffs would not move a hair's breadth. This somewhat annoyed me, as it muffled a little the steady flow of spanish, and even sometimes was a cause of considerable waste. Once or twice without success I attempted to move the cuff on my side away from the plate. Their ascendancy over him and their indolence was profound.

But I was not content merely to work him for his mother-tongue inertly, as it were. I wished to see it in use: to watch this stream of castilian working the mill of general conversation, for instance. Although willing enough for himself, he had no chance in this Pension. On the third day, however, he invited me to come round to the Café after dinner and hear him play. Our dinners overlapped, he leaving early. So the meal over, I strolled round, alone.

The Café Pelayo was the only really parisian establishment in the town. It was the only one where the Madrilenos and the other Spaniards proper, resident in Pontaisandra, went regularly. I entered, peering round in a business-like way at its monotonously mirrored walls and gilded ceiling. I took up an advantageous position, and settled down to study the idiom.

In a lull of the music, my chef d'orchestre came over to me, and presented me to a large group of people, friends of his. It was an easy matter, from that moment, to become acquainted with every-body in the Café.

I did not approach Spaniards in general, I may say, with any very romantic emotion. Each man I met possessed equally an ancient and admirable tongue, however degenerate himself. He often appeared like some rotten tree, in which a swarm of highly evocative admirable words had nested. I, like a bee-cultivator, found it my business to transplant this vagrant swarm to a hive prepared. A language has its habits and idiosyncrasies just like a species of insect, as my first professor comfortably explained; its little world of symbols and parts of speech have to be most carefully studied and manipulated. But above all it is important to observe their habits and idiosyncrasies, and the pitch and accent that naturally accompanies them. So I had my hands full.

When the Café closed, I went home with Don Pedro, chef d'orchestre, to the Pension. Every evening, after dinner – and at lunch-time as well – I repaired there. This lasted for three or four days. I now had plenty of opportunity of talking castilian Spanish. I had momentarily forgotten my american enemy.

On the fifth evening, I entered the Café as usual, making towards my most useful and intelligent group. But then, with a sinking of the heart, I saw the rectangular form of my ubiquitous enemy, quartered with an air of demoniac permanence in their midst. A mechanic who finds an unaccountable lump of some foreign substance stuck in the very heart of his machinery – what simile shall I use for my dismay? To proceed somewhat with this image, as this unhappy engineer might dash to the cranks or organ stops of his machine, so I dashed to several of my formerly most willing listeners and talkers. I gave one a wrench and another a screw, but I found that already the machine had become recalcitrant.

I need not enumerate the various stages of my defeat on that evening. It was more or less a passive and moral battle, rather than one with any evident show of the secretly bitter and desperate nature of the passions engaged. Of course, the inclusion of so many people unavoidably caused certain brusqueries here and there. The gradual cooling down of the whole room towards me, the disaffection that swept over the chain of little drinking groups from that centre of mystical hostility, that soul that recognized in me something icily antipodean too, no doubt; the immobile figure of America's newest and most mysterious child, apparently emitting these strong waves without effort, as naturally as a fountain: all this, with great vexation, I recognized from the moment of the intrusion of his presence. It almost seemed as though he had stayed away from this haunt of his foreseeing what would happen. He had waited until I had comfortably settled myself and there was something palpable to attack. His absence may have had some more accidental cause.

What exactly it was, again, he found to say as regards me I never discovered. As at Bayonne, I saw the mouth working and experienced the social effects, only. No doubt it was the subtlest and most electric thing that could be found; brief, searching and annihilating. Perhaps something seemingly crude – that I was a spy – may have recommended itself to his ingenuity. But I expect it was a meaningless blast of disapprobation that he blew upon me, an eerie and stinging wind of convincing hatred. He evidently enjoyed a great ascendancy in the Café Pelayo. This would be explained no doubt by his commercial prestige. But it was due, I am sure, even more to his extraordinary character – moulded by the sublime force of his illusion. His inscrutable immobility, his unaccountable self-control (for such a person, and feeling as he did towards me), were of course the american or anglo-saxon phlegm and sang-froid as reflected, or interpreted, in this violent human mirror.

I left the Café earlier than usual, before the chef d'orchestre. It was the following morning at lunch when I next saw him. He was embarrassed. His eyes wavered in my direction, fascinated and inquisitive. He found it difficult to realize that his respect for me had to end and give place to another feeling.

'You know Monsieur de Valmore?' he asked.

'That little ape of a Frenchman, do you mean?'

I knew this description of my wonderful enemy was only vulgar and splenetic. But I was too discouraged to be more exact.

This way of describing Monsieur de Valmore appeared to the chef d'orchestre so eccentric, apart from its vulgarity, that I lost at once in Don Pedro's sympathy. He told me, however, all about him; details that did not touch on the real constituents of this life.

'He owns the Burgaleza and many houses in Pontaisandra. Ships, too – Es Americano,' he added.

Vexations and hindrances of all sorts now made my stay in Pontaisandra useless and depressing. Don Pedro had generally almost finished when we came to dinner, and I was forced to close down, so to say, the mine. Nothing more was to be extracted, at length, except disobliging monosyllables. The rest of the boarders remained morose and inaccessible. I went once more to the Café Pelayo, but the waiters even seemed to have come beneath the hostile spell. The new Café I chose yielded nothing but gallego chatter, and the garçon was not talkative.

There was little encouragement to try another Pension and stay on in Pontaisandra. I made up my mind to go to Corunna. This would waste time and I was short of money. But there is more gallego than spanish spoken in Galicia, even in the cities. Too easily automatic a conquest as it may seem, Monsieur de Valmore had left me nothing but the Gallegos. I was not getting the practice in spanish I needed, and this sudden deprivation of what I had mainly come into Spain for, poisoned for me the whole air of the place. The task of learning this tiresome language began to be burdensome. I even considered whether I should not take up gallego instead. But I decided finally to go to Corunna. On the following day, some hours before the time for the train, I paraded the line of streets towards the station, with the feeling that I was no longer there. The place seemed cooling down beneath my feet and growing prematurely strange. But the miracle happened. It declared itself with a smooth suddenness. A more exquisite checkmate never occurred in any record of such warfare.

The terrible ethnological difference that existed between Monsieur de Valmore and myself up till that moment, showed every sign of ending in a weird and revolting defeat for me. The 'moment' I refer to was that in which I turned out of the High Street, into the short hilly avenue where the post office lay. I thought I would go up to the Correo and see for the last time if a letter for which I had been waiting had arrived.

On turning the corner I at once became aware of three anomalous figures walking just in front of me. They were all three of the proportions known in America as 'husky.' When I say they were walking, I should describe their movements more accurately as *wading* – wading through the air, evidently towards the post office. Their carriage was slightly rolling, like a ship under way. They occasionally bumped into each other, but did not seem to mind this. Yet no one would have mistaken these three young men for drunkards. But I daresay you will have already guessed. It would under other circumstances have had no difficulty in entering my head. As it was, there seemed a certain impediment of consciousness or inhibition with me which prevented me from framing to myself the word 'American.' These three figures were three Americans! This seems very simple, I know: but this very ordinary fact trembled and lingered before completely entering into my consciousness. The extreme rapidity of my mind in another sense – in seeing all that this fact, if verified, might signify to me – may have been responsible for that. Then one of them, on turning his head, displays the familiar features of Taffany, a Mississippi friend of mine. I simultaneously recognized Blauenfeld and Morton, the other two members of a trio. A real trio, like real twins, is rarer than one thinks. This one was the remnant of a quartet, however. I had met it first in Paris. Poor Bill (Borden Henneker) was killed in a motor accident. These three had mourned him with insatiable drinking, to which I had been a party for some days the year before. And my first feeling was complicated with a sense of their forlornness, as I recognized their three backs, rolling heavily and mournfully.

In becoming, from any three Americans, three friends of mine, they precipitated in an immediate inrush of the most full-blooded hope the sense of what might be boldly anticipated from this meeting. Two steps brought me up with them: my cordiality if anything exceeded theirs.

'Why, if it isn't Cairo! Look at this! Off what Christmas-tree did you drop? Gee, I'm glad to see you, Kire!' shouted Taffany. He was the irrepressible Irishman of the three.

'Why, it's you, that's swell. We looked out for you in Paris. You'd just left. How long have you been round here?' Blauenfeld ground out cordially. He was the rich melancholy one of the three.

'Come right up to the Correo and interpret for us, Cairo. You know the idioma, I guess. Feldie's a washout,' said Morton, who was the great debauchee of the three.

Optimism, consciousness of power (no wonder! I reflected) surged out of them, my simple-hearted friends. Ah, the kindness! the *overwhelming* kindness. I bathed voluptuously in this american greeting – this real american greeting. Nothing naturalized about *that*. At the same time I felt almost awe at the thought of the dangerous nationality. These good fellows I knew and liked so well, seemed for the moment to have some inter-mixture of the strangeness of Monsieur de Valmore. However, I measured with enthusiasm their egregious breadth of shoulder, the exorbitance of their 'pants.' I examined with some disappointment these signs of nationality. How english they looked, compared to de Valmore. They were by no means american enough for my taste. Had they appeared in a star-stripe swallow-tail suit like the cartoons of Uncle Sam, I should not have been satisfied.

But I felt rather like some ambitious eastern prince who, having been continually defeated in battle by a neighbour because of the presence in the latter's army of a half-dozen elephants, suddenly becomes possessed of a couple of dozen himself.

I must have behaved oddly. I enquired anxiously about their plans. They were not off at once? No. That was capital. I was most awfully glad that they were not departing at once. I was glad that they had decided to stop. They had booked their rooms? Yes. That was good. So they were here for the night at all events? That was as it should be! You should always stop the night. Yes, I would with very great pleasure interpret for them at the Correo. – I cherished my three Americans as no Americans before have ever been cherished. I was inclined to shelter them as though they were perishable, to see that they didn't get run over, or expose themselves unwisely to the midday sun. Each transatlantic peculiarity of speech or gesture I received with something approaching exultation. Morton was soon persuaded that I was tight. All thoughts of Corunna disappeared. I did not ask at the Poste Restante for my letter.

First of all, I took my trio into a little Café near the post office. There I told them briefly what was expected of them.

'You have a most distinguished compatriot here,' I said.

'Oh. An American?' Morton asked seriously.

'Well, he deserves to be. But he began too late in life, I think. He hails from the southern part of France, and americanism came to him as a revelation when youth had already passed. He repented sincerely of his misguided early nationality. But his years spent as a Frenchman have left their mark. In the meantime, he won't leave Englishmen alone. He persecutes them, apparently, wherever he finds them.'

'He mustn't do that!' Taffany said with resolution. 'That won't do at all.'

'Why, no, I guess he mustn't do that. What makes him want to do that? What's biting him anyway? Britishers are harmless enough, aren't they?' said Blauenfeld.

'I knew you'd look at the matter in that light,' I said. 'It's a rank abuse of authority; I knew it would be condemned at headquarters. Now if you could only be present, unseen, and witness how I, for instance, am oppressed by this fanatic fellow-citizen of yours; and if you could issue forth, and reprove him, and tell him not to do it again, I should bless the day on which you were born in America.'

'I wasn't born there anyway,' said Morton. 'But that's of no importance I suppose. Well, unfold your plan, Cairo.'

'I don't see yet what we can do. Do you owe the guy any money? How does it come that he persecutes you like this?' Taffany asked.

'I'm very sorry you should have to complain, Mr. Ker-Orr, of treatment of that sort – but what sort is it anyway?'

I gave a lurid picture of my tribulations, to the scandal and indignation of my friends. They at once placed themselves, and with a humorous modesty their americanism – any quantity of that mixture in their 'organisms' – at my disposal.

It appeared to me, to start with, of the first importance that Monsieur de Valmore should not get wind of what had happened. I took my three Americans cautiously out of the Café, reconnoitring before allowing them outside. As their hotel was near the station and not near the enemy's haunts, I encouraged their going back to it. I also supposed that they would wish to make some toilet for the evening, and relied on their good sense to put on their largest clothes, though Taffany was the only one of the three that seemed at all promising from that point of view. The scale of his buttocks did assure a certain outlandish girth that would at once reveal to M. de Valmore the presence of an American.

My army was in excellent form. A robust high spirits possessed them. I kept them out of the way till nightfall, and then after an early dinner, by a circuitous route, approached the Café Pelayo.

Morton was by this time a little screwed: he showed signs that he might become difficult. He insisted on producing a packet of obscene photographs, which he held before him fan-wise, like a hand of cards, some of them upside down. The confused mass of bare legs and arms of the photographs, distorted by this method of holding them, with some highly indecent details occurring here and there, produced the effect of a siamese demon. Blauenfeld was grinning over his shoulder, and seemed likely to forget the purpose for which he was being brought to the Pelayo.

'I know that coon,' he insisted, pointing to one of the photos. 'I swear I know that coon.'

My idea was that the three Americans should enter the Café Pelayo without me. There they would establish themselves, and I had told them where to sit and how to spot their man. They should become acquainted with Monsieur de Valmore. Almost certainly the latter would approach his fellow citizens at once. But if there was any ice to break, it must be broken quickly by Taffany. They must ply him with imitation high-balls or some other national drink, which they must undertake to mix for him. For this they could hand the bill to me afterwards. When the ground was sufficiently prepared, Taffany was to sign to me from the door, and I would then, after a further interval, put in my appearance.

Morton was kissing one of the photographs. Should he continue to produce, in season and out of season, his objectionable purchases, and display them, perhaps, to the customers of the Pelayo, although he might gain an ill-deserved popularity, he would certainly convey an impression of a different sort to that planned by me for this all-american evening. After considerable drunken argument I persuaded him to let me hold the photographs until the *coup* had been brought off. That point of discipline enforced, I sent them forward, sheltering, myself, in an archway in an adjoining street, and watched them enter the swing door 'ra-raing,' as ordered. But I had the mortification of seeing Morton fall down as he got inside, tripping, apparently, over the mat. Cursing this intemperate clown, I moved with some stealth to a small gallego Café within sight of the door of the Pelayo to await events.

I fixed my eyes on the brilliantly lighted windows of the Café. I imagined the glow of national pride, the spasm of delighted recognition, that would invade Monsieur de Valmore, on hearing the 'ra-ra' chorus. Apart from the sentimental reason – its use as a kind of battle-song – was the practical one that this noisy entrance would at once attract my enemy's attention. Ten minutes passed. I knew that my friends had located Monsieur de Valmore, even if they had not begun operations. Else they would have returned to my place of waiting. I wallowed naïvely in a superb indifference. Having set the machinery going, I turned nonchalantly away, paying no more attention to it. But the stage analogy affected me, in the sense that I became rather conscious of my appearance. I must await my cue, but was sure of my reception. I was the great star that was not expected. I was the unknown quantity. Meantime I pulled out the photographs and arranged them fantastically as Morton had done. From time to time I glanced idly down the road. At last I saw Blauenfeld making towards me, his usual american swing of the body complicated by rhythmical upheavals of mirth into tramplings, stumblings and slappings of his thigh. He was being very american in a traditional way as he approached me. He was a good actor, I thought: I was grateful to him. I paid for my coffee while he was coming up.

'Is it O.K.? Is he spitted?'

'Yep! we've got him fine! Come and have a look at him.'

'Did he carry out his part of the programme according to my arrangements?'

'Why, yes. We went right in, and all three spotted him at the same time. Taffany walked round and showed himself: he was the decoy. Morty and me coquetted round too, looking arch and *very american*. We could see his old pop-eyes beginning to stick out of his old head, and his old mouth watering. At last he could hold himself no longer. He roared at us. We bellowed at him. Gee, it was a great moment in american history! We just came together with a hiss and splutter of joy. He called up a trayful of drinks, to take off the rawness of our meeting. He can't have seen an American for months. He just gobbled us up. There isn't much left of poor old Taff. He likes him best and me next. Morty's on all fours at present, tickling his legs. He doesn't much care for Morty. He's made us promise to go to his hotel to-night.'

I approached the palmy terrace, my mouth a little drawn and pinched, eyebrows raised, like a fastidious expert called in at a decisive moment. I entered the swing door with Blauenfeld, and looked round in a cold and business-like way, as a doctor might, with the dignified enquiry, 'Where is the patient?' The patient was there right enough, surrounded by the nurses I had sent. There he sat in as defenceless a condition of beatitude as possible. He stared at me with an incredulous grin at first. I believe that in this moment he would have been willing to extend to me a temporary pardon – a passe-partout to his Café for the evening. He was so happy I became a bagatelle. Had I wished, an immediate reconciliation was waiting for me. But I approached him with impassive professional rapidity, my eye fixed on him, already making my diagnosis. I was so carried away by the figure of the physician, and adhered so faithfully to the bedside manner that I had decided upon as the most appropriate for the occasion, that I almost began things by asking him to put out his tongue. Instead I sat down carefully in front of him, pulling up my trousers meticulously at the knee. I examined his flushed and astounded face, his bristling moustache, his blood-shot eyes in silence. Then I very gravely shook my head.

No man surprised by his most mortal enemy in the midst of an enervating debauch, or barely convalescent from a bad illness, could have looked more nonplussed. But Monsieur de Valmore turned with a characteristic blank childish appeal to his nurses or boon companions for help, especially to Taffany. Perhaps he was shy or diffident of taking up actively his great rôle, when more truly great actors were present. Would not the divine America speak, or thunder, through them, at this intruder? He turned a pair of solemn, appealing, outraged dog's-eyes upon Taffany. Would not his master repulse and chastise this insolence?

'I guess you don't know each other,' said Taffany. 'Say, Monsieur de Valmore, here's a friend of mine, Mr. Ker-Orr from London.'

My enemy pulled himself together as though the different parts of his body all wanted to leap away in different directions, and he found it all he could do to prevent such disintegration. An attempt at a bow appeared as a chaotic movement, the various parts of his body could not come together for it. It had met other movements on the way, and never became a bow at all. An extraordinary confusion beset his body. The beginning for a score of actions ran over it blindly and disappeared.

'Guess Mr de Valmore ain't quite comfortable in that chair, Morty. Give him yours.'

Then in this chaotic and unusual state he was hustled from one chair to the other, his muffled expostulations being in french, I noticed.

His racial instinct was undergoing the severest revolution it had yet known. An incarnation of sacred America herself had commanded him to take me to his bosom. And, as the scope of my victory dawned upon him, his personal mortification assumed the proportions of a national calamity. For the first time since the sealing of his citizenship he felt that he was only a Frenchman from the Midi – hardly as near an American, in point of fact, as is even a poor god-forsaken Britisher.

The Soldier of Humour is chivalrous, though implacable. I merely drank a bottle of champagne at his expense; made Don Pedro and his orchestra perform three extras, all made up of the most intensely national english light comedy music. Taffany, for whom Monsieur de Valmore entertained the maximum of respect, held him solemnly for some time with a detailed and fabulous enumeration of my virtues. Before long I withdrew with my forces to riot in barbarous triumph at my friends' hotel for the rest of the evening.

During the next two days I on several occasions visited the battlefield, but Monsieur de Valmore had vanished. His disappearance alone would have been sufficient to tell me that my visit to Spain was terminated. And in fact two days later I left Pontaisandra with the Americans, parting with them at Tuy, and myself continuing on the Leon–San Sebastian route back to France, and eventually to Paris. The important letter which I had been expecting had arrived at last and contained most unexpected news. My presence was required, I learnt, in Budapest.

Arrived at Bayonne, I left the railway station with what people generally regard as a premonition. It was nothing of course but the usual mechanical working of inference within the fancy. It was already night-time. Stepping rapidly across the square, I hurried down the hall-way of the Fonda del Mundo. Turning brusquely and directly into the dining-room of the inn I gazed round me almost shocked not to find what I now associated with that particular scene. Although Monsieur de Valmore had not been there to greet me, as good or better than his presence seemed to be attending me on my withdrawal from Spain. I still heard in this naked little room, as the wash of the sea in the shell, the echo of the first whisperings of his weird displeasure. Next day I arrived in Paris, my spanish nightmare shuffled off long before I reached that humdrum spot.

# Beau Séjour

On arrival at *Beau Séjour*, in the country between Roznoën and the littoral, I was taken by the proprietress, Mademoiselle Péronnette, for a 'Pole.'* She received my first payment with a smile. At the time I did not understand it. I believe that she was preparing to make a great favourite of me.

The 'Poles,' who in this case were mostly Little Russians, Finns and Germans, sat at the table d'hôte, at the head of the table. They smoked large pipes and were served first. They took the lion's share. If it was a chicken they stripped it, and left only the legs and bones for the rest of the company. This was a turbulent community. The quarrels of the permanent boarders with Mademoiselle Péronnette affected the quality of the food that came to the table.

The master-spirit was a man named Zoborov. This is probably not the way to spell it. I never saw it written. That is what I called him, and he answered to it when I said it. So the sound must have been true enough, though as I have written it down possibly no russian eye would recognize it.

This man was a discontented 'Pole.' He always spoke against the 'Polonais,' I noticed, I could not make out why. Especially to me he would speak with great contempt of all people of that sort. But he also spoke harshly of Mademoiselle Péronnette and her less important partner, Mademoiselle Maraude. He was constantly stirring up his fellow pensionnaires against them.

*An account of the 'Pole' will be found at the end of this story. The 'Pole' is a national variety of Pension-sponger, confined as far as I know to France, and to the period preceding the Russian Revolution.

Zoborov at first sight was a perfect 'Pole.' He was exceedingly quiet. He wandered stealthily about and yawned as a cat does. Sometimes he would get up with an abrupt intensity, like a cat, and walk steadily, strongly and rhythmically away out of sight. He may have had a date with another 'Pole,' of course, or have wanted exercise. But he certainly did succeed in conveying in a truly polesque manner that it was a more mysterious thing that had disturbed him. Every one has experienced those attractive calls that lead people to make impulsive visits, which result in some occurrence or meeting that, looking back on it, seems to have lain behind the impulse. Scenes and places, at least other things than men, an empty seashore, an old horse tethered in a field, some cavernous armorican lane, under some special aspect and mood, had perhaps the power of drawing these strange creatures towards it, as though it had something to impart. Yet as far as Zoborov was concerned, although certainly he succeeded in conveying the correct sensation at the time, when you thought about it afterwards you felt you had been deceived. The date or exercise seemed more likely in retrospect than the mysterious messages from arrangements of objects, or the attractive electrical dreaming of landscapes. In the truth-telling mind of after-the-event this crafty and turbulent personage was more readily associated with man-traps and human interests than with natural magic.

Zoborov was touchy, and he affected to be more so and in a different sense than actually he was. He wished you to receive a very powerful impression of his *independence*. To effect this he put himself to some pains. First he attempted to hypnotize you with his isolation. Yet everything about him proved 'the need of a world of men' for him. Are not people more apt to bestow things on a person who is likely to spurn them? you suspected him of reflecting: his gesture of spurning imaginary things recurred very often. So you gradually would get a notion of the sort of advantageous position he coveted in your mind.

After dinner in conversing with you he always spoke in a hoarse whisper, or muttered in an affected bass. He scarcely parted his lips, often whistling his words through his teeth inside them. Whether he were telling you what a hypocrite Mademoiselle Péronnette was, or, to give you a bit of romance and savagery, were describing how the Caucasians ride standing on their horses, and become so exultant that they fling their knives up in the air and catch them – he never became audible to any one but you. He had a shock of dark hair, was dark-skinned, his eyes seemed to indicate drugs and advertised a profound exhaustion. He had the smell of a tropical plant: the vegetation of his body was probably strong and rank. Through affecting not to notice people, to be absorbed in his own very important thoughts, or the paper or the book he was reading, the contraction of his eyebrows had become permanent. He squinted slightly. He had bow-legs and protruding ears and informed me that he suffered from haemorrhoids. His breath stank; but as he never opened his mouth more than he could help, this concerned only himself.

He was a great raconteur. He had a strongly marked habit of imitating his own imitations. In telling a story in which he figured (his stories were all designed to prove his independence) he had a colourless formula for his interlocutor. A gruff, half-blustering tone was always used to represent himself. Gradually these two voices had coalesced and had become his normal conversational voice. He was short, thick-set and muscular. His physical strength must have been considerable. He exploited it in various ways. It was a confirmation of his independence. His 'inferiority complex' brought forward his tremendous chest, when threatened, with above it his cat-like face seeming to quizz, threaten and go to sleep all at once, with his mouth drawn to a point, in a purring position. His opponent would be in doubt as to whether he was going to hit him, laugh or sneeze.

French visitors he always made up to. Seeing him with the friend of the moment, talking confidentially apart, making signs to him at table, you would have supposed him an exclusive, solitary man, who 'did not make friends easily.' Aloofness towards the rest of the company was always maintained. You would not guess that he knew them except to nod to. When about to take up with a new-comer, his manner became more severe than ever, his aloofness deepened. As he passed the salt to him, he scarcely showed any sign of realizing what he was doing, or that he had a neighbour at all. His voice became gruffer. As though forcing himself to come out of himself and behave with decent neighbourliness, he would show the new guest a stiff politeness.

He was from twenty-five to thirty years old. In women he took no interest, I think, and disliked exceedingly Mademoiselle Péronnette and Mademoiselle Maraude. I thought he was a eunuch. No homosexuality was evident. He often spoke of a friend of his, a Russian like himself. This man was exceedingly independent: he was also prodigiously strong; far stronger than Zoborov. This person's qualities he regarded as his own, however, and he used them as such. The shadowy figure of this gigantic friend seemed indeed superimposed upon Zoborov's own form and spirit. You divined an eighth of an inch on all sides of the contour of his biceps and pectorals, another contour – the visionary contour of this friend's even larger muscles. And beyond even the sublime and frowning pinnacles of his own independence, the still loftier summits of his friend's pride, of a piece with his.

His friend was in the Foreign Legion. In recent fighting with the Moors he had displayed unusual powers of resistance. Because of his extraordinary strength he was compelled on the march to carry several of his comrades' rifles in addition to his own. Zoborov would read his african letters apart, with an air of absorbed and tender communion, seeking to awaken one's jealousy. He repeated long dialogues between his friend and himself. When it came to his friend's turn to speak, he would puff his chest out, and draw himself up, until the penumbra of visionary and supernatural flesh that always accompanied him was almost filled by his own dilated person. He would assume a debonair recklessness of manner, his moustaches would flaunt upwards over his laughing mouth, and even the sombre character of his teeth and his strong breath would be momentarily forgotten. His gestures would be those of an open-handed and condescending prince. He would ostentatiously make use of the personal pronoun 'thou' (in his french it had a finicky lisping sound), to make one eager to get on such terms with him oneself.

I never got on those terms with him. One day he remained at table after the others had left. He was waiting to be asked to go for a walk. Off my guard, I betrayed the fact that I had noticed this. Several such incidents occurred, and he became less friendly.

Many of Zoborov's tales had to do with Jews. The word 'juif' with him appeared as a long, juicy sound, 'jouiive,' into which, sleepily blinking his eyes, he injected much indolent contempt. When he used it he made a particular face – sleepy, faraway, heavy-lidded, allowing his almost immobile mouth to flower rather dirtily, drawn down to a peculiarly feline point. He mentioned Jews so often that I wondered if he were perhaps a Jew. On this point I never came to any definite conclusion.

My second night at *Beau Séjour* there was a scene outside my room, which I witnessed. My bedroom was opposite that of Mademoiselle Péronnette. Hearing the shattering report of a door and sounds of heavy breathing, I got up and looked out.

'Va-t'en! Tu n'es-qu'un vaurien! Va-t'en! Tu m'entends? Tu m'agaces! Va-t'en!'

The voice of the proprietress clappered behind her locked door. A long white black-topped lathe was contorted against it. It was the most spoilt of all our 'Poles,' a german giant, now quite naked. With his bare arms and shoulders he strained against the wood. As I appeared he turned round enquiring breathlessly with farcical fierceness:

'Faurien! Faurien! Elle m'abelle faurien!'

His eyes blazed above a black-bearded grin, with clownesque incandescence. He was black and white, dazzling skin and black patches of hair alternating. His thin knees were unsteady, his hands were hanging in limp expostulation, his grin of protest wandered in an aimless circle, with me for centre.

'Faurien,' he repeated.

'Veux-tu t'en aller? Je te défends de faire un scandale, tu entends,

Charles? Va-t'en!' The voice of the proprietress energetically rattled on the other side of the door.

'Sgantal?' he asked helplessly and incredulously, passing one hand slowly in front of his body, with heavy facetious prudery. The floor boards groaned to the right, a stumpy figure in stocking feet, but otherwise clothed, emerged in assyrian profile, in a wrestling attitude, flat hands extended, rolling with professional hesitation, with factitious rudeness seized the emaciated nudity of the german giant beneath the waist, then disappeared with him bodily down the passage to the left. It was Zoborov in action. The word 'faurien' came escaping out of the dark in a muzzy whistle, while the thump thump of the stocking feet receded. I closed the door.

This gave me an insight at once into the inner social workings of the Pension. Carl had slept with the proprietress from the start, but that was not among Zoborov's accomplishments. He intrigued in complete detachment. Carl and he never clashed, they both sucked up to each other.

Next morning I had a look at Carl. He was about six foot two, with a high, narrow, baldish black head and long black beard. His clothes hung like a sack on his thin body. He gave me an acid grin. Zoborov frowned, blinked stupidly in front of him, and swallowed his coffee with loud, deep-chested relish. He then wiped his moustache slowly, rose, and stamped heavily out into the garden in his sabots, rolling, husky peasant fashion, from side to side. Carl's lank black hair curled in a ridge low on his neck: a deep smooth brow surmounted the settled unintelligent mockery of the rest of his face. The general effect was that of an exotic, oily, south-german Royal Academician. He had an italian name. Essaying a little conversation, I found him surly.

A week later Zoborov, sitting in the orchard with his back against a tree, whittling a stick, obliged me with his views of Carl.

'Where did you take him?' I said, referring to the night scene.

Zoborov knitted his brows and muttered in his most rough and blustering voice:

'Oh, he was drunk. I just threw him on his bed, and told him to shut his head and go to sleep. He bores me, Carl does.'

'He's on good terms with Mademoiselle Péronnette?'

'Is he? I don't know if he is now. He was. She was angry with him that night because she'd found him with the bonne, in the bonne's room. That's why Maria left – the little bonne that waited at table when you came. He sleeps with all the bonnes.'

'I slept with the new one last night,' I said.

He looked up quickly, wrinkling his eyes, and puffed out in his sturdiest, heartiest bass, puffed through his closed teeth, that is, in his spluttering buzz:

'Did you? With Antoinette? She's rather a pretty girl. But all bonnes are dirty!' He expressed distaste with his lips. 'A girl who works as a bonne never has time to wash. Maria *stank*. There's no harm in his sleeping with the bonnes. But truly he gets so drunk, too drunk – all the time. He's engaged to Mademoiselle Péronnette, you know.' He laughed softly, gently fluttering his moustaches, heaving up his square protruding chest, and making a gruff rumble in it.

'Engaged – what is that?'

'Why, engaged to be married.' He laughed, throwing his eyes coquettishly up. 'He *was*. I don't know if they're still supposed to be. *He* says she's always trying to marry him. Last year she lent him some money and they became engaged.' He never raised his eyes, except to laugh, and went on whittling the stick.

'She paid him for the engagement?' I said at last.

'Ye-es!' he drawled, with soft shaking chuckles. 'And that's all she'll ever get out of old Carl! – But I don't think she wants to marry him now. I think she wants the money back. I wish he'd take himself off!' He frowned and became gruff. 'He's a good fellow all right, but he's always making scandals. I *think* – he wants her to lend him more money. That's what I think he wants. All these scandals – they disgust me, both of them. I'd leave here to-morrow if I had any money to get out with.'

He hooked his eyebrows down in a calm and formal frown, and surveyed his finger nails. They were short and thick. Putting down the stick he turned his attention to them. He chipped indolently at their edges, then bit the corners off.

I was frequently the witness of quarrels between Carl and Mademoiselle Péronnette. A few days after my conversation in the orchard I entered the kitchen of the Pension, but noticing that Carl was holding Mademoiselle Péronnette by the throat, and was banging her head on the kitchen table, I withdrew. As I closed the door I heard Mademoiselle Péronnette, as I supposed, crash upon the kitchen floor. Dull sounds that were probably kicks followed, and I could hear Carl roaring, 'Gourte! Zale gourte!' When enraged he always made use of the word *gourte*. It was, I think, a corruption of the french word *gourd*, which means a calabash.

As I was leaving Antoinette's bedroom one night I thought I noticed something pale moving in the shadow of the staircase. Five minutes afterwards I returned to her room to remind her to wake me early, and as I got outside I heard voices. She was saying, 'Allez-vous-en, Charles! Non, je ne *veux* pas! J'ai sommeil! Laisse-moi tranquille. Non!' There was a scuffling and creaking of the bed, accompanied by a persuasive and wheedling rumble that I recognized as belonging to Carl.

Then suddenly there was a violent commotion, Antoinette's voice exploded in harsh breton-french:

'Sacré *garce*, fiche-moi donc la paix, veux-tu! *Laisse*-moi tranquil, nom de dieu de dieu –'

The door flew open and Carl, quite naked again, came hotly flopping into my arms, his usual grin opening his beard and suffusing his eyes. He lay in my arms a moment grinning, then stood up.

'Nothing doing to-night?' I said. I was going back to my room when a furious form brushed past me, and I heard a violent slap, followed by the screaming voice of our proprietress:

'Ah, satyr, tu couches avec les bonnes? Tu ne peux pas laisser les femmes tranquilles la nuit, sale bête? C'est ainsi que tu crois toujours débaucher les bonnes après avoir trahi la patronne, espèce de salopris! Prends ça pour ton rhume – et ça. Fumier! Oui, sauve-toi, sale bête!'

The doors began opening along the passage: a few timid little slav pensionnaires and a couple of Parisians began appearing in their openings; I could see the unsteady nudity of Carl staggering beneath slaps that resounded in him, as though she had been striking a hollow column. I hastened to my room. A moment later the precipitate tread of Zoborov passed my door *en route* for the scene of the encounter. The screaming voice of Antoinette then made itself heard amongst the others. I went to my door: I was glad to hear that Antoinette was giving Mademoiselle Péronnette more than she was receiving, delivering herself of some trenchant reflections on the standard of the *mœurs* obtaining in the *Beau Séjour*, on employers that it was impossible to respect, seeing that they were not respectable, and I then once more closed my door. A few moments later Mademoiselle Péronnette's door crashed, the other doors quietly closed, the returning tread of Zoborov passed my wall. So that night's events terminated.

The two Parisians on our landing left next morning to seek more respectable quarters, and Antoinette the same. Carl was at breakfast as usual. He grinned at me when I sat down. Zoborov frowned at the table, drank his coffee loudly, rose, pushing his chair back and standing for a moment in a twisted overbalanced posture, then, his sabots falling heavily on the parquet floor, his body rolling with the movement of a husky peasant, he went out of the window into the garden. The food grew worse. Two days later I told the proprietress that I was leaving.

Next night I was sitting in the kitchen reading *l' Éclair de l' Ouest*. Mademoiselle Péronnette and Mademoiselle Maraude were sitting near the lamp on the kitchen table and mending the socks of several pensionnaires, when Carl came in at the door, shouted:

'Gourte! Brend za bour don rhume!' . . . and fired three shots from a large revolver at Mademoiselle Péronnette. Two prolonged screams rose from the women, rising and falling through a diapason at each fresh shot. Mademoiselle Péronnette fell to the floor. Carl withdrew. Mademoiselle Péronnette slowly rose from the floor, her hands trembling, and burst into tears. A little Pole who had been curled up asleep on the bench by the fire, and who no doubt had escaped Carl's notice, got up, and limped towards the table. He had been hit in the calf by a bullet. The women had not been hit, and they rolled up his trousers with execrations of the 'bandit,' Carl, and washed and dressed the wound, which was superficial. I went to look for Zoborov, whose presence I thought was probably required. I found him at the bottom of the orchard with two other 'Poles,' in the moonlight, playing a flute. As he lifted his little finger from a stop and released a shrill squeak, he raised one eyebrow, which he lowered again when, raising another finger, he produced a lower note. I sat down beside them. Zoborov finished the tune he was playing. His companions lay at right angles to each other, their heads propped on their bent forearms.

'Carl has broken out,' I said.

'Ah. He is always doing that,' Zoborov said.

'He's been firing a pistol at the proprietress.'

Zoborov lifted one eyebrow, as he had when he released the squeak on the flute.

'That doesn't surprise me,' he said.

'No one was hurt except a pensionnaire, who was asleep at the time. He hit him in the calf.'

'Who was it?'

'I don't know his name.'

Zoborov turned in my direction, and falling down on his side, propped his head like the other two 'Poles,' on his bent forearm, while he puffed out his heavy chest. His voice became rough and deep.

'Écoutez!' he began, with the sound like a voice blowing in a comb covered with tissue paper. 'Écoutez, mon ami. – This Pension will never be quiet until that imbecile Carl leaves. He's not a bad fellow (il n'est pas mauvais camarade), he's a bad hat (il est mauvais sujet). You understand, he's not straight about money. He's a chap with money, his father's a rich brewer. A brewer, yes, my friend,

53

you may laugh! It's not without its humour. He'd have to brew a lot to satisfy old Carl! He is an inveterate boozer. Why? Why does a man drink so much as that? Why?' His voice assumed the russian sing-song of pathetic enquiry, the fine gnat-like voice rapidly ascending and dropping again in an exhausted complaint. 'Because he is a german brute! That is the reason. He thinks because his father is a rich brewer that people should give him drink for nothing – it is a strange form of reasoning! He is always dissatisfied. – Now he has shot a pensionnaire. It is not the first time that he has fired at Mademoiselle Péronnette. But he never hits her! He doesn't want to hit her. He just fires off his revolver to make her excited! Then he tries to borrow more money!'

The three of them now remained quite immobile, stretched out on the dewy grass in different directions. I got up. With a gruff and blustering sigh, Zoborov exclaimed:

'Ah yes, my friend, that is how it is!'

I walked back to the house. As I passed the kitchen, I heard a great deal of noise, and went in.

The little shot pensionnaire was once more back on the bench, by the fire, with his bare leg, bandaged, stretched out horizontally in front of him, his two hands behind his head. At the table sat Carl, his face buried in a large handkerchief, which he held against his forehead, his shoulders heaving. A great volume of sound rose from him, a rhythmical bellowing of grief.

Mademoiselle Péronnette was standing a few yards away from him, a denunciatory forefinger stabbing the air in the direction of his convulsions.

'There he sits, the wretch. Mon dieu, he is a pretty sight! And to reflect that that is a fellow of good family, who comes from a home cracking with every luxury! Ça fait pitié! – Is there anything I haven't done for you, Charles? Say, Charles, can you deny I have done all a woman can?' she vociferated. 'I have given you my youth' (tremblingly and tenderly), 'my beauty! – I have shamed myself. I have offered myself to the saucy scorn of mere bonnes, I have made every sacrifice a woman can make! With what result I should like to know? Ah yes, you may well hide your face! You outrage me at every moment, you take my last halfpenny, and when you have soaked yourself in a neighbouring saloon, you come back here and debauch my bonnes! Any dirty peasant girl serves your turn. Is not that true, Charles? Answer! Deny it if you dare! That is what you do! That is how you repay all my kindness!'

Observing my presence, she turned expansively towards me.

'Tenez, ce monsieur-là peut te le dire, il a été le témoin de tes indignes caprices. – Had you not, sir, occasion to observe this ruffian, as naked as he came into the world, issuing from the bedroom of the good-for-nothing harlot, Antoinette? Is not that the case, sir? Without a stitch of clothing, this incontinent ruffian—'

The french tongue, with its prolix dignity for such occasions, clamoured on. As I was drawn into the discussion, a section of Carl's face appeared from behind the handkerchief, enough to free the tail of his eye for an examination of that part of the kitchen that was behind him. Our boche exhibitionist ascertained who it was had witnessed his last nocturnal contretemps. He thrust his head back deeper into the handkerchief. A roar of mingled disapproval and grief broke from him.

'Ah yes, now you suffer! But you never consider how you have made me suffer!'

But her discourse now took a new direction.

'I don't say, Charles, that you are alone – there are others who are even more guilty than you. I could name them if I wished! There is that dirty sneaking individual Zoborov, for instance. Ah, how he irritates me, that man! He is an extremely treacherous personage, that! *I* have heard the things he says about me. He thinks I don't know. I know very well. I am informed of all his manœuvres. *That* is the guilty party in this affair. He is the person who poisons the air of this establishment! I would get rid of him tomorrow if I could! Yes, Charles, I know that you, in comparison with such a crapulous individual as that Zoborov, are at least frank. At least you are a gentleman, a man of good family, accustomed to live in ease – what do I say, in luxury: and your faults are the faults of your station. *Tu es un fils de papa*, mon pauvre garçon – you are a spoilt darling. You are not a *dirty moujik*, like that Zoborov!'

I noticed at this point, the face of Zoborov peering in at the window with his gascon frown, his one hooked-down and angrily-anchored eyebrow, and fluffy cavalier moustache, above his steady inscrutable feline pout. Mademoiselle Péronnette observed him at the same moment.

'Yes, I see you, sir! *Toujours aux écoutes!* Always eavesdropping! What eavesdroppers hear of themselves they deserve to hear. I hope you are satisfied, that's all I can say!'

'La ferme! La ferme!' Zoborov's gruff railing voice puffed in at the window. He made his hand into a duck's bill, and worked it up and down to make it quack, as he turned away.

'He insults me, you know, that dirty *type*, he treats me as though I were the last of creatures! Yet what is he? He is nothing but a dirty moujik! He actually boasts of it. He's not a credit to the house – you should see the Parisians looking at him. He has driven pension-naires away with his rudeness – and his dirt! He doesn't mind what he says. Then he abuses me to *everybody*, from morning till night. C'est une mauvaise langue!'

'En effet!' Mademoiselle Maraude agreed. 'He has a bad tongue. He does this house no good.'

The 'Pole' with the bandaged leg began giggling. The two women turned to him.

'What is it, mon petit? Is your leg hurting you?'

Carl's head had sunk upon the table. The heat inside the hand-kerchief, the effects of the brandy he had been drinking, and the constant music of Mademoiselle Péronnette's voice, had overcome him. Now prolonged and congested snores rose from him, one especially vicious and intense crescendo making Mademoiselle Péronnette, who was examining the bandage on the leg of the pensionnaire, jump.

'Mon dieu!' she said. 'I wondered whatever it was.' The door opened, and Zoborov entered, advancing down the kitchen with as much noise as he could extract from his weight, his clumsiness, and the size of his sabots.

As he came, expanding his chest and speaking in his deepest voice, he said, bluff and 'proletarian':

'Écoutez, Mademoiselle Péronnette! I don't like the way you talk about me. You are absurd! What have I done to cause you to speak about me like that? I spend half my time keeping the peace between you and Carl; and when anything happens you turn on me! You are not reasonable!'

He spoke in an indolent sing-song, his eyes half closed, scarcely moving his lips, and talking through his teeth. He knelt down beside his wounded compatriot and put his hand gently upon his bandaged leg, speaking to him in russian.

'I only say what I know, sir!' Mademoiselle Péronnette hotly replied.

Zoborov continued speaking in russian to the injured pensionnaire, who replied in accents of mild musical protest.

'Your intrigues are notorious! You are always making mischief. I detest you, and wish you had never entered this house!'

Zoborov had unwound the bandage. He rose with a face of frowning indignation.

'Écoutez, Mademoiselle! If instead of amusing yourself by blowing off steam in that way, you did something for this poor chap who has just been injured through no fault of his own, you would be showing yourself more humane, yes, more humane! Why have you not at once put him to bed? He should see a doctor. His wound is in a dangerous condition! If it is not attended to blood-poisoning will set in.'

Mademoiselle Péronnette faced him, eye flashing; Mademoiselle Maraude had risen and moved towards the injured figure.

'It isn't true!' Mademoiselle Maraude said. 'He is not seriously hurt –'

'No, you are lying, Zoborov! He has been attended to,' Mademoiselle Péronnette said. 'It doesn't hurt, does it, mon petit?' she appealed coaxingly. 'It was nothing but a scratch, was it? – No. It was nothing but a scratch.'

'For a scratch there's a good deal of blood,' Zoborov said. 'Fetch a basin and some hot water. I will go for a doctor.'

The women looked at each other.

'A doctor? Why? You must be off your head! There's no occasion for a doctor! Do you wish for a doctor, mon petit?'

The injured pensionnaire smiled indulgently, with an amused expression, as though an elder taking part in a children's game, and shook his head.

'No. He does not wish for a doctor. Of course he doesn't! He ought to know best himself.'

'Écoutez!' said Zoborov sleepily. 'It's for your sake, Mademoiselle Péronnette, as much as his— You don't want anything to happen to him? No. These wounds are dangerous. You should get a doctor.'

Mademoiselle Péronnette stared at him in impotent hatred. She turned quickly to Mademoiselle Maraude, and said:

'Run quickly, Marie, and get some ice – down at Cornic's.'

Zoborov started rolling with ungainly speed towards the door, saying over his shoulder, 'I will go. I shall be back in a few minutes. Bathe his leg.'

As the door closed Mademoiselle Péronnette stared glassily at Mademoiselle Maraude.

'Quel homme! Quel homme! Mon dieu, quel malhonnête individu que celui-là! You saw how he put the blame on us? any one would think that we had neglected this poor boy here. My god, what a man!'

An obscene and penetrating trumpeting rose from the prostrate Carl – it rose shrieking and strong, sank to a purr, then rose again louder and stronger, sank to a gurgling purr again, then rose to a brazen crow, higher and higher.

Mademoiselle Péronnette put her fingers in her ears. 'My god, my god! As though it were not enough to have caused all this trouble –'

She sprang over, and seizing Carl by the shoulders shook him nervously.

'Go and sleep off your booze somewhere else – do you hear? Be off! Get out! Allez – vite! Marchez! Assez, assez! Fiche-moi la paix! *Enfin!*'

Carl rose unsteadily, a malevolent eye fixed on Mademoiselle Péronnette, and staggered out of the room. Mademoiselle Péronnette drew Mademoiselle Maraude aside, and began whispering energetically to her. I withdrew.

That night the bedroom door of the proprietress opened and shut it seemed incessantly. Between four and five, as it was getting light, I woke and heard a scuffle in the passage. The voice of Mademoiselle Péronnette insisted in a juicy whisper:

'Dis, Charles, tu m'aimes? M'aimes-tu, chéri? Dis!'

A sickly rumble came in response. Then more scuffling. Sucking and patting sounds and the signs of disordered respiration, with occasional rumbles, continued for some time. I got down to the bottom of the bed and turned the key in the door. I expected our german exhibitionist to enter my room at any moment with the nude form of Mademoiselle Péronnette in his arms, and perhaps edify me with the final phases of his heavy adieus. The sound of the key in the lock cut short whatever it was, and gradually the sounds ceased.

Next evening, at the request of Carl, we all collected in the kitchen for a little celebration. Whether it was to mark the rupture of the engagement, an approaching marriage, or what, was not made clear to us. Carl, with the courtliness of the South of Germany, his thin academic black locks and lengthy beard conferring the air of a function upon the scene, was very attentive to Mademoiselle Péronnette.

Zoborov was the gallant moujik. He toasted, with rough plebeian humour, the happy couple.

'Aux deux tourtereaux!' he rolled bluffly out, lifting his glass, and rolling the r's of 'tourtereau' with a rich russian intensity. Placing his heavy sinewy brown hand before his mouth he whispered to me:

'Old Carl has relieved her of a bit more of her dough!' He shook his shoulders and gurgled in the bass.

'Do you think that's it?'

'*Zurement!*' he lisped. 'He's got the secret of the safe! He knows the combination!' He chuckled, bawdy and bluff. 'Old Carl will clean her out, you see.'

'He's an exceedingly noisy burglar. He woke me up last night in the course of his operations.'

Zoborov chuckled contentedly.

'He's mad!' he said. 'Still, he gets what he goes for. Good luck to him, I say.'

'Is Mademoiselle Péronnette rich?' I asked him. He squinted and hooked his left eyebrow down, then burst out laughing and looked in my face.

'I don't know,' he said. 'I shouldn't think so. Have you seen the safe?' he laughed again.

'No.'

'She has the safe in her bedroom. Carl rattles it when he's very screwed. Once he tried to carry it out of the room.' Zoborov laughed with his sly shaking of his big diaphragm. The recollection of this event tickled him. Then he said to me: 'If you ask me, all she's got is in that safe, that's what I think.'

A piano had been brought in. A pensionnaire was playing the 'Blue Danube.'

Carl and Mademoiselle Péronnette danced. She was a big woman, about thirty. Her empty energetic face was pretty, but rather dully and evenly laid out. Her back when *en fête* was a long serpentine blank with an embroidered spine. When she got up to dance she held herself forward, bare arms hanging on either side, two big meaty handles, and she undulated her *nuque* and back while she drew her mouth down into the tense bow of an affected kiss. While she held her croupe out stiffly in the rear, in muscular prominence, her eyes burnt at you with traditional gallic gallantry, her eyebrows arched in bland acceptance (a static '*Mais oui, si vous voulez!*') of french sex-convention, the general effect intended to be 'witty' and sugges-tive, without vulgarity. I was very much disgusted by her for my part: what she suggested to me was something like a mad butcher, who had put a piece of bright material over a carcase of pork or mutton, and then started to ogle his customers, owing to a sudden shuffling in his mind of the respective appetites. Carl on this occasion behaved like the hallucinated customer of such a pantomime, who, come into the shop, had entered into the spirit of the demented butcher, and proceeded to waltz with his sex-promoted food. The stupid madness, or commonplace wildness, that always shone in his eyes was at full blast as he jolted uncouthly hither and thither, while the proprietress undulated and crackled in complete independence, held roughly in place merely by his two tentacles.

With the exception of Mademoiselle Maraude and the bonne amie of a parisian schoolmaster on his vacation, all the guests were men. They danced together timidly and clumsily; Zoborov, frowning and squinting, stamped over to the schoolmaster's girl, and with a cross gruff hauteur invited her to dance. He rolled his painful proletarian weight once or twice round the room. The 'Blue Danube' rolled on; Carl poured appreciative oily light into Mademoiselle Péronnette's eyes, she redoubled her lascivious fluxions, until Carl, having exhausted all the superlatives of the language of the eyes, cut short their rhythmical advance and, becoming immobile in the middle of the room, clasped her in his arms, where she hung like a dying wasp, Carl devouring with much movement the lower part of her face, canted up with abandon. The pensionnaire at the piano broke into a cossack dance. Zoborov, who had handed the lady back to her schoolmaster again, with ceremony, and had returned to sit at my side, now rose and performed a series of gargantuan movements up and down the kitchen (flinging the less weighty couples to left and right) studiously devoid of any element of grace or skill. At regular intervals he stamped in his sabots and uttered a few gruff cries, while the pianist trumped upon the piano. Then, head back and his little moustache waving above his mouth, he trundled down the room, with a knees-up gymnastic movement. Satisfied that he had betrayed nothing but the completest barbaric uncouthness, he resumed his seat, grinning gravely at me.

His compatriots applauded, the piano stopped.

'That is a *typical* dance, mon ami, of the Don Cossacks!' he said, puffing a little. '*Typical*' (Tee-peek!), in his slow mincing french. In using this word his attitude was that I had a well-known curiosity about everything cossack, and that now, by the purest chance, I had heard a characteristic Don dance, and seen it interpreted with a racy savagery that only a Cossack could convey: and that, at the same time, he, Zoborov, had been astonished, he was bound to admit, at this happening in such an informative way as it had. In fine, I was lucky.

'Typical!' he said again. 'But I am out of practice.' Then he dropped the subject. The piano struck up again, with a contemporary Berlin dance-tune, and the floor was soon full of bobbing shapes, attempting to time their feet to the music. Long before the end the forms of Carl and Mademoiselle Péronnette, head and shoulders above the rest of the company, were transfixed in the centre of the room, Carl like a lanky black spider, always devouring but never making an end of his meal provided by the palpitating wasp in his arms while the others bobbed on gently around them.

Zoborov fixed his frown of quizzical reproof upon them, and stuttered thickly in the beard that was not there:

'Les deux tourrterreaux!'

The cider was of good quality, and it was plentiful, being drawn from a large cask. Carl and Mademoiselle Péronnette in the intervals of the music remained in a deep embrace by the side of the fire. At length, when the fête had been in progress for perhaps half an hour, they withdrew, so coiled about one another that they experienced some difficulty in getting out of the door.

Zoborov drew my attention to their departure.

'The two doves are going to their nest to lie down for a little while!' he remarked, with the bluff rolling jocosity of Zoborov celebrating.

Zoborov now took charge, and the party became all-russian. He fetched his flute and another pensionnaire had an accordion: a concert of russian popular music began. The Volga Boat Song was chorally rendered, with Zoborov beating time.

At the end of a quarter of an hour Mademoiselle Péronnette and Carl reappeared. Carl was pale and Mademoiselle Péronnette very red. She affected to fan herself. Carl's monotonous grin attached itself to the faces of the company with its unfailing brutal confession, hang-dog to stress its obscene message, while his sleek and shining black hair curled venerably behind, where a hasty brush and comb had arranged it.

'Qu'il fait *chaud*!' exclaimed Mademoiselle Péronnette, and drew down a window.

Zoborov took no notice of the reappearance of the turtle doves, but continued his concert. After a while Mademoiselle Péronnette showed signs of impatience. She got up, and advancing towards her choir of pensionnaires, who were gathered round the fire in a half-circle, she exclaimed:

'What do you say to another dance, now, my friends? Let somebody play the piano. Your russian music is very pretty but it is so sad. It always makes me sad. Let us have something more cheerful.'

A pensionnaire got up and went to the piano. Zoborov remained near the fire. The dance began half-heartedly. Zoborov went on playing the flute to himself, his little peaked mouth drawn down to the mouthpiece, his little finger remaining erect while he sampled the feeble sound.

The 'Poles' of the Pension sat and gazed, like a group of monks bowed down with many vows, at their proprietress and her german lover, while one of their number made music for this voluptuous couple, so strangely different from them. Their leader, Zoborov, continued to draw a few notes out of his flute, the skeleton of a melancholy air. Then two or three rose and embraced each other awkwardly, and began to move round the room, shuffling their feet, out of consideration for their worldly hostess. The parisian schoolmaster and his bonne amie also accommodated.

The kitchen door opened and a group of eleven Russians entered, friends of Zoborov, whom he had invited. They had come over from a neighbouring Pension. He rose and greeted them in impressive gutturals, lurching huskily about. They moved to the bottom of the kitchen, were provided with cups, and drew cider from the barrel. There were now about thirty Russians in the room. A few were dancing languidly. Mademoiselle Péronnette and Carl were indulging in a deep kiss midway in their career. Zoborov, when his visitors had refreshed themselves, crossed the kitchen with them and they left. He was going to show them over the establishment.

'I ask you!' said Mademoiselle Péronnette to Mademoiselle Maraude. 'Quel toupet, quand même!'

Mademoiselle Maraude, to whom I had been talking, gazed after Zoborov.

'En effet!' she said.

'One would think that the house belonged to him!' exclaimed Mademoiselle Péronnette. 'He brings a band of strangers in here— I might not exist at all, for all I am consulted! What an ill-mannered individual!'

'C'est un paysan, quoi!' Mademoiselle Maraude folded her hands in her lap with dignified deliberation. Carl grinned at both of them in turn. Zoborov returned with his friends. Mademoiselle Péronnette burst out:

'Monsieur! One would say that you have forgotten to whom this house belongs! You bring your friends in here and take no more notice of me than if I were the bonne. I am the proprietress of this establishment, gentlemen, and this,' turning to Carl, 'my fiancé, is now my partner.'

Zoborov advanced sleepily towards Mademoiselle Péronnette, a blustering complaint blowing from his mouth as he came, rolling and blowing lazily before him.

'But, Mademoiselle Péronnette. I don't understand you, really. You asked us to invite anybody we liked. – These are good friends of mine. I have just shown them over the house out of kindness to *you*. I was advertising your Pension!'

'I'm quite capable of doing that myself, Monsieur Zoborov!'

'You can't have too much advertisement!' said Zoborov genially.

Carl, who had stood with his dark sheepish grin on his face, gave a loud and unexpected laugh. Quickly raising his arm, he brought his hand down on Zoborov's back. He then kneaded with his long white fingers Zoborov's muscular shoulder.

'Zagré Zoborov!' he exclaimed, shaking with guttural mirth, 'that's capital! I and my partner appoint you as our agent!'

Rolling gently in contact with the hearty mannerisms of his german friend, glancing up quickly with shrewd conciliation, Zoborov blustered out pleasantly:

'Good! I'll be your factor. That's fixed. – Congratulations, old fellow, on your promotion! – What is my salary?'

'We pay by results!' grinned Carl.

'Well, here is one gentleman already who wishes to come round and reside here.'

He pointed to a ragged figure lurking absentmindedly in the rear of the group. 'I shall expect my commission when he moves in.'

Mademoiselle did not like this conversation, and now said:

'I've got quite enough Russians here already. I should be more obliged to you if you found a few Parisians or Americans. That's what I should like.'

'En effet!' said Mademoiselle Maraude distinctly, under her breath.

The tactful pensionnaire at the piano began playing a viennese waltz. Mademoiselle Péronnette, still boiling, drew Carl away, saying:

'C'est trop fort! How that man irritates me, how he irritates me! He's *malin*, also, he is treacherous! He always has an answer, have you noticed? He's never without an answer. He's as rusé as a peasant – but, anyhow, he *is* a peasant, so that's to be expected. How he irritates me!'

Carl rumbled along incoherently beside her, bending down, his arms dangling, his stoop accentuated.

'Oh, he means no harm!' he said.

'Not so. He's a treacherous individual, I tell you!'

Carl put his arm around her waist, and kicking his large flat feet about for a few moments, jerked her into a brisk dance, which with reluctant and angry undulations she followed. As they flew round, in angular sweeps, describing a series of rough squares, a discontented clamour still escaped from her.

A little later the Russians began singing the Volga Boat Song, at the bottom of the room, Zoborov again acting as conductor. Mademoiselle Péronnette put her fingers in her ears.

'Mon dieu, quelle vilaine musique que celle-là!' she exclaimed.

'En effet!' said Mademoiselle Maraude, 'elle n'est pas bien belle!'

'En effet!' said Mademoiselle Péronnette.

Carl was pouring himself out a cognac, and in a blunt and booming bass was intoning the air with the others. Mademoiselle Péronnette left the room. After an interval Carl followed her.

I went over and talked by the fire to the pensionnaire who usually played the piano. Zoborov came up, his chest protruding, and his eyes almost closed, and sat down heavily beside us.

'Well, my friend, what do you think of Mademoiselle Péronnette's new *partner*?' he laughed with a gruff gentle rattle.

'Carl, do you mean?'

'Why yes, Carl!' he again gave way to soft rumbling laughter. 'I wish them luck of their partnership. They are a likely pair, I am bound to say!'

The pianist gazed into the fire.

'What time do you leave in the morning?' he asked.

'At ten.' We talked about Vannes, to which I was going first. He seemed to know Brittany very well. He gave several yawns, gazing over towards his animated crowd of compatriots.

'It's time we went to bed. I shall get rid of this lot,' he said, getting up. 'Come along, my children,' he exclaimed. 'To bed! We're going to bed!'

Several hurried up to him excitedly. They talked for some minutes in russian. Again he raised his voice.

'Let's go to bed, my friends! It's late.'

Mademoiselle Péronnette entered the kitchen. Zoborov, without looking in her direction, put out his hand and switched off the lights. A roar of surprise, laughter and scuffling ensued. The fire lighted up the faces of those sitting near us, and a restless mass beyond.

'Will you be so kind, Monsieur Zoborov, as to put on the lights at once!' the voice of Mademoiselle Péronnette clamoured. 'Monsieur Zoborov, do you hear me? Put on the lights immediately!' Suddenly the lights were switched on again. Mademoiselle Péronnette had done it herself.

'Will you allow me, Monsieur Zoborov, to manage my own house? At last I have had enough of your ways! You are an insolent personage. You are an ill-conditioned individual!'

Zoborov's eyes were now completely closed, apparently with sleep that could not be put off. He blustered plaintively back without opening them:

'But, Mademoiselle! I thought you'd gone to bed! Some one had to get all these people out! I don't understand you. Truly I don't understand you at all! Still, now that you're here I can go to bed! I'm dropping with sleep! Good-night! Good-night!' he sang gruffly as he rolled out, raising his brawny paw several times in farewell.

'Quel homme que celui-là! Quel homme!' said Mademoiselle Péronnette, gazing into the eyes of Mademoiselle Maraude, who had come up.

'En effet!' said Mademoiselle Maraude. 'For a pensionnaire who never pays his "pension," he is a cool hand!'

That night the new partners had their first business disagreement in the bedroom of the proprietress. I heard their voices booming and rattling for a long time before the door opened. It burst open at last. Mademoiselle Péronnette shouted:

'Bring me the fifteen thousand francs you have stolen from me, you indelicate personage, and I will then return you your papers. If your father knew of your conduct what would he think? Do you suppose he would like to think that he had a son who was nothing but a crook? Yes, crook! Our partnership begins from the moment of the first *versement* that you have promised, do you understand? And I require the money at once, you hear? At once!'

A furious rumble came from outside my door.

'No, I have heard that before! Enough! I will hear no more.'

A second rumble answered.

'What, you accuse me of that? You ungrateful individual, you have the face to—'

A long explanatory muted rumble followed.

'Never!' she screamed. 'Never, while I live! I will sign nothing! That's flat! I would never have believed it possible—'

A rumble came from a certain distance down the passage.

'Yes, you had better go! You do well to slink away! But I'll see you don't get far, my bird. You will be held for *escroquerie*, yes, *escroquerie!* at the nearest commissariat! Don't make any mistake!'

A distant note sounded, like the brief flatulence of an elephant. I took it to be 'Gourte!'

'Ah yes, my pretty bird!' vociferated Mademoiselle Péronnette. 'Wait a bit! You may vilify me now. That is the sort of person you are! That I should have expected! But we shall see! We shall see!'

There was no answer. There was a short silence. Mademoiselle Péronnette's door crashed to.

The next morning I left at ten.

A year later I went to the Pardon at Rot. I was sitting amongst the masses of black-clothed figures at a minor wedding, when I saw a figure approaching that appeared familiar. Five peasants were rolling along in their best sabots and finest flat black hats, one in the middle holding the rest with some story he was telling, with heavy dare-devil gestures, as they closed in deferentially upon him as they walked. In the middle one I recognized Zoborov. He was now dressed completely as a breton peasant, in black cloth a half-inch thick, of the costliest manufacture. He rocked from side to side, stumbling at any largish cobble, chest up and out, a double chin descending spoon-shaped and hard beneath upon his short neck, formed as a consequence of the muscular arrangements for the production of his deep bass. His mouth protruded like the mouths of stone masks used for fountains.

As he shouldered his way impressively forward, he made gestures of condescending recognition to left and right, as he caught sight of somebody he knew. His fellow peasants responded with eager salutes or flattering obeisances.

As he caught sight of me he stumbled heartily towards me, his mouth belled out, as though mildly roaring, one large rough hand held back in readiness to grasp mine.

'Why, so you are back again in this part of the country, are you? I am glad to see you! How are you?' he said. 'Come inside, I know the patronne here. I'll get her to give us some good cider.'

We all went in. The patronne saw us and made her way through the crowd at once to Zoborov. Her malignant white face, bald at the sides, as usual with the breton woman, shone with sweat; she came up whining deferentially. With his smiling frown, and the gruff caress of his artificial roar, Zoborov greeted her, and went with her into a parlour next to the kitchen. We followed.

'Bring us three bottles of the best cider, Madame Mordouan,' he said.

'Why yes, Monsieur Zoborov, certainly, immediately,' she said, and obsequiously withdrew.

Zoborov was fatter. The great thickness of the new suiting made him appear very big indeed. The newness and stiffness of the breton fancy dress, the shining broadcloth and velvet, combined with the noticeable filling out of his face, resulted in a disagreeable impression of an obese doll or gigantic barber's block.

'You look prosperous,' I said.

'Do you think so? I'm *en breton* now, you see! When are you coming over to see us at *Beau Séjour*? This gentleman was at *Beau Séjour*,' he said, turning to his friends. 'Are you stopping in the neighbourhood? I'll send the trap over for you.'

'The trap? Have they a trap now?'

'A trap? Why yes, my friend. There have been great changes since you were at *Beau Séjour*!'

'Indeed. Of what kind?'

'Of *every* kind, my friend!'

'How is Mademoiselle Péronnette?'

'Oh, she's gone, long ago!'

'Indeed!'

'Why yes, she and old Carl left soon after you.' He paused a moment. 'I am the proprietor now!'

'You!'

'Why yes, my friend, me! Mademoiselle Péronnette went bust. *Beau Séjour* was sold at auction as it stood. It was not expensive. I took the place on. – Mais oui, mon ami, je suis maintenant le propriétaire!' He seized me by the shoulder, then lightly tapped me there. 'C'est drôle, n'est-ce pas?'

I seemed to hear the voice of Mademoiselle Maraude replying, 'En effet.'

'En effet!' I said.

He offered himself banteringly as the comic proprietor. Fancy Zoborov being the proprietor of a french hotel! He turned, frowning menacingly, however, towards the peasants, and raised his glass with solemn eye. I raised mine. They raised their glasses like a peasant chorus.

'What has become of Carl?' I asked.

'Carl? Oh I don't know what's become of Carl! He's gone to the devil, I should think!'

I saw that I was obtruding other histories upon the same footing with his, into a new world where they had no place. They were a part of the old bad days.

'How are the Russians, "les Polonais"?'

He looked at me for a moment, his eyes closing in his peculiar withdrawal or sleep.

'Oh, I've cleared all that rubbish out! I've got a chic hotel now! It is really quite comfortable. You should come over. I have several Americans, there's an Englishman, Kenyon, do you know him? His father is a celebrated architect. – I only have three Russians there now. I kept them on, poor devils. They help me with the work. Two act as valets. – I know what Russians are, being one myself, you see! I have no wish to go bankrupt like Mademoiselle Péronnette.'

I was rather richly dressed at the time, and I was glad. I ordered for the great 'peasant' and his satellites another bottle of the ceremonious cider.

## *The Pole*

In pre-war Europe, which was also even more the Europe of before the Russian Revolution, a curious sect was established in the watering-places of Brittany. Its members were generally known by the peasants as 'Poles.' The so-called 'Pole' was a russian exile or wandering student, often coming from Poland. The sort that collected in such great numbers in Brittany were probably not politicians, except in the sentimental manner in which all educated Russians before the Revolution were 'radical' and revolutionary. They had banished themselves, for purely literary political reasons, it is likely, rather than been banished. Brittany became a heavenly Siberia for masses of middle-class russian men and women who made 'art' the excuse for a never-ending holiday. They insensibly became a gentle and delightful parasite upon the French. Since the Revolution (it being obvious that they cannot have vast and lucrative estates, which before the Revolution it was easy for them to claim) they have mostly been compelled to work. The Paris taxi-driver of to-day, lolling on the seat of his vehicle, cigarette in mouth, who, without turning round, swiftly moves away when a fare enters his cab, is what in the ancien régime would have been a 'Pole.' If there is a communist revolution in France, this sort of new nomad will move down into Spain perhaps. He provides for the countries of Europe on a very insignificant scale a new version, to-day, of the 'jewish problem.' His indolence, not his activity, of course, makes him a 'problem.'

The pre-war method of migration was this. A 'Pole' in his home in Russia would save up or borrow about ten pounds. He then left his native land for ever, taking a third-class ticket to Brest. This must have become an almost instinctive proceeding. At Brest he was in the heart of the promised land. He would then make the best of his way to a Pension de Famille, already occupied by a phalanstery of 'Poles.' There he would have happily remained until the crack of doom, but for the Bolshevik Revolution. He had reckoned without Lenin, so to speak.

He was usually a 'noble,' very soberly but tactfully dressed. He wore suède gloves: his manners were graceful. The proprietress had probably been warned of his arrival and he was welcome. His first action would be to pay three months' board and lodging in advance; that would also be his last action of that sort. With a simple dignity that was the secret of the 'Pole,' at the end of the trimestre, he remained as the guest of the proprietress. His hostess took this as a matter of course. He henceforth became the regular, unobtrusive, respected inhabitant of the house.

If the proprietress of a Pension de Famille removed her establishment from one part of the country to another, took a larger house, perhaps (to make room for more 'Poles'), her 'Poles' went with her without comment or change in their habits. Just before the war, Mademoiselle T. still sheltered in her magnificent hotel, frequented by wealthy Americans, some of these quiet 'Poles,' who had been with her since the day when she first began hotel-keeping in a small wayside inn. Lunching there you could observe at the foot of the table a group of men of a monastic simplicity of dress and manner, all middle-aged by that time, indeed even venerable in several instances, talking among themselves in a strange and attractive tongue. Mademoiselle T. was an amiable old lady, and these were her domestic gods. Any one treating them with disrespect would have seen the rough side of Mademoiselle T.'s tongue.

Their hosts, I believe, so practical in other ways, became superstitious about these pensive inhabitants of their houses. Some I know would no more have turned out an old and ailing 'Pole' who owed them thirty years' board and lodging, than many people would get rid of an aged and feeble cat.

For the breton peasant, 'Polonais' or 'Pole' sufficed to describe the member of any nation whom he observed leading anything that resembled the unaccountable life of the true slav parasite with which he had originally familiarized himself under the name of 'Pole.'

Few 'Poles,' I think, ever saw the colour of money once this initial pin-money that they brought from Russia was spent. One 'Pole' of my acquaintance did get hold of three pounds by some means, and went to spend a month in Paris. After this outing, his prestige considerably enhanced, he came back and resumed his regular life, glad to be again away from the *siècle* and its metropolitan degradation. In pre-war Paris, 'Poles' were to be met, very much *de passage*, seeing some old friends (*en route* for Brest) for the last time.

A woman opened a smart hotel of about thirty beds not far from *Beau Séjour*. I was going over to see it. She advertised that any artist who would at once take up his quarters there would receive his first six months gratis. Referring to this interesting event in the hearing of a 'Pole,' he told me he had been over there the previous day. He had found no less than twelve 'Poles' already installed, and there was a considerable waiting list. 'If you like to pay you can go there all right,' he said, laughing.

The general explanation given by the 'Pole' of the position in which he found himself, was that his hosts, after six or nine months, were afraid to let him go, for fear of losing their money. He would add that he could confidently rely on more and more deference the longer he stopped, and the larger the amount that he represented in consequence. Ordinary boarders, he would tell you, could count on nothing like so much attention as he could.

That such a state of affairs should ever have occurred, was partly due perhaps to the patriarchal circumstances of the breton agricultural life. This new domestic animal was able to insinuate himself into its midst because of the existence of so many there already. Rich peasants, and this applied to the proprietors of country inns, were accustomed in their households to suffer the presence of a number of poor familiars, cousinly paupers, supernumeraries doing odd jobs on the farm or in the stables. The people not precisely servants who found a place at their hearth were not all members of the immediate family of the master.

But there was another factor favouring the development of the 'Pole.' This was that many of them were described as painters. They seldom of course were able to practise that expensive art, for they could not buy colours or canvases: in their visitors' bulletins, however, they generally figured as that. But after the death of Gauguin, the dealer, Vollard, and others, came down from Paris. They ransacked the country for forgotten canvases: when they found one they paid to the astonished peasants, in the heat of competition, very considerable sums. Past hosts of the great french romantic had confiscated paintings in lieu of rent. The least sketch had its price. The sight of these breathless collectors, and the rumours of the sums paid, made a deep impression on the local people. The 'Poles' on their side were very persuasive. They assured their hosts that Gauguin was a mere cipher compared to them. – These circumstances told in favour of the 'Pole.'

But no such explanations can really account for the founding of this charming and whimsical order. Whether there are still a few 'Poles' surviving in Brittany or not, I have no means of knowing. In the larger centres of *villégiature* the *siècle* was already paramount before the war.

The Russian with whom translations of the russian books of tsarist Russia familiarized the West was an excited and unstable child. We have seen this society massacred in millions without astonishment. The russian books prepared every Western European for that consummation. All the cast of the *Cherry Orchard* could be massacred easily by a single determined gunman. This defencelessness of the essential Slav can, under certain circumstances, become an asset. Especially perhaps the French would find themselves victims of such a harmless parasite, so different in his nature to themselves. A more energetic parasite would always fail with the gallic nature, unless very resolute.

# Bestre

As I walked along the quay at Kermanac, there was a pretty footfall in my rear. Turning my head, I found an athletic frenchwoman,
of the bourgeois class, looking at me.

The crocket-like floral postiches on the ridges of her head-gear
looked crisped down in a threatening way: her nodular pink veil
was an apoplectic gristle round her stormy brow; steam came out
of her lips upon the harsh white atmosphere. Her eyes were dark,
and the contiguous colour of her cheeks of a redness quasi-
venetian, with something like the feminine colouring of battle. This
was surely a feline battle-mask, then; but in such a pacific and
slumbrous spot I thought it an anomalous ornament.

My dented *bidon* of a hat – cantankerous beard – hungarian
boots, the soles like the rind of a thin melon slice, the uppers in
stark calcinous segments; my cassock-like blue broadcloth coat
(why was I like this? – the habits of needy travel grew this composite
shell), this uncouthness might have raised in her the question of
defiance and offence. I glided swiftly along on my centipedal boots,
dragging my eye upon the rough walls of the houses to my right
like a listless cane. Low houses faced the small vasey port. It was
there I saw Bestre.

This is how I became aware of Bestre.

The detritus of some weeks' hurried experience was being dealt
with in my mind, on this crystalline, extremely cold walk through
Kermanac to Braspartz, and was being established in orderly heaps.
At work in my untidy hive, I was alone: the atmosphere of the
workshop dammed me in. That I moved forward was no more

strange than if a carpenter's shop or chemist's laboratory, installed in a boat, should move forward on the tide of a stream. Now, what seemed to happen was that, as I bent over my work, an odiously grinning face peered in at my window. The impression of an intrusion was so strong, that I did not even realize at first that it was I who was the intruder. That the window was not my window, and that the face was not peering in but out: that, in fact, it was I myself who was guilty of peering into somebody else's window: this was hidden from me in the first moment of consciousness about the odious brown person of Bestre. It is a wonder that the curse did not at once fall from me on this detestable inquisitive head. What I did do was to pull up in my automatic progress, and, instead of passing on, to continue to stare in at Bestre's kitchen window, and scowl at Bestre's sienna-coloured gourd of a head.

Bestre in his turn was nonplussed. He knew that some one was looking in at his kitchen window, all right: he had expected some one to do so, some one who in fact had contracted the habit of doing that. But he had mistaken my steps for this other person's; and the appearance of my face was in a measure as disturbing to him as his had been to me. My information on these points afterwards became complete. With a flexible imbrication reminiscent of a shutter-lipped ape, a bud of tongue still showing, he shot the latch of his upper lip down in front of the nether one, and depressed the interior extremities of his eyebrows sharply from their quizzing perch – only this monkey-on-a-stick mechanical pull – down the face's centre. At the same time, his arms still folded like bulky lizards, blue tattoo on brown ground, upon the escarpment of his vesicular middle, not a hair or muscle moving, he made a quick, slight motion to me with one hand to get out of the picture without speaking – to efface myself. It was the suggestion of a theatrical sportsman. I was in the line of fire. I moved on: a couple of steps did it. That lady was twenty yards distant: but nowhere was there anything in sight evidently related to Bestre's gestures. 'Pension de Famille?' What prices? – and how charmingly placed! I remarked the vine: the building, of one storey, was exceedingly long, it took some time to pass along it. I reached the principal door. I concluded this entrance was really disused, although more imposing. So emerging on the quay once more, and turning along the front of the house, I again discovered myself in contact with Bestre. He was facing towards me, and down the quay, immobile as before, and the attitude so much a replica as to make it seem a plagiarism of his kitchen piece. Only now his head was on one side, a verminous grin had dispersed the equally unpleasant entity of his shut mouth. The new facial arrangement and angle for the head imposed on what seemed his stock pose for the body, must mean: 'Am I not rather smart? Not just a little bit smart? Don't you think? A little, you will concede? You did not expect that, did you? That was a nasty jar for you, was it not? Ha! my lapin, that was unexpected, that is plain! Did you think you would find Bestre asleep? He is always awake! He watched you being born, and has watched you ever since. Don't be too sure that he did not play some part in planting the little seed from which you grew into such a big, fine (many withering ex-clamation marks) boy (or girl). He will be in at your finish too. But he is in no hurry about that. He is never in a hurry! He bides his time. Meanwhile he laughs at you. He finds you a little funny. That's right! Yes! I am still looking!'

His very large eyeballs, the small saffron ocellation in their centre, the tiny spot through which light entered the obese wilderness of his body; his bronzed bovine arms, swollen handles for a variety of indolent little ingenuities; his inflated digestive case, lent their combined expressiveness to say these things; with every tart and biting condiment that eye-fluid, flaunting of fatness (the well-filled), the insult of the comic, implications of indecency, could provide. Every variety of bottom-tapping resounded from his dumb bulk. His tongue stuck out, his lips eructated with the incredible indecorum that appears to be the monopoly of liquids, his brown arms were for the moment genitals, snakes in one massive twist beneath his mamillary slabs, gently riding on a pancreatic swell, each hair on his oil-bearing skin contributing its message of porcine affront.

Taken fairly in the chest by this magnetic attack, I wavered. Turning the house corner it was like confronting a hard meaty gust. But I perceived that the central gyroduct passed a few feet clear of me. Turning my back, arching it a little, perhaps, I was just in time to receive on the boko a parting volley from the female figure of the obscure encounter, before she disappeared behind a rock which brought Kermanac to a close on this side of the port. She was evidently replying to Bestre. It was the rash grating philippic of a battered cat, limping into safety. At the moment that she vanished behind the boulder, Bestre must have vanished too, for a moment later the quay was empty. On reaching the door into which he had sunk, plump and slick as into a stage trap, there he was inside – this grease-bred old mammifer – his tufted vertex charging about the plank ceiling – generally ricochetting like a dripping sturgeon in a boat's bottom – arms warm brown, ju-jitsu of his guts, tan canvas shoes and trousers rippling in ribbed planes as he darted about – with a filthy snicker for the scuttling female, and a stark cock of the eye for an unknown figure miles to his right: he filled this short tunnel with clever parabolas and vortices, little neat stutterings of triumph, goggle-eyed hypnotisms, in retrospect, for his hearers.

'T'as vu? T'as vu? Je l'ai fichu c'es' qu'elle n'attendait pas! Ah, la rosse! Qu'elle aille raconter ça à sa crapule de mari. Si, si, s'il vient ici, tu sais—'

His head nodded up and down in batches of blood-curdling affirmations; his hand, pudgy hieratic disc, tapped the air gently, then sawed tenderly up and down.

Bestre, on catching sight of me, hailed me as a witness. 'Tiens! Ce monsieur peut vous le dire: il était là. Il m'a vu là-dedans qui l'attendait!'

I bore witness to the subtleties of his warlike ambush. I told his sister and two boarders that I had seldom been privy to such a rich encounter. They squinted at me, and at each other, dragging their eyes off with slow tosses of the head. I took a room in this house immediately – the stage-box in fact, just above the kitchen. For a week I was perpetually entertained.

Before attempting to discover the significance of Bestre's proceedings when I clattered into the silken zone of his hostilities, I settled down in his house; watched him idly from both my windows – from that looking on to the back – (cleaning his gun in the yard, killing chickens, examining the peas), from the front one – rather shyly sucking up to a fisherman upon the quay. I went into his kitchen and his shed and watched him. I realized as little as he did that I was patting and prodding a subject of these stories. There was no intention in these stoppages on my zigzag course across Western France of taking a human species, as an entomologist would take a Distoma or a Narbonne Lycosa, to study. Later, at the time of my spanish adventure (which was separated by two years from Bestre), I had grown more professional. Also, I had become more conscious of myself and of my powers of personally provoking a series of typhoons in tea-cups. But with my Bretons I was very new to my resources, and was living in a mild and early millennium of mirth. It was at the end of a few months' roaming in the country that I saw I had been a good deal in contact with a tribe, some more and some less generic. And it is only now that it has seemed to me an amusing labour to gather some of these individuals in retrospect and group them under their function, to which all in some diverting way were attached.

So my stoppage at Kermanac, for example, was because Bestre was a little excitement. I had never seen brown flesh put to those uses. And the situation of his boarding-house would allow of unlimited pococurantism, idling and eating, sunning myself in one of my windows, with Berkeley or Cudworth in my hand, and a staring eye that lost itself in reveries that suddenly took on flesh and acted some obstinate little part or other, the phases of whose dramatic life I would follow stealthily from window to window, a book still in my hand, shaking with the most innocent laughter. I was never for a minute unoccupied. Fête followed fête, fêtes of the mind. Then, as well, the small cliffs of the scurfy little port, its desertion and queer train of life, reached a system of very early dreams I had considered effaced. But all the same, although not self-conscious, I went laughing after Bestre, tapping him, setting traps for the game that he decidedly contained for my curiosity. So it was almost as though Fabre could have established himself within the masonries of the bee, and lived on its honey, while investigating for the human species: or stretched himself on a bed of raphia and pebbles at the bottom of the Lycosa's pit, and lived on flies and locusts. I lay on Bestre's billowy beds, drank his ambrosial cider, fished from his boat; he brought me birds and beasts that he had chased and killed. It was an idyllic life of the calmest adventure. We were the best of friends: he thought I slapped him because contact with his fat gladdened me, and to establish contact with the feminine vein in his brown-coated ducts and muscles. Also he was Bestre, and it must be nice to pat and buffet him as it would be to do that with a dreadful lion.

He offered himself, sometimes wincing coquettishly, occasionally rolling his eyes a little, as the lion might do to remind you of your natural dread, and heighten the luxurious privilege.

Bestre's boarding-house is only open from June to October: the winter months he passes in hunting and trapping. He is a stranger to Kermanac, a Boulonnais, and at constant feud with the natives. For some generations his family have been strangers where they lived; and he carries on his face the mark of an origin even more distant than Picardy. His great-grandfather came into France from the Peninsula, with the armies of Napoleon. Possibly his alertness, combativeness and timidity are the result of these exilings and difficult adjustments to new surroundings, working in his blood, and in his own history.

He is a large, tall man, corpulent and ox-like: you can see by his movements that the slow aggrandizement of his stomach has hardly been noticed by him. It is still compact with the rest of his body, and he is as nimble as a flea. It has been for him like the peculations of a minister, enriching himself under the nose of the caliph; Bestre's kingly indifference can be accounted for by the many delights and benefits procured through this subtle misappropriation of the general resources of the body. Sunburnt, with large yellow-white moustache, little eyes protruding with the cute strenuosity already noticed, when he meets any one for the first time his mouth stops open, a cigarette end adhering to the lower lip. He will assume an expression of expectancy and repressed amusement, like a man accustomed to nonplussing: the expression the company wears in those games of divination when they have made the choice of an object, and he whose task it is to guess its nature is called in, and commences the cross-examination. Bestre is jocose; he will beset you with mocking thoughts as the blindfold man is danced round in a game of blind man's buff. He may have regarded my taps as a myopic clutch at his illusive person. He gazes at a new acquaintance as though this poor man, without guessing it, were entering a world of astonishing things! A would-be boarder arrives and asks him if he has a room with two beds. Bestre fixes him steadily for twenty seconds with an amused yellow eye. Without uttering a word, he then leads the way to a neighbouring door, lets the visitor pass into the room, stands watching him with the expression of a conjurer who has just drawn a curtain aside and revealed to the stupefied audience a horse and cart, or a life-size portrait of the Shah of Persia, where a moment ago there was nothing.

Suppose the following thing happened. A madman, who believes himself a hen, escapes from Charenton, and gets, somehow or other, as far as Finisterre. He turns up at Kermanac, knocks at Bestre's door and asks him with a perfect stereotyped courtesy for a large, airy room, with a comfortable perch to roost on, and a little straw in the corner where he might sit. Bestre a few days before has been visited by the very idea of arranging such a room: all is ready. He conducts his demented client to it. Now his manner with his everyday client would be thoroughly appropriate under these circumstances. They are carefully suited to a very weak-minded and whimsical visitor indeed.

Bestre has another group of tricks, pertaining directly to the commerce of his hospitable trade. When a customer is confessing in the fullest way his paraesthesias, allowing this new host an engaging glimpse of his nastiest propriums and kinks, Bestre behaves, with unconscious logic, as though a secret of the most disreputable nature were being imparted to him. Were, in fact, the requirements of a vice being enumerated, he could not display more plainly the qualms caused by his rôle of accessory. He will lower his voice, whisper in the client's ear; before doing so glance over his shoulder apprehensively two or three times, and push his guest roughly into the darkest corner of the passage or kitchen. It is his perfect understanding – is he not the only man who does, at once, forestall your eager whim: there is something of the fortune-teller in him – that produces the air of mystery. For his information is not always of the nicest, is it? He must know more about you than I daresay you would like many people to know. And Bestre will in his turn mention certain little delicacies that he, Bestre, will see that you have, and that the other guests will not share with you. So there you are committed at the start to a subtle collusion. But Bestre means it. Every one he sees for the first time he is thrilled about, until they have got used to him. He would give you anything while he is still strange to you. But you see the interest die down in his eyes, at the end of twenty-four hours, whether you have assimilated him or not. He only gives you about a day for your meal. He then assumes that you have finished him, and he feels chilled by your scheduled disillusion. A fresh face and an enemy he depends on for that 'new' feeling – or what can we call this firework that he sends up for the stranger, that he enjoys so much himself – or this rare bottle he can only open when hospitality compels – his own blood?

I had arrived at the master-moment of one of Bestre's campaigns. These were long and bitter affairs. But they consisted almost entirely of dumb show. The few words that passed were generally misleading. A vast deal of talking went on in the different camps. But a dead and pulverizing silence reigned on the field of battle, with few exceptions.

It was a matter of who could be most silent and move least: it was a stark stand-up fight between one personality and another, unaided by adventitious muscle or tongue. It was more like phases of a combat or courtship in the insect-world. The Eye was really Bestre's weapon: the ammunition with which he loaded it was drawn from all the most skunk-like provender, the most ugly mucins, fungoid glands, of his physique. Excrement as well as sputum would be shot from this luminous hole, with the same certainty in its unsavoury appulsion. Every resource of metonymy, bloody mind transfusion or irony were also his. What he selected as an arm in his duels, then, was the Eye. As he was always the offended party, he considered that he had this choice. I traced the predilection for this weapon and method to a very fiery source – to the land of his ancestry – Spain. How had the knife dropped out of his outfit? Who can tell? But he retained the *mirada* whole and entire enough to please any one, all the more active for the absence of the dagger. I pretend that Bestre behaved as he did directly because his sweet forebears had to rely so much on the furious languishing and jolly conversational properties of their eyes to secure their ends at all. The spanish beauty imprisoned behind her casement can only roll her eyes at her lover in the street below. The result of these and similar Eastern restraints develops the eye almost out of recognition. Bestre in his kitchen, behind his casement, was unconsciously employing this gift from his semi-arabian past. And it is not even the unsupported female side of Bestre. For the lover in the street as well must keep his eye in constant training to bear out the furibond jugular drops, the mettlesome stamping, of the guitar. And all the haughty chevaleresque habits of this bellicose race have substituted the eye for the mouth in a hundred ways. The Grandee's eye is terrible, and at his best is he not speechless with pride? Eyes, eyes: for defiance, for shrivelling subordinates, for courtesy, for love. A 'spanish eye' might be used as we say, 'Toledo blade.' There, anyway, is my argument; I place on the one side Bestre's eye; on the other I isolate the iberian eye. Bestre's grandfather, we know, was a Castilian. To show how he was beholden to this extraction, and again how the blood clung to him, Bestre was in no way grasping. It went so far that he was noticeably careless about money. This, in France, could not be accounted for in any other way.

Bestre's quarrels turned up as regularly as work for a good shoe-maker or dentist. Antagonism after antagonism flashed forth: became more acute through several weeks: detonated in the dumb pyrotechnic I have described; then wore itself out with its very exhausting and exacting violence. – At the passing of an enemy Bestre will pull up his blind with a snap. There he is, with his insult stewing lusciously in his yellow sweat. The eyes fix on the enemy, on his weakest spot, and do their work. He has the anatomical instinct of the hymenopter for his prey's most morbid spot; for an old wound; for a lurking vanity. He goes into the other's eye, seeks it, and strikes. On a physical blemish he turns a scornful and care-less rain like a garden hose. If the deep vanity is on the wearer's back, or in his walk or gaze, he sluices it with an abundance you would not expect his small eyes to be capable of delivering.

But the *mise en scène* for his successes is always the same. Bestre is *discovered* somewhere, behind a blind, in a doorway, beside a rock, when least expected. He regards the material world as so many ambushes for his body.

Then the key principle of his strategy is provocation. The enemy must be exasperated to the point at which it is difficult for him to keep his hands off his aggressor. The desire to administer the blow is as painful as a blow received. That the blow should be taken back into the enemy's own bosom, and that he should be stifled by his own oath – *that* Bestre regards as so many blows, and so much abuse, of *his*, Bestre's, although he has never so much as taken his hands out of his pockets, or opened his mouth.

I learnt a great deal from Bestre. He is one of my masters. When the moment came for me to discover myself – a thing I believe few people have done so thoroughly, so early in life and so quickly – I recognized more and more the beauty of Bestre. I was only prevented from turning my eye upon myself even at that primitive period of speculative adolescence by that one-sidedness that only the most daring tamper with.

The immediate quay-side neighbours of Bestre afford him a constant war-food. I have seen him slipping out in the evening and depositing refuse in front of his neighbour's house. I have seen a woman screeching at him in pidgin french from a window of the débit two doors off, while he pared his nails a yard from his own front door. This was to show his endurance. The subtle notoriety, too, of his person is dear to him. But local functionaries and fishermen are not his only fare. During summer, time hangs heavy with the visitor from Paris. When the first ennui comes upon him, he wanders about desperately, and his eye in due course falls on Bestre.

It depends how busy Bestre is at the moment. But often enough he will take on the visitor at once in his canine way. The visitor shivers, opens his eyes, bristles at the quizzing pursuit of Bestre's œillade; the remainder of his holiday flies in a round of singular plots, passionate conversations and prodigious encounters with this born broiler.

Now, a well-known painter and his family, who rented a house in the neighbourhood, were, it seemed, particularly responsive to Bestre. I could not – arrived, with some perseverance, at the bottom of it – find any cause for his quarrel. The most insignificant pretext was absent. The pretentious peppery Paris Salon artist, and this Boulogne-bred Breton inhabited the same village, and they grew larger and larger in each other's eyes at a certain moment, in this armorican wilderness. As Bestre swelled and swelled for the painter, he was seen to be the possessor of some insult incarnate, that was an intolerable factor in the life of so lonely a place. War was inevitable. Bestre saw himself growing and growing, with the glee of battle in his heart, and the flicker of budding affront in his little eye. He did nothing to arrest this alarming aggrandizement. Pretexts could have been found: but they were dispensed with, by mutual consent. This is how I reconstructed the obscure and early phases of that history. What is certain, is that there had been much eye-play on the quay between Monsieur Rivière and Monsieur Bestre. And the scene that I had taken part in was the culmination of a rather humiliating phase in the annals of Bestre's campaigns.

The distinguished painter's wife, I learnt, had contracted the habit of passing Bestre's kitchen window of a morning when

Mademoiselle Marie was alone there – gazing glassily in, but never looking at Mademoiselle Marie. This had such a depressing effect on Bestre's old sister, that it reduced her vitality considerably, and in the end brought on diarrhœa. Why did Bestre permit the war to be brought into his own camp with such impunity? The only reason that I could discover for this was, that the attacks were of very irregular timing. He had been out fishing in one or two cases, employed in his garden or elsewhere. But on the penultimate occasion Madame Rivière had practically finished off the last surviving female of Bestre's notable stock. As usual, the wife of the parisian Salon master had looked into the kitchen; but this time she had looked *at* Mademoiselle Marie, and in such a way as practically to curl her up on the floor. Bestre's sister had none of her brother's ferocity, and in every way departed considerably from his type, except in a mild and sentimental imitation of his colouring. The distinguished painter's wife, on the other hand, had a touch of Bestre about her. Bestre did not have it all his own way. Because of this, recognizing the redoubtable and Bestre-like quality of his enemy, he had resorted no doubt to such extreme measures as I suspect him of employing. She had chosen her own ground – his kitchen. That was a vast mistake. On that ground, I am satisfied, Bestre was invincible. It was even surprising that there any trump should have been lavished.

On that morning when I drifted into the picture what happened to induce such a disarray in his opponent? What superlative shaft, with deadly aim, did he direct against her vitals? She would take only a few seconds to pass the kitchen window. He had brought her down with a stupendous rush. In principle, as I have said, Bestre sacrifices the claims any individual portion of his anatomy might have to independent expressiveness to a tyrannical appropriation of all this varied battery of bestial significance by his *eye*. The eye was his chosen weapon. Had he any theory, however, that certain occasions warranted, or required, the auxiliary offices of some unit of the otherwise subordinated mass? Can the sex of his assailant give us a clue? I am convinced in my own mind that another agent was called in on this occasion. I am certain that he struck the death-blow with another engine than his eye. I believe that the most savage and obnoxious means of affront were employed to cope with the distinguished painter's wife. His rejoinder would perhaps be of that unanswerable description, that it would be stamped on the spot, for an adversary, as an authentic last word. No further appeal to arms of that sort would be rational: it must have been right up against litigation and physical assault.

Monsieur Rivière, with his painting-pack and campstool, came along the quay shortly afterwards, going in the same direction as his wife. Bestre was at his door; and he came in later, and let us know how he had behaved.

'I wasn't such a fool as to insult him: there were witnesses; let him do that. But if I come upon him in one of those lanes at the back there, you know . . . I was standing at my door; he came along and looked at my house and scanned my windows' (this is equivalent in Bestre-warfare to a bombardment). 'As he passed I did not move. I thought to myself, "Hurry home, old fellow, and ask Madame what she has seen during her little walk!" *I looked him in the white of the eyes.* He thought I'd lower mine; he doesn't know me. And, after all, what is he, though he's got the Riband of the Legion of Honour? I don't carry my decorations on my coat! I have mine marked on my body. Did I ever show you what I've got here? No; I'm going to show you.' He had shown all this before, but my presence encouraged a repetition of former successes. So while he was speaking he jumped up quickly, undid his shirt, bared his chest and stomach, and pointed to something beneath his arm. Then, rapidly rolling up his sleeves, he pointed to a cicatrice rather like a vaccination mark, but larger. While showing his scars he slaps his body, with a sort of sneering rattle or chuckle between his words, his eyes protruding more than usual. His customary wooden expression is disintegrated: this compound of a constant foreboded reflection of the expression of astonishment your face will acquire when you learn of his wisdom, valour, or wit: the slightest shade of sneering triumph, and a touch of calm relish at your wonder. Or he seems teaching you by his staring grimace the amazement you should feel: and his grimace gathers force and blooms as the full sense of what you are witnessing, hearing, bursts upon you, while your gaping face conforms more and more to Bestre's prefiguring mask.

As to his battles, Bestre is profoundly unaware of what strange category he has got himself into. The principles of his strategy are possibly the possession of his libido, but most certainly not that of the bulky and surface citizen, Bestre. On the contrary, he considers himself on the verge of a death struggle at any moment when in the presence of one of his enemies.

Like all people who spend their lives talking about their deeds, he presents a very particular aspect in the moment of action. When discovered in the thick of one of his dumb battles, he has the air of a fine company promoter, concerned, trying to corrupt some sombre fact into shielding for an hour his unwieldy fiction, until some fresh wangle can retrieve it. Or he will display a great empirical expertness in reality, without being altogether at home in it.

Bestre in the moment of action feels as though he were already talking. His action has the exaggerated character of his speech, only oddly curbed by the exigencies of reality. In his moments of most violent action he retains something of his dumb passivity. He never seems quite entering into reality, but observing it. He is looking at the reality with a professional eye, so to speak: with a professional liar's.

I have noticed that the more cramped and meagre his action has been, the more exuberant his account of the affair is afterwards. The more restrictions reality has put on him, the more unbridled is his gusto as historian of his deeds, immediately afterwards. Then he has the common impulse to avenge that self that has been perishing under the famine and knout of a bad reality, by glorifying and surfeiting it on its return to the imagination.

# The Cornac and His Wife

I met in the evening, not far from the last inn of the town, a cart containing the rough professional properties, the haggard offspring, of a strolling circus troupe from Arles, which I had already seen. The cornac and his wife tramped along beside it. Their talk ran on the people of the town they had just left. They both scowled. They recalled the inhabitants of the last town with nothing but bitterness.

Against the people to whom they played they had an implacable grudge. With the man, obsessed by ill-health, the grievance against fortune was associated with the more brutal hatred that almost choked him every time he appeared professionally.

With their children the couple were very demonstrative. Mournful caresses were showered upon them: it was a manner of conspicuously pitying themselves. As a fierce reproach to the onlooker these unhandsome gytes were publicly petted. Bitter kisses rained upon their heads. The action implied blows and ill-treatment at the hands of an anonymous adversary; in fact, the world at large. The children avoided the kisses as though they had been blows, wailing and contorting themselves. The animosity in the brutal lips thrust down upon their faces was felt by them, but the cause remained hidden for their inexperience. Terror, however, they learnt to interpret on all hands; even to particularly associate it with love towards the offspring. When the clown made a wild grimace in their blubbering faces, they would sometimes howl with alarm. This was it, perhaps! They concluded that this must be the sign and beginning of the terrible thing that had so long been covertly menacing them; their hearts nearly hopped out of their throats, although what occurred passed off in a somersault and a gush of dust as the clown hurled his white face against the earth, and got up rubbing his sides to assure the spectators that he was hurt.

Setting up their little tent in a country town this man and his wife felt their anger gnawing through their reserve, like a dog under lock and key. It was maddened by this other animal presence, the perspiring mastodon that roared at it with cheap luxurious superiority. Their long pilgrimage through this world inhabited by 'the Public' (from which they could never escape) might be interpreted by a nightmare image. This was a human family, we could say, lost in a land peopled by sodden mammoths possessed of a deeply-rooted taste for outdoor performances of a particularly depressing and disagreeable nature. These displays involved the insane contortions of an indignant man and his dirty, breathless wife, of whose ugly misery it was required that a daily mournful exhibition should be made of her shrivelled legs, in pantomime hose. She must crucify herself with a scarecrow abandon, this iron and blood automaton, and affect to represent the factor of sex in a geometrical posturing. These spells were all related in some way to physical suffering. Whenever one of these monsters was met with, which on an average was twice a day, the only means of escape for the unfortunate family was to charm it. Conduct involving that never failed to render the monster harmless and satisfied. They then would hurry on, until they met another. Then they would repeat just the same thing over again, and once more hasten away, boiling with resentment.

The first time I saw them, the proprietress stood straddling on a raised platform, in loose flesh-tights with brown wrinkled knee-caps, *espadrilles*, brandy-green feathers arching over her almost naked head; while clutched in her hands aloft she supported a rigid child of about six. Upon this child stood three others, each provided with a flag. The proprietor stood some distance away and observed this event as one of the public. I leant on the barrier near him, and wondered if he ever willed his family to fall. I was soon persuaded, on observing him for a short while, that he could never be visited by such a mild domestic sensation. He wished steadily and all the time, it was quite certain, that the earth would open with a frantic avulsion, roaring as it parted, decorated with heavy flames, across the middle of the space set aside for his performance; that everybody there would immediately be hurled into this chasm, and be crushed flat as it closed up. The Public on its side, of course, merely wished that the entire family might break their necks one after the other, the clown smash his face every time he fell, and so on.

To some extent Public and Showman understood each other. There was this amount of give and take, that they both snarled over the money that passed between them, or if they did not snarl it was all the worse. There was a unanimity of brutal hatred about that. Producer and consumer both were bestially conscious of the passage of coppers from one pocket to another. The public lay back and enjoyed itself hardly, closely, and savagely. The showman contorted himself madly in response. His bilious eye surveyed its grinning face, his brow sweated for its money, his ill-kept body ached. He made it a painful spectacle; he knew how to make it painful. He had the art of insisting on the effort, that foolish effort. The public took it in the contrary spirit, as *he* felt, on purpose. It was on purpose, as he saw it, that it took its recreation, which was coarse. It deliberately promoted his misery and affected to consider him a droll gay bird.

So this by no means exceptional family took its lot: it dressed itself up, its members knocked each other about, tied their bodies in diabolical knots before a congregation of Hodges, who could not even express themselves in the metropolitan tongue, but gibbered in breton, day in, day out. That was the situation. Intimately, both Showman and Public understood it, and were in touch more than, from the outside, would be at once understood. Each performance always threatened to end in the explosion of this increasing volume of rage. (This especially applied to its fermentation within the walls of the acrobatic vessel known as the 'patron,' who was Monsieur Jules Montort.) Within, it flashed and rumbled all the time: but I never heard of its bursting its continent, and it even seemed of use as a stimulus to gymnastics after the manner of Beethoven with a fiery composition.

So there those daily crowds collected, squatted and watched, 'above the mêlée,' like *aristos* or gentlepeople. But they did pay for their pleasure (and such pleasure!): they were made to part with their sous, strictly for nothing, from the performers' standpoint. That would be the solitary bright spot for the outraged nomad. At least to that extent they were being got the better of. Had you suggested to the Showman that the Public paid for an idea, something it drew out of itself, that would have been a particularly repugnant thought. The Public depends upon him, that the primitive performer cannot question. And if women for instance find it hard to look on their own beauty as their admirer does (so that a great number of their actions might be traced to a contempt for men, who become so passionate about what they know themselves to be such an ordinary matter – namely themselves), so it was perhaps their contempt that enabled this fierce couple to continue as they did.

This background of experience was there to swell out my perception of what I now saw – the advancing caravan, with the familiar forms of its owners approaching one of their most hated haunts, but their heads as yet still full of the fury aroused by the last midday encounter. I followed them, attempting to catch what they were saying: but what with the rumbling of the carriages and the thick surge of the proprietor's voice, I could not make out much except expletives. His eye, too, rolled at me so darkly that I fell behind. I reflected that his incessant exercise in holding up his family ranged along his extended arm, though insipid to watch, must cause him to be respected on a lonely road, and his desperate nature and undying resentment would give his ferocity an impact that no feeling I then experienced could match. So I kept my eyes to myself for the time and closed down my ears, and entered the town in the dust of his wagons.

But after my evening meal I strolled over the hill bisected by the main street, and found him in his usual place on a sort of square, one side of which was formed by a stony breton brook, across which went a bridge. Drawn up under the beeches stood the brake. Near it in the open space the troupe had erected the trapeze, lighted several lamps (it was after dark already), and placed three or four benches in a narrow semicircle. When I arrived, a large crowd already pressed round them. 'Fournissons les bancs, Messieurs et M'dames! fournissons les bancs, et alors nous commençons!' the proprietor was crying.

But the seats remained unoccupied. A boy in tights, with his coat drawn round him, shivered at one corner of the ring. Into the middle of this the Showman several times advanced, exhorting the coy Public to make up its mind and commit itself to the extent of sitting down on one of his seats. Every now and then a couple would. Then he would walk back, and stand near his cart, muttering to himself. His eyebrows were hidden in a dishevelled frond of hair. The only thing he could look at without effort was the ground, and there his eyes were usually directed. When he looked up they were heavy – vacillating painfully beneath the weight of their lids. The action of speech with him resembled that of swallowing: the dreary pipe from which he drew so many distressful sounds seemed to stiffen and swell, and his head to strain forward like a rooster about to crow. His heavy under-lip went in and out in sombre activity as he articulated. The fine natural resources of his face for inspiring a feeling of gloom in his fellows, one would have judged irresistible on that particular night. The bitterest disgust disfigured it to a high degree.

But *they* watched this despondent and unpromising figure with glee and keen anticipation. This incongruity of appearance and calling was never patent to them at all, of course. That they had no wish to understand. When the furious man scowled they gaped delightedly; when he coaxed they became grave and sympathetic. All his movements were followed with minute attention. When he called upon them to occupy their seats, with an expressive gesture, they riveted their eyes on his hand, as though expecting a pack of cards to suddenly appear there. They made no move at all to take their places. Also, as this had already lasted a considerable time, the man who was fuming to entertain them – they just as incomprehensible to him as he was to them from that point of view – allowed the outraged expression that was the expression of his soul to appear more and more in his face.

Doubtless they had an inspired presentiment of what might shortly be expected of the morose figure before them. The chuckling exultation with which an amateur of athletics or fight-fan would examine some athlete with whose prowess he was acquainted, yet whose sickly appearance gives no hint of what is to be expected of him, it was with that sort of enlightened and hilarious knowingness that they responded to his melancholy appeals.

His cheerless voice, like the moaning bay of solitary dogs, conjured them to occupy the seats.

'Fournissons les bancs!' he exhorted them again and again. Each time he retired to the position he had selected to watch them from, far enough off for them to be able to say that he had withdrawn his influence, and had no further wish to interfere. Then, again, he stalked forward. This time the exhortation was pitched in as formal and matter-of-fact a key as his anatomy would permit, as though this were the first appeal of the evening. Now he seemed merely waiting, without discreetly withdrawing – without even troubling to glance in their direction any more, until the audience should have had time to seat themselves, – absorbed in briefly rehearsing to himself, just before beginning, the part he was to play. These tactics did not alter things in the least. Finally, he was compelled to take note of his failure. No words more issued from his mouth. He glared stupidly for some moments at the circle of people, and they, blandly alert, gazed back at him.

Then unexpectedly, from outside the periphery of the potential audience, elbowing his way familiarly through the wall of people, burst in the clown. Whether sent for to save the situation, or whether his toilet were only just completed, was not revealed.

'B-o-n-soir, M'sieurs et M'dames,' he chirruped and yodeled, waved his hand, tumbled over his employer's foot. The benches filled as if by magic. But the most surprising thing was the change in the proprietor. No sooner had the clown made his entrance, and, with his assurance of success as the people's favourite, and comic familiarity, told the hangers-back to take their seats, than a brisk dialogue sprang up between him and his melancholy master. It was punctuated with resounding slaps at each fresh impertinence of the clown. The proprietor was astonishing. I rubbed my eyes. This lugubrious personage had woken to the sudden violence of a cheerful automaton. In administering the chastisement his irrepressible friend perpetually invited, he sprang nimbly backwards and forwards as though engaged in a boxing match, while he grinned appreciatively at the clown's wit, as though in spite of himself, nearly knocking his teeth out with delighted blows. The audience howled with delight, and every one seemed really happy for the moment, except the clown. The clown every day must have received, I saw, a little of the *trop-plein* of the proprietor.

In the tradition of the circus it is a very distinct figure, the part having a psychology of its own – that of the man who invents posers for the clown, wrangles with him, and against whom the laugh is always turned. One of the conventions of the circus is, of course, that the physical superiority of this personage should be legendary and indisputable. For however numerous the clowns may be, they never attack him, despite the brutal measures he adopts to cover his confusion and meet their ridicule. He seems to be a man with a marked predilection for evening dress. As a result he is a far more absurd figure than his painted and degenerate opponent. It may be the clown's superstitious respect for rank, and this emblem of it, despite his consciousness of intellectual superiority, that causes this ruffianly dolt to remain immune.

In playing this part the pompous dignity of attitude should be preserved in the strictest integrity. The actor should seldom smile. If so, it is only as a slight concession, a bid to induce the clown to take a more serious view of the matter under discussion. He smiles to make it evident that he also is furnished with this attribute of man – a discernment of the ridiculous. Then, with renewed gusto and solemnity, he asks the clown's *serious* opinion of the question by which he seems obsessed, turning his head sideways with his ear towards his droll friend, and closing his eyes for a moment.

Or else it is the public for whom this smile is intended, and towards whom the discomfited 'swell' in evening dress turns as towards his peers, for sympathy and understanding, when 'scored off' anew, in, as the smile would affirm, this low-bred and unanswerable fashion. They are appealed to, as though it were their mind that was being represented in the dialogue, and constantly discomfited, and he were merely their mouthpiece.

Originally, no doubt, this throaty swell stood in some sense for the Public. Out of compliment to the Public, of course, he would be provided with evening dress. It would be tacitly understood by the courteous management, that although many of those present were in billycocks, blouses and gaiters, shawls and reach-me-downs, their native attire was a ceremonial evening outfit.

The distinguished Public would doubtless still further appreciate the delicacy of touch in endowing its representative with a high-born inability to understand the jokes of his inferiors, or be a match for them in wit. In the better sort of circus, his address is highly genteel, throaty and unctuous.

In the little circuses, such as the one I am describing, this is a different and a very lonely part. There are none of those appeals to the Public – as the latter claim, not only community of mind, but of class, with the clown. It becomes something like a dialogue between mimes, representing employer and employee, although these original distinctions are not very strictly observed.

A man without a sense of humour, the man in the toff's part, finds himself with one whose mischievous spirit he is aware of, and whose ridicule he fears. Wishing to avoid being thought a bore, and racking his brains for a means of being entertaining, he suddenly brings to light a host of conundrums, for which he seems endowed with a stupefying memory. Thoroughly reassured by the finding of this powerful and traditional aid, with an amazing persistence he presses the clown, making use of every 'gentlemanly' subterfuge, to extract a grave answer. 'Why is a cabbage like a soul in purgatory?' or, 'If you had seven pockets in your waistcoat, a hip pocket, five ticket-pockets, and three other pockets, how many extra buttons would you need?' So they follow each other. Or else some anecdote (a more unmanageable tool) is remembered. The clown here has many opportunities of displaying his mocking wit.

This is the rôle of honour usually reserved for the head showman, of course. The part was not played with very great consistency in the case in question. Indeed, so irrepressible were the comedian's spirits, and so unmanageable his vitality at times, that he seemed to be turning the tables on the clown. In his cavernous baying voice, he drew out of his stomach many a caustic rejoinder to the clown's pert but stock wit. The latter's ready-made quips were often no match for his strange but genuine hilarity. During the whole evening he was rather 'hors de son assiette,' I thought. I was very glad I had come, for I had never seen this side of him, and it seemed the most unaccountable freak of personality that it was possible to imagine. Before, I had never spent more than a few minutes watching them, and certainly never seen anything resembling the present display.

This out-of-door audience was differently moved from the audiences I have seen in the little circus tents of the breton fairs. The absence of the mysterious hush of the interior seemed to release them. Also the nearness of the performers in the tent increases the mystery. The proximity of these bulging muscles, painted faces and novel garbs, evidently makes a strange impression on the village clientèle. These primitive minds do not readily dissociate reality from appearance. However well they got to know the clown, they would always think of him the wrong way up, or on all-fours. The more humble suburban theatre-goer would be twice as much affected at meeting the much-advertised star with whose private life he is more familiar than with her public display, in the wings of the theatre, as in seeing her on the stage. Indeed, it would be rather as though at some turning of an alley at the Zoo, you should meet a lion face to face – having gazed at it a few minutes before behind its bars. So the theatre, the people on the stage and the plays they play, is part of the surface of life, and is not troubling. But to get behind the scenes and see these beings out of their parts, would be not merely to be privy to the workings and 'dessous' of the theatre, but of life itself.

Crowded in the narrow and twilight pavilion of the saltimbanques at the breton Pardon, the audience will remain motionless for minutes together. Their imagination is awakened by the sight of the flags, the tent, the drums, and the bedizened people. Thenceforth it dominates them, controlling their senses. They enter the tent with a mild awe, in a suggestive trance. When a joke is made that requires a burst of merriment, or when a turn is finished, they all begin moving themselves, as though they had just woken up, changing their attitude, shaking off the magnetic sleep.

Once I had seen this particular troupe in a fair with their tent up. I had gone in for a short while, but had not paid much attention to them individually and soon left. But the clown, I remember, conducted everything – acting as interpreter of his own jokes, tumbling over and getting up and leading the laugh, and explaining with real conscientiousness and science the proprietor's more recondite conundrums. He took up an impersonal attitude. He was a friend who had dropped in to see the 'patron'; he appreciated quite as one of the public the curiosities of the show. He would say, for instance: 'Now this is very remarkable: this little girl is only eleven, and she can put both her toes in her mouth,' etc., etc. Had it not been for his comments, I am persuaded that the performance would have passed off in a profound, though not unappreciative, silence.

Returning to the present occasion, some time after the initial bout between the clown and his master, and while some chairs were being placed in the middle of the ring, I became aware of a very grave expression on the latter's face. He now mounted upon one of the chairs. Having remained impressively silent till the last moment, from the edge of the chair, as though from the brink of a precipice, he addressed the audience in the following terms:

'Ladies and gentlemen! I have given up working for several years myself, owing to ill-health. As far as some of my most important tricks are concerned, my little girl has taken my place. But Monsieur

le Commissaire de Police would not give the necessary permission
for her to appear. – Then I will myself perform!'

A grievance against the police would, of course, any day of the
week, drive out everything else with any showman. The Public
momentarily benefited. At these words M. Montort jerked himself
violently over the back of the chair, the unathletic proportions of
his stomach being revealed in this movement, and touched the
ground with his head. Then, having bowed to the audience, he
turned again to the chairs and grasping them, with a gesture of
the utmost recklessness, heaved his body up into the air. This was
accompanied by a startling whir proceeding from his corduroys,
and a painful crepitation of his joints. Afterwards he accomplished
a third feat, suspending himself between two chairs; and then a
fourth, in which he gracefully lay on all three, and picked up a
handkerchief with his face reversed. At this sensational finish, I
thought it appropriate to applaud: a *feu nourri* of clapping broke
from me. Unfortunately the audience was spellbound and my
demonstration attracted attention. I was singled out by the
performer for a look of individual hatred. He treated all of us coldly:
he bowed stiffly, and walked back to the cart with the air of a man
who has just received a bullet wound in a duel, and refusing the
assistance of a doctor walks to his carriage.

He had accomplished the feats that I have just described with a
bitter dash that revealed once more the character that from former
more casual visits I recognized. He seemed courting misfortune. 'Any
mortal injury sustained by me, M. le Commissaire, during the
performance, will be at your door! The Public must be satisfied. I
am the servant of the Public. You have decreed that it shall be me
(all my intestines displaced by thirty years of contortions) that shall
satisfy them. Very well! I know my duty, if you don't know yours.
Good! It shall be done as you have ordered, M. le Commissaire!'

The drama this time was an *internal* one, therefore. It was not a
question of baiting the public with a broken neck. We were invited
to concentrate our minds upon what was going on *inside*. We had
to visualize a colony of much-twisted, sorely-tried intestines, screwed

this way and that, as they had never been screwed before. It was an anatomical piece.

The unfortunate part was that the public could not *see* these intestines as they could see a figure suspended in the air, and liable to crash. A mournful and respectful, a *dead* silence, would have been the ideal way, from his point of view, for the audience to have greeted his pathetic skill. Instead of that, salvos of muscular applause shook the air every time he completed one of the phases of this painful trick. Hearing the applause, he would fling himself wildly into his next posture, with a whistling sneer of hatred. The set finished, the last knot tied and untied, he went back and leant against the cart, his head in the hollow of his arm, coughing and spitting. A boy at my side said, 'Regarde – donc; il souffre!' This refusal of the magistrate to let his little girl perform was an event that especially outraged him: it wounded his french sense of the dignity of a fully-enfranchised person. His wife was far less affected, but she seconded him with a lofty scowl. Shortly afterwards, she provided a new and interesting feature of the evening's entertainment.

Various insignificant items immediately succeeded the showman's dramatic exploit, where he deputized for his daughter. A donkey appeared, whose legs could be tied into knots. The clown extracted from its middle-class comfortable primness of expression every jest of which it was susceptible. The conundrums broke out again; they only ceased after a discharge that lasted fully a quarter of an hour. There was a little trapeze. For some time already we had been aware of a restless figure in the background. A woman with an expression of great dissatisfaction on her face, stood with muffled arms knotted on her chest, holding a shawl against the cold air. Next, we became aware of a harsh and indignant voice. This woman was slowly advancing, talking all the while, until she arrived in the centre of the circle made by the seats. She made several slow gestures, slightly raising her voice. She spoke as a person who had stood things long enough. 'Here are hundreds of people standing round, and there are hardly a dozen sous on the carpet! We give you entertainment, but it is not for nothing! We do not work for nothing! We have our living to make as well as other people! This is the third performance we have given to-day. We are tired and have come a long way to appear before you this evening. You want to enjoy yourselves; but you don't want to pay! If you want to see any more, loosen your purse-strings a little!'

While delivering this harangue her attitude resembled that seen in the London streets, when women are quarrelling – the neck strained forward, the face bent down, and the eyes glowering upwards at the adversary. One hand was thrust stiffly out. In these classes of action the body, besides, is generally screwed round to express the impulse of turning on the heel in disgust and walking away. But the face still confronts whoever is being apostrophized, and utters its ever-renewed maledictory post-scriptums.

Several pieces of money fell at her feet. She remained silent, the arms fiercely folded, the two hands bitterly dug into her sides. Eventually she retired, very slowly, as she had advanced, as it were indolently, her eyes still flashing and scowling resentfully round at the crowd as she went. They looked on with amiable and gaping attention. They took much more notice of her than of the man; she thoroughly interested them, and they conceded to her unconditionally their sympathy. There was no response to her attack – no gibing or discontent; only a few more sous were thrown. Her husband, it appeared, had been deeply stimulated by her speech. One or two volcanic conundrums followed closely upon her exit. The audience seemed to relish the entertainment all the more after this confirmation from the proprietress of its quality, instead of being put in a more critical frame of mind.

Her indignant outburst carried this curious reflection with it; it was plain that it did not owe its tone of conviction to the fact that she conceived a high opinion of their performance. Apparently it was an axiom of her mind that the public paid, for some obscure reason, not for its proper amusement, but for the trouble, inconvenience, fatigue, and in sum for all the ills of the showman's lot. Or rather did *not* pay, sat and watched and did not pay. Ah ça! –

that was trying the patience too far. This, it is true, was only the reasoning every gesture of her husband forcibly expressed, but explicit, in black and white, or well-turned forcible words.

Peasant audiences in latin countries, and no doubt in most places, are herded to their amusements like children; the harsh experts of fun barbarously purge them for a few pence. The spectacles provided are received like the daily soup and weekly cube of tobacco of the convict. Spending wages, it seems, is as much a routine as earning them. So in their entertainment, when buying it with their own money, they support the same brow-beating and discipline as in their work. Of this the outburst of the proprietress was a perfect illustration. Such figures represent for the spectators, for the moment, authority. In consequence a reproof as to their slackness in spending is received in the same spirit as a master's abuse at alleged slackness in earning it.

I have described the nature of my own humour – how, as I said, it went over into everything, making a drama of mock-violence of every social relationship. Why should it be so *violent* – so mock-violent – you may at the time have been disposed to enquire? Everywhere it has seemed to be compelled to go into some frame that was always a simulacrum of mortal combat. Sometimes it resembled a dilution of the Wild West film, chaplinesque in its violence. Why always *violence*? However, I have often asked that myself.

For my reply here I should go to the modern Circus or to the Italian Comedy, or to Punch. Violence is of the essence of *laughter* (as distinguished of course from smiling wit): it is merely the inversion or failure of *force*. To put it in another way, it is the *grin* upon the Deathshead. It must be extremely primitive in origin, though of course its function in civilized life is to keep the primitive at bay. But it hoists the primitive with its own explosive. It is a realistic firework, reminiscent of war.

These strolling players I am describing, however, and their relation to their audience, will provide the most convincing illustration of what I mean. The difference and also the inevitable consanguinity between my ideal of humour, and that of any other man whatever, will become plain. For the primitive peasant audience the comic-sense is subject to the narrowest convention of habit. Obviously a peasant would not see anything ridiculous in, or at least never amuse himself over, his pigs and chickens: his constant sentiment of their utility would be too strong to admit of another. Thus the disintegrating effect of the laughing-gas, and especially the fundamentals of the absurd, that strike too near the life-root, is instinctively isolated. A man who succeeds in infuriating us, again, need never fear our ridicule, although he may enhance our anger by his absurdity. A countryman in urging on his beast may make some disobliging remark to it, really seizing a ludicrous point in its appearance to envenom his epithet: but it will be caustic and mirthless, an observation of his intelligence far removed from the irresponsible emotion of laughter. It will come out of his anger and impatience, not his gaiety. You see in the peasant of Brittany and other primitive districts of France a constant tendency to sarcasm. Their hysterical and monotonous voices – a variety of the 'celtic' screech – are always with the Bretons pitched in a strain of fierce raillery and abuse. But this does not affect their mirth. Their laughter is sharp and mirthless and designed usually to wound. With their grins and quips they are like armed men who never meet without clashing their weapons together. Were my circus-proprietor and his kind not so tough, this continual howl or disquieting explosion of what is scarcely mirth would shatter them.

So (to return to the conventions of these forms of pleasure) it could be said that if the clown and the manager consulted in an audible voice, before cracking each joke – in fact, concocted it in their hearing – these audiences would respond with the same alacrity. Any rudiment of décor or makeshift property, economy in make-up, or feeble trick of some accredited acrobat, which they themselves could do twice as well, or mirthless patter, is not enough to arouse criticism in them, who are so critically acute in other matters. To criticize the amusements that Fate has provided, is an anarchy to which they do not aspire.

The member of a peasant community is trained by Fate, and his law is to accept its manifestations – one of which is comic, one of love, one of work, and so on. There is a little flowering of tenderness for a moment in the love one. The comic is always strenuous and cruel, like the work. It never flowers. The intermediary, the showman, knows that. He knows the brutal *frisson* in contact with danger that draws the laughter up from the deepest bowel in a refreshing unearthly gush. He knows why he and the clown are always black and blue, his children performing dogs, his wife a caryatid. He knows Fate, since he serves it, better than even the peasant.

The educated man, like the true social revolutionary, does not *accept* life in this way. He is in revolt, and it is the laws of Fate that he sets out to break. We can take another characteristic fatalism of the peasant or primitive man. He can never conceive of anybody being anything else but just what he is, or having any other name than that he is known by. John the carpenter, or Old John (or Young John) the carpenter, is not a person, but, as it were, a fixed and rigid communistic convention. One of our greatest superstitions is that the plain man, being so 'near to life,' is a great 'realist.' In fact, he seldom gets close to reality at all, in the way, for instance, that a philosophic intelligence, or an imaginative artist, does. He looks at everything from the outside, reads the labels, and what he *sees* is what he has been told to see, that is to say, what he expects. What he does not expect, he, of course, does not see. For him only the well-worn and general exists.

That the peasant, or any person living under primitive conditions, does not appreciate the scenery so much as, say, John Keats, is a generally accepted truth, which no available evidence gives us any reason to question. His contact with the quickest, most vivid, reality, if he is averagely endowed, is muffled, and his touch upon it strangely insensitive; he is surrounded by signs, not things. It is for this reason that the social revolutionary, who wishes to introduce the unexpected and to awaken a faculty of criticism, finds the peasant such unsatisfactory material.

Just as the peasant, then, has little sense of the beauty of his life, so his laughter is circumscribed. The herd-bellow at the circus is always associated with mock-violent events, however, and his true laughter is always torn out of a tragic material. How this explains my sort of laughter is that both our patterns are cut or torn out of primitive stuff. The difference is that pure physical action usually provides him with his, whereas mine deal with the phantoms of action and the human character. For me *everything* is tragically primitive: whereas the peasant only feels 'primitively' at stated times. But both our comedies are comedies of action, that is what I would stress.

This particular performance wound up rather strangely. The showman's wife had occasion to approach and lash the public with her tongue again, in the final phase. As the show approached its conclusion, the donkey was led in once more, pretended to die, and the clown made believe to weep disconsolately over it. All was quiet and preparation for a moment.

Then, from an unexpected quarter, came a sort of dénouement to our evening. Every one's attention was immediately attracted to it. A small boy in the front row began jeering at the proprietor. First, it was a constant muttering, that made people turn idly to that quarter of the ring. Then it grew in volume and intensity. It was a spontaneous action it appeared, and extremely sudden. The outraged showman slouched past him several times, looking at him from the tail of his eye, with his head thrust out as though he were going to crow. He rubbed his hands as he was accustomed to do before chastising the clown. Here was a little white-faced clown, an unprofessional imp of mischief! He would slap him in a moment. He rubbed his horny hands but without conviction. This had no effect: the small voice went steadily on like a dirge. This unrehearsed number found him at a loss. He went over to the clown and complained in a whisper. This personage had just revealed himself as a serious gymnast. Baring his blacksmith's arms, and discarding his ludicrous personality, he had accomplished a series of mild feats on the trapeze. He benefited, like all athletic clowns, by his traditional foolish incompetence. The public were duly impressed. He now surveyed them with a solemn and pretentious eye. When his master came up to him, supposing that the complaint referred to some disorderly booby, he advanced threateningly in the direction indicated. But when he saw who was the offender, finding a thoughtful-looking little boy in place of an intoxicated peasant, he was as nonplussed as had been his master. He looked foolishly round, and then fell to jeering back, the clown reasserting itself. Then he returned with a shrug and grimace to his preparations for the next and final event.

It is possible that this infant may never have thought comically before. Or he may, of course, have visited travelling shows for the purpose of annoying showmen, advertising his intelligence, or even to be taken on as a clown. But he may have been the victim of the unaccountable awakening of a critical vein, grown irresponsibly active all at once. If the latter, then he was launched on a dubious career of offence. He had one of the handsome visionary breton faces. His oracular vehemence, though bitterly sarcastic, suggested the more romantic kind of motivation. The showman prowled about the enclosure, grinning and casting sidelong glances at his poet: his vanity tickled in some fashion, perhaps: who knows? the boy persevering blandly, fixing him with his eye. But suddenly his face would darken, and he would make a rush at the inexplicable juvenile figure. Would this boy have met death with the exultation of a martyr rather than give up his picture of an old and despondent mountebank – like some stubborn prophet who would not forgo the melodrama forged by his orderly hatreds – always of the gloom of famine, of cracked and gutted palaces, and the elements taking on new and extremely destructive shapes for the extermination of man?

At last that organism, 'the Public,' as there constituted, fell to pieces, at a signal: the trapeze collapsed, the benches broke the circle described for the performance, and were hurried away, the acetylene lamps were extinguished, the angry tongues of the saltimbanques began their evil retrospective clatter. There had been *two* Publics, however, this time. It had been a good show.

# The Death of the Ankou

'And Death once dead, there's no more dying then.'
William Shakespeare

*Ervoanik Plouillo* – meaning the death-god of Ploumilliau; I said
over the words, and as I did so I saw the death-god. – I sat in a
crowded inn at Vandevennec, in the *argoat*, not far from Rot, at
the Pardon, deafened by the bitter screech of the drinkers, finishing
a piece of cheese. As I avoided the maggots I read the history of the
Ankou, that is the armorican death-god. The guide-book to the
antiquities of the district made plain, to the tourist, the ancient
features of this belief. It recounted how the gaunt creature
despatched from the country of death traversed at night the breton
region. The peasant, late on the high-road and for the most part
drunk, staggering home at midnight, felt around him suddenly the
atmosphere of the shades, a strange cold penetrated his tissues,
authentic portions of the *Néant* pushed in like icy wedges within
the mild air of the fields and isolated him from Earth, while rapid
hands seized his shoulders from behind, and thrust him into the
ditch. Then, crouching with his face against the ground, his eyes
shut fast, he heard the hurrying wheels of the cart. Death passed
with his assistants. As the complaint of the receding wheels died
out, he would cross himself many times, rise from the ditch, and
proceed with a terrified haste to his destination.

There was a midnight mass at Ploumilliau, where the Ankou,
which stood in a chapel, was said to leave his place, pass amongst
the kneeling congregation, and tap on the shoulders those he

proposed to take quite soon. These were memories. The statue no longer stood there, even. It had been removed some time before by the priests, because it was an object of too much interest to local magicians. They interfered with it, and at last one impatient hag, disgusted at its feebleness after it had neglected to assist her in a deadly matter she had on hand, introduced herself into the chapel one afternoon and, unobserved by the staff, painted it a pillar-box red. This she imagined would invigorate it and make it full of new mischief. When the priest's eyes in due course fell upon the red god, he decided that that would not do: he put it out of the way, where it could not be tampered with. So one of the last truly pagan images disappeared, wasting its curious efficacy in a loft, dusted occasionally by an ecclesiastical *bonne*.

Such was the story of the last authentic plastic Ankou. In ancient Brittany the people claimed to be descended from a redoubtable god of death. But long passed out of the influence of that barbarity, their early death-god, competing with gentler images, saw his altars fall one by one. In a semi-'parisian' parish, at last, the cult which had superseded him arrived in its turn at a universal decline, his ultimate representative was relegated to a loft to save it from the contemptuous devotions of a disappointed sorceress. Alas for Death! or rather for its descendants, thought I, a little romantically: that chill in the bone it brought was an ancient tonic: so long as it ran down the spine the breton soul was quick with memory. So, *alas!*

But I had been reading after that, and immediately prior to my encounter, about the peasant in the ditch, also the blinding of the god. It was supposed, I learnt, that formerly the Ankou had his eyesight. As he travelled along in his cart between the hedges, he would stare about him, and spot likely people to right and left. One evening, as his flat, black, breton peasants' hat came rapidly along the road, as he straddled attentively bolt-upright upon its jolting floor, a man and his master, in an adjoining field, noticed his approach. The man broke into song. His scandalized master attempted to stop him. But this bright bolshevik continued to sing an offensively carefree song under the nose of the supreme authority. The scandal did not pass unnoticed by the touchy destroyer. He shouted at him over the hedge, that for his insolence he had eight days to live, no more, which perhaps would teach him to sing etcetera! As it happened St. Peter was there. St. Peter's record leaves little question that a suppressed communist of an advanced type is concealed beneath the archangelical robes. It is a questionable policy to employ such a man as doorkeeper, and many popular airs in latin countries facetiously draw attention to the possibilities inherent in such a situation. In this case Peter was as scandalized at the behaviour of the Ankou as was the farmer at that of his farm-hand.

'Are you not ashamed, strange god, to condemn a man in that way, *at his work*?' he exclaimed. It was the *work* that did it, as far as Peter was concerned. Also it was his interference with work that brought his great misfortune on the Ankou. St. Peter, so the guide-book said, was as touchy as a captain of industry or a demagogue on that point. Though how could poor Death know that work, of all things, was sacred? Evidently he would have quite different ideas as to the attributes of divinity. But he had to pay immediately for his blunder. The revolutionary archangel struck him blind on the spot – struck Death blind; and, true to his character, that of one at all costs anxious for the applause of the *muchedumbre*, he returned to the field, and told the astonished labourer, who was still singing – because in all probability he was a little soft in the head – that he had his personal guarantee of a very long and happy life, and that not many miles away. *Ervoanik Plouillo* – still to be seen for threepence: and while I was making plans for the necessary journey, my mind was powerfully haunted by that blind and hurrying apparition which had been so concrete there.

It was a long room where I sat, like a gallery: except during a Pardon it was not so popular. When I am reading something that interests me, the whole atmosphere is affected. If I look quickly up, I see things as though they were a part of a dream. They are all penetrated by the particular medium I have drawn out of my mind. What I had last read on this occasion, although my eyes at the moment were resting on the words *Ervoanik Plouillo*, was the account of how it affected the person's fate at what hour he met the Ankou. The din and smoke in the dark and crowded gallery was lighted by weak electricity, and a wet and lowering daylight beyond. Crowds of umbrellas moved past the door which opened on to the square. Whenever I grew attentive to my surroundings, the passionate movement of whirling and striking arms was visible at the tables where the play was in progress, or a furious black body would dash itself from one chair to another. The 'celtic screech' meantime growing harsher and harsher, sharpening itself on caustic snarling words, would soar to a paroxysm of energy. 'Garce!' was the most frequent sound. All the voices would clamour for a moment together. It was a shattering noise in this dusky tunnel. – I had stopped reading, as I have said, and I lifted my eyes. It was then that I saw the Ankou.

With revulsed and misty eyes almost in front of me, an imperious figure, apparently armed with a club, was forcing its way insolently forward towards the door, its head up, an eloquently moving mouth hung in the air, as it seemed, for its possessor. It forced rudely aside everything in its path. Two men who were standing and talking to a seated one flew apart, struck by the club, or the sceptre, of this king amongst afflictions. The progress of this embodied calamity was peculiarly straight. He did not deviate. He passed my table and I saw a small, highly coloured, face, with waxed moustaches. But the terrible perquisite of the blind was there in the staring, milky eyeballs: and an expression of acetic ponderous importance weighted it so that, mean as it was in reality, this mask was highly impressive. Also, from its bitter immunity and unquestioned right-of-way, and from the habit of wandering through the outer jungle of physical objects, it had the look that some small boy's face might acquire, prone to imagine himself a steam-roller, or a sightless Juggernaut.

The blinded figure had burst into my daydream so unexpectedly and so pat, that I was taken aback by this sudden close-up of so trite a tragedy. Where he had come was compact with an emotional medium emitted by me. In reality it was a private scene, so that this overweening intruder might have been marching through my mind with his taut convulsive step, club in hand, rather than merely traversing the eating-room of a hotel, after a privileged visit to the kitchen. Certainly at that moment my mind was lying open so much, or was so much exteriorized, that almost literally, as far as I was concerned, it was inside, not out, that this image forced its way. Hence, perhaps, the strange effect.

The impression was so strong that I felt for the moment that I had met the death-god, a garbled version with waxed moustaches. It was noon. I said to myself that, as it was noon, that should give me twelve months more to live. I brushed aside the suggestion that day was not night, that I was not a breton peasant, and that the beggar was probably not Death. I tried to shudder. I had not shuddered. His attendant, a sad-faced child, rattled a lead mug under my nose. I put two sous in it. I had no doubt averted the omen, I reflected, with this bribe.

The weather improved in the afternoon. As I was walking about with a fisherman I knew, who had come in twenty miles for this Pardon, I saw the Ankou again, collecting pence. He was strolling now, making a leisurely harvest from the pockets of these religious crowds. His attitude was, however, peremptory. He called out hoarsely his requirements, and turned his empty eyes in the direction indicated by his acolyte, where he knew there was a group who had not paid. His clothes were smart, all in rich, black broadcloth and black velvet, with a ribboned hat. He entered into every door he found open, beating on it with his club-like stick. I did not notice any *Thank you!* pass his lips. He appeared to snort when he had received what was due to him, and to turn away, his legs beginning to march mechanically like a man mildly shell-shocked.

The fisherman and I both stood watching him. I laughed.

'Il ne se gêne pas!' I said. 'He does not *beg*. I don't call that a *beggar.*'

'Indeed, you are right. – That is Ludo,' I was told.

'Who is Ludo, then?' I asked.

'Ludo is the king of Rot!' my friend laughed. 'The people round here spoil him, according to my idea. He's only a beggar. It's true he's blind. But he takes too much on himself.'

He spat.

'He's not the only blind beggar in the world!'

'Indeed, he is not,' I said.

'He drives off any other blind beggars that put their noses inside Rot. You see his stick? He uses it!'

We saw him led up to a party who had not noticed his approach. He stood for a moment shouting. From stupidity they did not respond at once. Turning violently away, he dragged his attendant after him.

'He must not be kept waiting!' I said.

'Ah, no. With Ludo you must be nimble!'

The people he had left remained crestfallen and astonished.

'Where does he live?' I asked.

'Well, he lives, I have been told, in a cave, on the road to Kermarquer. That's where he lives. Where he banks I can't tell you!'

Ludo approached us. He shouted in breton.

'What is he saying?'

'He is telling you to get ready; that he is coming!' said my friend. He pulled out a few sous from his pocket, and said: 'Faut bien! Needs must!' and laughed a little sheepishly.

I emptied a handful of coppers into the mug.

'Ludo!' I exclaimed. 'How are you? Are you well?'

He stood, his face in my direction, with, except for the eyes, his mask of an irritable Jack-in-office, with the waxed moustaches of a small pretentious official.

'Very well! And you?' came back with unexpected rapidity.

'Not so bad, touching wood!' I said. 'How is your wife?'

'Je suis garçon! I am a bachelor!' he replied at once.

'So you are better off, old chap!' I said. 'Women serve no good purpose, for serious boys!'

'You are right,' said Ludo. He then made a disgusting remark. We laughed. His face had not changed its expression. Did he try, I wondered, to picture the stranger, discharging remarks from empty blackness, or had the voice outside become for him or had it always been what the picture is to us? If you had never seen any of the people you knew, but had only talked to them on the telephone – what under these circumstances would So-and-So be as a voice, I asked myself, instead of mainly a picture?

'How long have you been a beggar, Ludo?' I asked.

'Longtemps!' he replied. I had been too fresh for this important beggar. He got in motion and passed on, shouting in breton.

The fisherman laughed and spat.

'Quel type!' he said. 'When we were in Penang, no it was at Bankok, at the time of my service with the fleet, I saw just such another. He was a blind sailor, an Englishman. He had lost his sight in a shipwreck. – He would not beg from the black people.'

'Why did he stop there?'

'He liked the heat. He was a *farceur*. He was such another as this one.'

Two days later I set out on foot for Kermarquer. I remembered as I was going out of the town that my friend had told me that Ludo's cave was there somewhere. I asked a woman working in a field where it was. She directed me.

I found him in a small, verdant enclosure, one end of it full of half-wild chickens, with a rocky bluff at one side, and a stream running in a bed of smooth boulders. A chimney stuck out of the rock, and a black string of smoke wound out of it. Ludo sat at the mouth of his cave. A large dog rushed barking towards me at my approach. I took up a stone and threatened it. His boy, who was cooking, called off the dog. He looked at me with intelligence.

'Good morning, Ludo!' I said. 'I am an Englishman. I met you at the Pardon, do you remember? I have come to visit you, in passing. How are you? It's a fine day.'

'Ah, it was you I met? I remember. You were with a fisherman from Kermanec?'

'The same.'

'So you're an Englishman?'

'Yes.'

'Tiens!'

I did not think he looked well. My sensation of mock-superstition had passed. But although I was now familiar with Ludo, when I looked at his staring mask I still experienced a faint reflection of my first impression, when he was the death-god. That impression had been a strong one, and it was associated with superstition. So he was still a feeble death-god.

The bodies of a number of esculent frogs lay on the ground, from which the back legs had been cut. These the boy was engaged in poaching.

'What is that you are doing them in?' I asked him.

'White wine,' he said.

'Are they best that way?' I asked.

'Why, that is a good way to do them,' said Ludo. 'You don't eat frogs in England, do you?'

'No, that is repugnant to us.'

I picked one up.

'You don't eat the bodies?'

'No, only the thighs,' said the boy.

'Will you try one?' asked Ludo.

'I've just had my meal, thank you all the same.'

I pulled out of my rucksack a flask of brandy.

'I have some eau-de-vie here,' I said. 'Will you have a glass?'

'I should be glad to,' said Ludo.

I sat down, and in a few minutes his meal was ready. He disposed of the grenouilles with relish, and drank my health in my brandy, and I drank his. The boy ate some fish that he had cooked for himself, a few yards away from us, giving small pieces to the dog.

After the meal Ludo sent the boy on some errand. The dog did not go with him. I offered Ludo a cigarette which he refused. We sat in silence for some minutes. As I looked at him I realized how the eyes mount guard over the face, as well as look out of it. The faces of the blind are hung there like a dead lantern. Blind people must feel on their skins our eyes upon them: but this sheet of flesh is rashly stuck up in what must appear far outside their control, an object in a foreign world of sight. So in consequence of this divorce, their faces have the appearance of things that have been abandoned by the mind. What is his face to a blind man? Probably nothing more than an organ, an exposed part of the stomach, that is a mouth.

Ludo's face, in any case, was *blind*; it looked the blindest part of his body, and perhaps the deadest, from which all the functions of a living face had gone. As a result of its irrelevant external situation, it carried on its own life with the outer world, and behaved with all the disinvolture of an internal organ, no longer serving to secrete thought any more than the foot. For after all to be lost *outside* is much the same as to be hidden in the dark *within*. – What served for a face for the blind, then? What did they have instead, that was expressive of emotion in the way that our faces are? I supposed that all the responsive machinery must be largely re-adjusted with them, and directed to some other part of the body. I noticed that Ludo's hands, all the movement of his limbs, were a surer indication of what he was thinking than was his face.

Still the face registered something. It was a health-chart perhaps. He looked very ill I thought, and by that I meant, of course, that his *face* did not look in good health. When I said, 'You don't look well,' his hands moved nervously on his club. His face responded by taking on a sicklier shade.

'I'm ill,' he said.

'What is it?'

'I'm indisposed.'

'Perhaps you've met the Ankou.' I said this thoughtlessly, probably because I had intended to ask him if he had ever heard of the Ankou, or something like that. He did not say anything to this, but remained quite still, then stood up and shook himself and sat down again. He began rocking himself lightly from side to side.

'Who has been telling you about the Ankou, and all those tales?' he suddenly asked.

'Why, I was reading about it in a guide-book, as a matter of fact, the first time I saw you. You scared me for a moment. I thought you might be he.'

He did not reply to this, nor did he say anything, but his face assumed the expression I had noticed on it when I first saw it, as he forced his way through the throngs at the inn.

'Do you think the weather will hold?' I asked.

He made no reply. I did not look at him. With anybody with a face you necessarily feel that they can see you, even if their blank eyes prove the contrary. His fingers moved nervously on the handle of his stick. I felt that I had suddenly grown less popular. What had I done? I had mentioned an extinct god of death. Perhaps that was regarded as unlucky. I could not guess what had occurred to displease him.

'It was a good Pardon, was it not, the other day?' I said.

There was no reply. I was not sure whether he had not perhaps moods in which, owing to his affliction, he just entered into his shell, and declined to hold intercourse with the outside. I sat smoking for five minutes, I suppose, expecting that the boy might return. I coughed. He turned his head towards me.

'Vous êtes toujours là?' he asked.

'Oui, toujours,' I said. Another silence passed. He placed his hand on his side and groaned.

'Is there something hurting you?' I asked.

He got up and exclaimed:

'Merde!'

Was that for me? I had the impression, as I glanced towards him to enquire, that his face expressed fear. Of what?

Still holding his side, shuddering and with an unsteady step, he went into his cave, the door of which he slammed. I got up. The dog growled as he lay before the door of the cave. I shouldered my rucksack. It was no longer a hospitable spot. I passed the midden on which the bodies of the grenouilles now lay, went down the stream, and so left. If I met the boy I would tell him his master was ill. But he was nowhere in sight, and I did not know which way he had gone.

I connected the change from cordiality to dislike on the part of Ludo with the mention of the Ankou. There seemed no other explanation. But why should that have affected him so much? Perhaps I had put myself in the position of the Ankou, even – unseen as I was, a foreigner and, so, ultimately dangerous – by mentioning the Ankou, with which he was evidently familiar. He may even have retreated into his cave, because he was afraid of me. Or the poor devil was simply ill. Perhaps the frogs had upset him: or maybe the boy had poisoned him. I walked away. I had gone a mile probably when I met the boy. He was carrying a covered basket.

'Ludo's ill. He went indoors,' I said. 'He seemed to be suffering.'

'He's not very well to-day,' said the boy. 'Has he gone in?'

I gave him a few sous.

Later that summer the fisherman I had been with at the Pardon told me that Ludo was dead.

# Franciscan Adventures

I found him in front of a crowd of awestruck children, the french vagabond, hoisting a box up under his arm, strapping it over his shoulder, and brandishing three ruined umbrellas. 'Ah, yes, say what you will, music, that is the art for me! Do you know, shall I tell you?' (he approached a little girl, who shrank abashed from his confidences). 'Shall I tell you, my little chicken?' he whispered, his voice sustaining in a sepulchral vibration the *dise* of 'veux-tu que je te *dise*?' and slobbering at 'poule,' which he puffed out from his vinous lips, eyes sodden, fixed and blank.

'*I am musical!*'

Waggling his head, he turned away and started down the road. Then he wheeled at their jeers. In big strides he hurried back: he saw himself as a giant in a fairy tale. The group of small children backed in a block, all eyes centering on the figure stalking towards them. He brought himself to a sudden halt, stiffened to lift himself still further above their lilliputian stature. 'Music!' he exclaimed: 'ah, yes, I am' (he paused, kneading them with his fiery eyes; then in a very confidential key) '*musical!*' He proceeded with that theme, but conversationally. In making use of certain expressions such as *pianissimo* and *contralto*, he would add, as a polite afterthought, 'that is a term in music.' Then, towering over his puny audience, arms extended, head thrown back, he would call out menacingly his maxims – all on the subject of music. Afterwards, dropping his voice once more, and turning his pompous and knowing eyes upon the nearest infant, he would add, in a manner suggestive of a favoured privacy, some further information or advice, 'Remember, the stomach is the womb! L'estomac, c'est la matrice! it is the stomach that sings! It comes out here.' He pointed to his mouth. He placed his hand midway on his person. 'It is born here.' Tall, slender and with graceful waving limbs, he wore a full beard, growing in a lustreless, grey-green cascade, while hair fell, curling at the ends, upon his shoulders. He had a handsome, fastidiously regular, thin and tanned face, in which his luminous black eyes recognized the advantage of their position; they rolled luxuriously on either side of his aristocratic nose. He would frequently pass his hands, of a 'musical' tenuity, over his canonical beard.

I thought I would stop and interrogate this shell. I watched his performance from a distance. He soon saw me and left the children. He passed, his hat struck down over his eyes, a drunken pout of watchful defiance lying like a burst plum in a nest of green bristle and mildewed down, his nose reddening at its fine extremity. From beneath the hat-brim he quizzed me, but offering alternatives, I thought.

I smiled at him broadly, showing him my big, white, expensive teeth, in perfect condition.

'Good-day!' I nodded.

He might pull up, or perhaps he was too drunk, or not in the mood: I thought I would leave it at that. He was not sure: the tail of his eye interrogated.

'Good-day!' I nodded more sharply, reassuringly.

An arch light replaced the quizzing scowl, but still he did not stop.

'Good-day!' I exclaimed. 'Yes!' I nodded with pointed affirmative.

'Good-day!'

He went on, his eyes trained sideways on me. I gave a salvo of emphatic nods in quick succession.

'Yes!' I coaxed. I showed my teeth again. 'Why yes!'

He was repelled by my shabby appearance, I saw. I opened my coat and showed him a rich coloured scarf. I smiled again, slowly and hypnotically, offering to his dazzled inspection the dangling scarf.

He suddenly wheeled in my direction, stopped, stretched out the hand with the scarecrow umbrellas, and began singing a patriotic song. I stopped. A half-dozen yards separated us. His voice was strong: it spent most of its time in his throat, wallowing in a juicy bellow. Sometimes by accident the sinuses were occupied by it, as it charged up the octave, and it issued pretty and flute-like from the well-shaped inside of his face. As he sang, his head was dramatically lowered, to enable him to fish down for the low notes; his eyes glared fixedly up from underneath. His mouth was stretched open to imitate the dark, florid aperture of a trumpet: from its lips rich sputum trickled. He would stop, and with an indrawn wheeze or a quick gasp, fetch it back as it was escaping. Then he would burst out violently again into a heaving flux of song. I approached him.

'That was not at all bad,' I remarked when he had done, and was gathering up stray drops the colour of brandy with his tongue.

'No?'

'Not at all. It was very musical. Quite good!'

'Ah!' he exclaimed, and his eyes rested blankly on my person. 'Musical! Ah!'

'Yes, I think so.'

'Ah!'

'By God and the Devil and what comes between, you have a voice that is not at all bad.'

'You are of that opinion?'

'My God, yes!'

'Truly?'

'That is what I hold for the moment. But I must hear more of it.'

He retreated a step, lowered his head, took a deep breath, and opened his mouth. I held up my hand. He closed his mouth, deflated his chest, and raised his head.

'Have a cigarette,' I said.

He eyed my luxurious new morocco cigarette case. He perceived the clean, pink shirt and collar as I drew it out. With a clear responsive functioning to delight 'Behavior,' he swung his box off his shoulder, put it down upon the road, and placed his umbrellas upon it. He felt stiff when that was off. He rattled himself about circumspectly.

'Thanks! Thanks!'

His fine amber and ebony finger-tips entered the case with suspicious decorum, and drew out the little body of a cigarette nipped between thumb and index.

'Thank you, old chap!'

The cigarette was stuck into the split plum, which came out in the midst of his beard – its dull-red hemispheres revolving a little, outward and then inward, to make way, gently closing upon it. I lighted it; he began sucking the smoke. A moment later it burst from his nostrils.

'What is the time, mon petit?' he asked.

He wanted to see my watch.

'Half-past hanging time,' I said. 'Will you have a drink? Tu prendras un petit coup, n'est-ce pas?'

'Mais! – je-ne-demande-pas-mieux!'

It was done. I led him to the nearby débit. We sat down in the excessive gloom and damp. I rattled on the tin table with the soucoupe of the last drinker.

I examined this old song-bird with scorn. Monotonous passion, stereotyped into a frenzied machine, he irritated me like an aimlessly howling wind. Had I been sitting with the wind, however, I should not have felt scorn. He was at the same time elemental and silly, that was the reason. What emotions had this automaton experienced before he accepted outcast life? In the rounded personality, known as Father Francis, the answer was neatly engraved. *The emotions provoked by the bad, late, topical sentimental songs of Republican France.* You could get no closer answer than that, and it accounted completely for him. He had become their disreputable embodiment. In his youth the chlorotic heroine of the popular lyrical fancy must have been his phantom mate. He became her ideal, according to the indications provided by the lying ballad. So he would lose touch more and more with unlyricized reality, which would in due course vomit him into the outcast void. That was the likeliest story of this shell I had arrested and attracted in here to inspect.

I settled down to watch. I flashed a few big smiles at him to warm him up. But he was very businesslike. A stranger would have supposed us engaged in some small but interesting negotiation. My rôle would have seemed that of a young, naïve, enthusiastic impresario. Francis was my 'find.' (I was evidently a musical impresario.)

After having been shown his throat, and having failed in my attempt to seize between my thumb and forefinger an imaginary vessel, which he insisted, with considerable violence, I should locate, our relations nearly terminated out of hand. I had cast doubt, involuntarily, upon a possession by which he set great store. He frowned. But he had other resources. I pursued song across this friend's anatomy to its darkest springs. Limited, possibly, to the field of his own body, he was a consummate ventriloquist. I have heard the endocrines uttering a C sharp, and there is nowhere in the intestines from which for me musical notes have not issued. Placing his hand upon his stomach, and convulsing himself solemnly, as though about to eat, his chin on his chest, he and I would sit and listen, and we would both hear a rich, musical sound an inch or so above the seat of the stool on which he sat.

He would then look up at me slowly, with a smile of naïve understanding.

I got tired of this, and said irrelevantly:

'Your hair is very long.'

He pushed in a brake – he had heard – he slowed down his speech, his eye doubtfully hooked on to mine: some sentences still followed. Then after a silence, releasing as it were with a snap all his face muscles so that his mask dropped into lines of preternatural gravity, he exclaimed:

'T'as raison mon pauv' gosse! – I will tell you. Here, I say, I will tell you. It's too long. My hair is too long!'

How vastly this differed from my own observation, though the words were the same, it is difficult to convey. If he had with irrefragable proofs confuted my statement for ever, it could not have been more utterly wiped out.

What was I? That did not exercise him. Once or twice he looked at me, not certainly with curiosity, but with a formal attention. An inscrutable figure had beckoned to him, and was now treating him for no reason beyond that he was. (This might be a strange circumstance. But it possessed no monopoly of strangeness.) His cigarettes, though not strong, were good. He was a foreigner. That was sufficient. François was not interested in other people, except as illustrations of elementary physics. Some people repelled him, violently on occasion, and set up interferences, resulting in hunger and thirst. He lived in outer space, outcast, and only came to earth to drink and get a crust. There people mattered, for a moment, but without identity.

The obstacles to be overcome if you were to establish profitable relations with this at first sight inaccessible mind, were many. Between it and the outer world many natural barriers existed. His conversation was obscure. My ignorance of the theory of music, the confusion caused in my mind by his prolonged explanation of difficult passages (full of what I supposed to be musicians' slang, confounded with thieves' slang and breton idiom); the destructive hiccups that engulfed so many of his phrases, and often ruined a whole train of thought, even nipped in the bud entire philosophies, the constant sense of insecurity consequent upon these repeated catastrophes, these were only a few of the disappointments. Another obstacle was that he spoke the major part of the time in a whisper. When I could not catch a single word, I yet often could judge, by the glances he shot at me, the scornful half-closing of his eyes, screwing up of his mouth and nose, all the horrid cunning of his expression and nodding of his head, the sort of thing that was occurring. At other times, his angry and defiant looks showed me that my respect was being peremptorily claimed. But it remained dumb show, often, his voice was pitched so low.

'Speak up, Francis. On Tibb's-eve you'll have to be louder than that.'

'I'm sorry, my poor friend. – It's the vocal cords. They function badly to-day.'

'Are you dry? Fill up.'

He forgot the next moment, and renewed his muttering.

The remembrance of injuries constantly stirred in him. Excited by his words, when he had found some phrase happier than another to express his defiant independence, he felt keenly the chance he had lost. But enemies melted into friends, and vice versa, in his mind, as they had in his experience. He turned and frankly enjoyed his verbal triumphs at my expense.

We had been together some time, and he had drunk a bottle of wine, when his thoughts began to run on a certain hotel-keeper of the neighbourhood, whom he suspected of wishing to sell his present business. The day before, or the week before, he had observed him looking up at a newly-constructed building in the main street of Rot.

When he first began about this, I supposed he was referring to the coarse eructations of some figure whom we had imperceptibly left, although I thought we were still with him. He dropped his voice, and looked behind him when he said 'Rot.' (Rot is a breton commune, and it also means a belch.) I sat over him with knitted brows for some time.

'Oui. Pour moi, c'est sa dame qui ne veut plus de Kermanec. – Que la vase pue là-bas – oh, là là! Quel odeur! Elle a raison! Qu'il aille à Rot! Qu'il y aille! Moi, je m'en foute! Tant pis pour lui. C'est un malin, tu sais.' He drank fiercely and continued (I will translate the sort of rigmarole that followed): 'He's like that. Once he gets an idea in his head. What's he want to leave Kermanec for? It's a good place: he has a fine trade. He's my cousin. He doesn't know me. I got behind the wall. It's not a bad house. It's been in that state for two years. What? Two years, I say, for certain; it may be three or four. There's no roof, but its first floor is in: – no staircase. It's dry. I don't say it's a Régina! They put a *flic* at the corner, but we got in the back way. There's waste-land – yes, waste. Of course. *Naturally*. I saw him. He was going in at the gate. I hid. He paced the frontage.' He put one sabot in front of the other to show the method. This was the innkeeper – not the *flic* – measuring the frontage of the half-built house, in the sheltered part of which tramps were accustomed to spend the night, under the nose of the sergent de ville. And this was the house on which, so it seemed, the landlord had his eye.

In the course of his recital, he repeatedly reverted to the proud spirit of this publican. On my catching the word 'vermin,' and showing interest, he repeated what he was saying a little louder.

'Any one seeing me as I am, without profession, poor, might suppose that I had vermin in my beard. Yes,' he added softly. We fell into a conversation at this point upon matters connected with the toilet. What a bore it was to wash! No great men had ever washed. There was a great sage in England called Shaw, I told him, he never washed. Doctor Johnson, another british sage, found washing repugnant. It was very unusual, I said, for *me* to wash, though I had, I said, washed that morning. Searching stealthily behind the unorganized panels of rags, which could be seen symmetrically depending when his greatcoat was opened, he produced the middle section of a comb. With this he made passes over his beard – without, however, touching it – which he shook scornfully. He looked at me steadily. I showed I was impressed. He replaced the comb. The dumb-show had been intended to reveal to my curiosity a characteristic moment of his toilet.

'Zut!' he said, coughing, 'I had a good brush. That rogue Charlot (ce chenapan de Charlot!) pinched it!' 'Charlot,' I heard, was so named among his brother vagabonds on account of his resemblance to Chaplin.

A story intervened in which he gave a glimpse of his physical resource and determination in moments of difficulty. The landlords of inns, and farmers, were his principal enemies. He told me how he treated them. First, it was in general, then particular figures suggested themselves. He dealt with them one by one.

'Je lui disais: Monsieur!' (Like Doctor Johnson all his addresses began with an emphatic and threatening 'Sir!') 'I said: Your views are not mine. It's no use my affecting to be in agreement with you. You say I'm a "rôdeur." I give you the lie. (– *I don't beat about the bush!* he said in an aside to me.) Je n'ai jamais rôdé. – Je ne bouge pas, moi – jamais! J'y suis, j'y reste! – That is my motto! That is my way, sir!'

A scene of considerable violence shortly took place. He stamped on the floor with his great sabots to render more vivid to himself this scene, also to supply the indispensable element of noise. Owing to emotion, his voice was incapable of providing this. He spoke with a dreadful intensity, glaring into my face. Eventually he sprang up; struggling and stamping about the room (overmatched at first) with an indomitable heave of the shoulders, and an irresistible rush, he then made believe to fling his antagonist out of the door. While engaged in this feat, panting and stamping, he had exclaimed where the action suggested it, 'Ah! veux-tu! Sale bête! Ah sacré gars! Et puis alors, quoi? Es-tu fou? Tu crois pétrir avec tes mains un tel que moi! Allons donc! Tu plaisantes! Ah! Je vois bien ton jeu! – Ah bah! le voilà foutu! Tant mieux! Con! Oui! Con! sale con! Ah!' He came back and sat down, his chest heaving, looking at me for a long time silently, with an air of insolent triumph.

It would have been difficult to blame him for the steps he had taken, for he evidently experienced a great relief at the eviction of this imaginary landlord. Probably he had thrown him out of every bar along the road. Ever since we had entered he had been restless. I was not sorry he had rid us of this phantom; but I looked with a certain anxiety towards the door from time to time. He now seemed enjoying the peace that he had so gallantly secured for himself. His limbs relaxed, his eyes were softer. The lips of the voluptuary were everted again, moving like gorged red worms in the hairs of his moustache and beard. He delicately fed them from his wine-glass. He proceeded now to show me his mild side. He could afford to. He assured me that he did not like turbulent people. 'J' n'aime pas l' monde turbulent!' And then he raised his voice, making the gesture of the teacher: 'Socrates said, "Listen, but do not strike!"' ('Socrate a dit: "Ecoutez, mais ne frappez pas."')

He abounded in a certain kind of catch-word (such as 'Il ne faut pas confondre la vitesse avec la précipitation! Non! il ne faut pas confondre la vitesse avec la précipitation!'). These sayings occurred to him hors d'à propos. Sometimes, finding them there on his tongue, he would just use them and leave it at that. Or he would boldly utter them and take them as a text for a new discourse. Another perhaps would turn up: he would drop the first and proceed triumphantly at a tangent.

'Do you go to Rumengol?' I asked him.

'Rumengol? Why, yes, I have gone to Rumengol.'

'It is the Pardon for men of your profession.'

He looked at me, saying absent-mindedly:

'Why, yes, perhaps.'

'It is called *le Pardon des chanteurs*, "the singer's Pardon," is not that so, I believe?'

His face lit up stupidly.

'Ah, is it called that?' he said. 'I didn't know it was called that. *Pardon des chanteurs*. That's jolly! Pardon des chanteurs!'

He began singing a catch.

'Is your beat mostly on the *armor*, or is it in the *argoat*?'

'Argouate?' he asked blankly. 'What is that? Argouate! I don't know it.'

Those are the terms for the littoral and the interior respectively. I was surprised to find he did not know them.

'Where do you come from?' I asked.

'I don't know. – Far from here,' he said briefly.

So he was not breton. The historic rôle of the vagabond in Armorica has almost imposed on him the advertisement of a mysterious origin. It was so much to his advantage, in the more superstitious centuries, to be a stranger, and seem not to know the breton tongue, if not deaf and mute. So he could slip into the legendary framework, and become, at need, Gabik or Gralon.

Something had struck his fancy particularly. This was connected with his name François. He told me how he had slept in the château of François I. at Chambord. It appeared that it was in giving information against his *bête noire*, the local innkeeper, that he had come to sleep there. I could not discover what connection these two facts might have. I expect they had none. It began suddenly with a picture of a wintry night in the forest. It was very cold and it blew. An inn put in its appearance. There an 'orgie' was in progress. He introduced himself. Without being exactly welcomed, he was suffered to remain. The account at this point became more and more fantastic and uncertain. He must have got drunk almost immediately. This I put down to his exposure to the cold: so I picked my way through his disordered words. His story staggered and came in flashes. He could not understand evidently why the material had, all of a sudden, grown so intractable. Once or twice he stopped. Living it again, he rolled his eyes and even seemed about to lose his balance on the stool. He wanted to go on telling it: but it began to sound absurd even to him. It still did not occur to him that at this point he had fallen down drunk. He gave it up.

But the inevitable wicked landlord put in his appearance, robbed him of his tobacco and other articles. He resisted this exploitation. Then we certainly reached the château. His face cleared up. We had arrived at the château. He became more composed. I asked him where he had slept in the château. He answered he had slept on a mattress, and had had *two* blankets. On second thoughts he concluded that this would tax my credulity too much, and withdrew one of the blankets. It was in the Château de Chambord that Molière played for the first time *Le Bourgeois Gentilhomme*, under the splendid ceiling covered then with freshly painted salamanders. But how did this Francis come to lodge there, if he ever did? Falubert's indignant account of the neglect into which, in his time, this celebrated castle had fallen, may afford some clue. He says of it: 'On l'a donné à tout le monde, comme si personne n'en voulait le garder. Il a l'air de n'avoir jamais presque servi et avoir été toujours trop grand. C'est comme une hôtellerie abandonnée où les voyageurs n'ont pas même laissé leurs noms aux murs.'

As it has been 'given to everybody,' and yet 'nobody has ever wanted it,' perhaps this 'derelict inn' was given to le père François for a night. When Flaubert and Maxime du Camp, already in a state of bellicose distress, gaze over the staircase into the central court, their indignant gaze falls on a humble female donkey, giving milk to a newly-born colt. 'Voilà ce qu'il y avait dans la cour d'honneur du Château de Chambord!' exclaims Flaubert: 'un chien qui joue dans l'herbe et un âne qui tette, ronfle et brait, fiente et gambade sur le seuil des rois . . .' Could Flaubert have observed le père François installed beneath his sumptuous blanket in the entrance court of kings, or addressing himself to his toilet, I feel certain that that impetuous man would have passinately descended the staircase and driven him out with his cane. But this account of Flaubert's does make the franciscan adventure of the Château de Chambord more likely: for if a dog and a donkey, why not a tramp?

There was no break in the story; but the château grew dim. He evidently rapidly fell asleep, owing to the unaccustomed blanket. He forgot the last landlord. He had been a robust man. He ran after the bonnes. He melted into a farmer. The farmer was robust. He ran after François. There was a dog. It fixed its teeth in his leg. He struggled madly with the dog, his back against the débit wall. Afterwards, when it was all over, he rolled up his trousers and we attempted to find a cicatrice. He wetted his thumb, with that he abraded a rectangular strip near the ankle: there was a little weal.

The saloon-keeper passed the table several times during this chain of stories. Once he said, stopping to listen for a moment, 'Ouf, a pack of lies!' 'Non pas!' replied Francis. 'You lie. You love falsehood! I can see it. Go away.' The man shrugged violently and went back to the bar. Some customers had come in. One sat listening to François with a heavy grin. I turned to him and said:

'He is original, le père François, don't you find that so?'

'Why, yes. He's mad.' The steady eyes of the smiling peasant continued to follow his movements with lazy attention.

'Yes, *original*, I am original!' François eagerly assented, as though in fear, then, that I should be converted to this other man's opinion.

'Original!' he insisted. 'I am original,'

Suddenly turning to me, with rapid condescension, he remarked:

'Je suis content de toi! I am satisfied with you!'

However, the horizon became anew overclouded. With him it never stood at Fair for long. He grew more and more violent. Often he sprang up and whirled round without reason, with the ecstasy of a dervish, his ruined umbrellas shaken at arm's length. Afterwards he sat down suddenly. He held his arm out stiffly towards me, looked at it, then at me, wildly, contracting his muscles, as if searching for some thought that this familiar instrument suggested, without finding it. Stretching his arm back swiftly as though about to strike, drawing his breath between his teeth, with the other hand he seized his forearm as though it were an independent creature, his fingers its legs, and stared at it. What did this mad arm want? Allons donc! He dropped it listlessly at his side, where it hung.

Night had fallen: the landlord had lighted the lamp over the bar. Francis grew steadily more noisy, singing and using the window as a drum, his arms on either side of it, tattooing and banging it, his head turned towards us. The landlord shouted at him at last, with great violence, 'Tais-toi, vieux imbécile!' The landlord was vexed. His wife slouched out from the kitchen, and directing the fine hostility of her gaze toward Francis, muttered heatedly with her husband for some minutes. They were afraid they would have to give him a night's lodging in the barn. Not long after this we were turned out. Francis went meekly: he ridiculed the event, in sotto voce conversation with himself. I was ready to go. At the door he cut a caper, and shouted at the landlord, bolder out of doors:

'Je vous remercie! Monsieur, adieu! Me v'là qui va me chauffer à la cheminée du roi René.'

'Plutôt à la belle étoile, mon pauv' viou!'

Francis looked up into the sky overhead and saw a bright star.

'Plutôt, en effet,' he said. 'Mais oui-là, t'as raison – il fait nuit! T'es intelligent, tu sais! N'est-ce pas, mon petit, qu'il est intelligent, le patron, quand même? Il n'en a pas l'air, par-bleu! Pauv' colas, va! Ah, bah! Tant pis! Les paysans de par-ici sont d'une bêtise! – c'est fantastique! Oui-dame: mais écoute! C'môme-là, tu sais: il n'est pas méchant; *mais* non! Il est trop bête! C'est à peine qu'il sait lire et écrire. C'est une brute, quoi! Tant pis! Ah! merde-alors, où sont donc mes photos – ?'

He stood drawn up to his full height, his hands hurrying dramatically into all the hiding-places of his person. First one hand, then the other, disappeared beneath his rags and leapt out empty.

'Rien! Ils ne sont pas là! Nom d'un nom! On m'a volé!'

He made as though to rush back to the débit. I held him by the arm.

'Come on! I'll give you a franc. You can buy some more.'

He was about to put into execution the immemorial tactic of the outcast in such a situation. Eviction from an eating and drinking house, first: then comes the retort of an accusation of theft. The indignant customary words raced on his tongue. He had been robbed! All his photographs had been pinched! What a house! What people! It was not safe for honest men to drink there! He would inform the Commissioner of Police when he reached Saint-Kaduan. They would see if he was to be robbed with impunity!

He shook his fist at the débit while I held him. The landlord had left the door. The road was deserted; a gilt moon (it was that he had mistaken for the sun, in a condition of partial eclipse) hung over the village a hundred yards away. Our shadows staggered madly for a moment, then the thought of the franc cut short this ceremony, and he came away towards the village. I gave him the franc. He came half way, then left me. Standing in the middle of the road, the moonlight converting him into a sickly figure of early republican romance, he sang to me as I walked away. With the franc, I supposed it was his intention to return to the débit.

In the 'granges' at the various farms, tramps usually find a night's lodging. They make arrangements to meet, and often spend several nights together in this way. The farm people take their matches and pipes away from them. Or they put them in the stable among the cattle, making a hole in the wet straw like a cradle for them. Two days later I saw him through an inn window for a moment, outside Braspartz. He was dancing in his heavy sabots, his shoulders drawn up to his ears, arms akimbo. 'I saw an Italian dance this way,' I heard him exclaim. 'It's true! This is the way the Italians dance!' A group of sullen peasants watched him, one laughing, to show he was not taken in. On noticing me, he began singing a love song, in a loud strong voice. Without interrupting the song, he stretched his hand through the window for a cigarette. There was no recognition in his face while he sang: his lips protruded eloquently in keeping with the sentiment. That is the last I saw of him.

# Brotcotnaz

Madame Brotcotnaz is orthodox: she is the breton woman at forty-five, from La Basse-Bretagne, the heart of Old Brittany, the region of the great Pardons. Frans Hals also would have passed from the painting of the wife of a petty burgess to Madame Brotcotnaz without any dislocation of his formulas or rupture of the time-sense. He would still have seen before him the black and white – the black broadcloth and white coiffe or caul; and for the white those virgated, slate-blue surfaces, the cold ink-black for the capital masses of the picture, would have appeared without a hitch. On coming to the face Frans Hals would have found his favourite glow of sallow-red, only deeper than he was accustomed to find in the flemish women. He would have gone to that part of the palette where the pigment lay for the men's faces at forty-five, the opposite end to the monticules of olive and sallow peach for the *juniores*, or the virgins and young wives.

The distillations of the breton orchard have almost subdued the obstinate yellow of jaundice, and Julie's face is a dull claret. In many tiny strongholds of eruptive red the more recent colour has entrenched itself. Her hair is very dark, parted in the middle, and tightly brushed down upon her head. Her eyebrows are for ever raised. She could not depress them, I suppose, any more, if she wanted to. A sort of scaly rigor fixes the wrinkles of the forehead into a seriated field of what is scarcely flesh, with the result that if she pulled her eyebrows down, they would fly up again the moment she released the muscles. The flesh of the mouth is scarcely more alive: it is parched and pinched in, so that she seems always hiding a faint snicker by driving it primly into her mouth. Her eyes are black and moist, with the furtive intensity of a rat. They move circumspectly in this bloated shell. She displaces herself also more noiselessly than the carefulest nun, and her hands are generally decussated, drooping upon the ridge of her waist-line, as though fixed there with an emblematic nail, at about the level of her navel. Her stomach is, for her, a kind of exclusive personal 'calvary.' At its crest hang her two hands, with the orthodox decussation, an elaborate ten-fingered symbol.

Revisiting the home of the Brotcotnazes this summer, I expected to find some change: but as I came down the steep and hollow ramp leading from the cliffs of the port, I was reassured at once. The door of the débit I perceived was open, with its desiccated bush over the lintel. Julie, with her head bound up in a large surgical bandage, stood there peering out, to see if there were any one in sight. No one was in sight, I had not been noticed; it was not from the direction of the cliffs that she redoubted interruption. She quickly withdrew. I approached the door of the débit in my noiseless *espadrilles* (that is, the hemp and canvas shoes of the country), and sprang quickly in after her. I snapped her with my eye while I shouted:

'Madame Brotcotnaz! Attention!'

She was behind the bar-counter, the fat medicine-glass was in the air, reversed. Her head was back, the last drops were trickling down between her gum and underlip, which stuck out like the spout of a cream-jug. The glass crashed down on the counter; Julie jumped, her hand on her heart. Beneath, among tins and flagons, on a shelf, she pushed at a bottle. She was trying to get it out of sight. I rushed up to her and seized one of her hands.

'I am glad to see you, Madame Brotcotnaz!' I exclaimed. 'Neuralgia again?' I pointed to the face.

'Oh, que vous m'avez fait peur, Monsieur Kairor!'

She placed her hand on her left breast, and came out slowly from behind the counter.

'I hope the neuralgia is not bad?'

She patted her bandage with a sniff.

'It's the erysipelas.'

'How is Monsieur Brotcotnaz?'

'Very well, thank you, Monsieur Kairor!' she said in a subdued sing-song. 'Very well,' she repeated, to fill up, with a faint prim smile. 'He is out with the boat. And you, Monsieur Kairor? Are you quite well?'

'Quite well, I thank you, Madame Brotcotnaz,' I replied, 'except perhaps a little thirsty. I have had a long walk along the cliff. Could we have a little glass together, do you think?'

'Why, yes, Monsieur Kairor.' She was more reserved at once. With a distant sniff, she turned half in the direction of the counter, her eyes on the wall before her. 'What must I give you now?'

'Have you any *pur jus*, such as I remember drinking the last time I was here?'

'Why, yes.' She moved silently away behind the wooden counter. Without difficulty she found the bottle of brandy, and poured me out a glass.

'And you, Madame? You will take one with me, isn't that so?'

'Mais, je veux bien!' she breathed with muted dignity, and poured herself out a small glass. We touched glasses.

'A votre santé, Madame Brotcotnaz!'

'A la vôtre, Monsieur Kairor!'

She put it chastely to her lip and took a decent sip, with the expression reserved otherwise for intercourse with the sacrament.

'It's good.' I smacked my lips.

'Why, yes. It is not at all bad,' she said, turning her head away with a faint sniff.

'It's good *pur jus*. If it comes to that, it is the best I have tasted since last I was here. How is it your *pur jus* is always of this high quality? You have taste where this drink is concerned, about that there can be no two opinions.'

She very softly tossed her head, wrinkled her nose on either side of the bridge, and appeared about to sneeze, which was the thing that came next before a laugh.

I leant across and lightly patted the bandage. She withdrew her head.

'It is painful?' I asked with commiseration.

My father, who, as I believe I have said, is a physician, once remarked in my hearing at the time my mother was drinking very heavily, prior to their separation, that for the management of alcoholic poisoning there is nothing better than koumiss.

'Have you ever tried a mixture of fermented mare's milk? Ordinary buttermilk will do. You add pepsin and lump sugar and let it stand for a day and a night. That is a very good remedy.'

She met this with an airy mockery. She dragged her eyes over my face afterwards with suspicion.

'It's excellent for erysipelas.'

She mocked me again. I told myself that she might at any moment find koumiss a useful drink, though I knew that she was wounded in the sex-war now only, and so required a management of another sort. I enjoyed arousing her veteran's contempt. She said nothing, but sat with resignation on the wooden bench at the table.

'I remember well these recurrent indispositions before, Madame Brotcotnaz,' I said. She looked at me in doubt for a moment, then turned her face quickly towards the door, slightly offended.

Julie was, of course, secretive, but as it had happened, she was forced to hug her secrets in public like two dolls that every one could see. I pretended to snatch first one, then the other. She looked at me and saw that I was not serious. She was silent in the way a child is: she just silently looked at me with a primitive coquetry of reproach, and turned her side to me. – Underneath the counter on the left hand of a person behind it was the bottle of eau-de-vie. When every one else had gone to the river to wash clothes, or had collected in the neighbouring inn, she approached the bottle on tiptoe, poured herself out several glasses in succession, which she drank with little sighs. Everybody knew this. That was the first secret. I had ravished it impetuously as described. Her second secret was the periodic beatings of Brotcotnaz. They were of very great severity. When I had occupied a room there, the crashing in the next apartment at night lasted sometimes for twenty minutes. The next day Julie was bandaged and could hardly limp downstairs. That was the erysipelas. Every one knew this, as well: yet her secretiveness had to exercise itself upon these scandalously exposed objects. I just thought I would stroke the second of them when I approached my hand to her bandaged face. These intrusions of mine into a *public* secret bored her only. She knew as well as I did when a thing was secret and when it was not. *Qu'est-ce qu'il a, cet homme?* she would say to herself.

'When do you expect Nicholas?' I asked.

She looked at the large mournful clock.

'Il ne doit pas tarder.'

I lifted my glass.

'To his safe return.'

The first muscular indications of a sneeze, a prim depression of the mouth, and my remark had been acknowledged, while she lifted her glass and took a solid sip.

Outside it was a white calm: I had seen a boat round the corner, with folded sails, beneath the cliff. That was no doubt Brotcotnaz. As I passed, they had dropped their oars out.

He should be here in a moment.

'Fill up your glass, Madame Brotcotnaz,' I said.

She did not reply. Then she said in an indifferent catch of the breath.

'Here he is!' Hands folded, or decussated as I have said they always were, she left him to me. She had produced him with her exclamation, 'Le v'là!'

A footfall, so light that it seemed nothing, came from the steps outside. A shadow struck the wall opposite the door. With an easy, dainty, and rapid tread, with a coquettishly supple giving of the knees at each step, and a gentle debonair oscillation of the massive head, a tall heavily-built fisherman came in. I sprang up and exclaimed:

'Ah! Here is Nicholas! How are you, old chap?'

'Why, it is Monsieur Kairor!' came the low caressing buzz of his voice. 'How are you? Well, I hope?'

137

He spoke in a low indolent voice. He smiled and smiled. He was dressed in the breton fashion.

'Was that you in the boat out there under the cliff just now?' I asked.

'Why, yes, Monsieur Kairor, that must have been us. Did you see us?' he said, with smiling interest.

I noted his child's pleasure at the image of himself somewhere else, in his boat, observed by me. It was as though I had said, Peep-oh! I see you, and we were back in the positions we then had occupied. He reflected a moment.

'I didn't see you. Were you on the cliff? I suppose you've just walked over from Loperec?'

His instinct directed him to account for my presence, here, and then up on the cliff. It was not curiosity. He wished to have cause and effect properly displayed. He racked his brains to see if he could remember having noticed a figure following the path on the cliff.

'Taking a little walk?' he added then.

He sat on the edge of a chair, with the symmetrical propriety of his healthy and powerful frame, the balance of the seated figure of the natural man, of the european type, found in the quattrocento frescoes. Julie and he did not look at each other.

'Give Monsieur Brotcotnaz a drink at once,' I said.

Brotcotnaz made a deprecatory gesture as she poured it, and continued to smile abstractedly at the table.

The dimensions of his eyes, and their oily suffusion with smiling-cream, or with some luminous jelly that seems still further to magnify them, are very remarkable. They are great tender mocking eyes that express the coquetry and contentment of animal fats. The sides of his massive forehead are often flushed, as happens with most men only in moments of embarrassment. Brotcotnaz is always embarrassed. But the flush with him, I think, is a constant affluence of blood to the neighbourhood of his eyes, and has something to do with their magnetic machinery. The tension caused in the surrounding vessels by this aesthetic concentration may account for it. What we call a sickly smile, the mouth remaining lightly drawn across the gums, with a slight painful contraction – the set suffering grin of the timid – seldom leaves his face.

The tread of this timid giant is softer than a nun's – the supple quick-giving at the knees at each step that I have described is the result no doubt of his fondness for the dance, in which he was so rapid, expert, and resourceful in his youth. When I first stayed with them, the year before, a man one day was playing a pipe on the cliff into the hollow of which the house is built. Brotcotnaz heard the music and drummed upon the table. Then, lightly springing up he danced in his tight-fitting black clothes a finicky hornpipe, in the middle of the débit. His red head was balanced in the air, face downwards, his arms went up alternately over his head, while he watched his feet like a dainty cat, placing them lightly and quickly here and there, with a ceremonial tenderness, and then snatching them away.

'You are fond of dancing,' I said.

His large tender steady blue eyes, suffused with the witchery of his secret juices, smiled and smiled: he informed me softly:

'J'suis maître danseur. C'est mon plaisir!'

The buzzing breton drawl, with as deep a 'z' as the dialect of Somerset, gave a peculiar emphasis to the *C'est mon plaisir!* He tapped the table, and gazed with the full benignity of his grin into my face.

'I am master of all the breton dances,' he said.

'The aubade, the gavotte—?'

'Why, yes, the breton gavotte.' He smiled serenely into my face. It was a blast of innocent happiness.

I saw as I looked at him the noble agility of his black faun-like figure as it must have rushed into the dancing crowd at the Pardon, leaping up into the air and capering to the *biniou* with grotesque elegance, while a crowd would gather to watch him. Then taking hands, while still holding their black umbrellas, they would spread out in chains, jolting in a dance confined to their rapidly moving feet. And still like a black fountain of movement, its vertex the flat, black, breton hat, strapped under the chin, he would continue his isolated performance. – His calm assurance of mastery in these dances implied such a position in the past in the festal life of the pagan countryside.

'Is Madame fond of dancing?' I asked.

'Why, yes. Julie can dance.'

He rose, and extending his hand to his wife with an indulgent gallantry, he exclaimed:

'Viens donc, Julie! Come then. Let us dance.'

Julie sat and sneered through her vinous mask at her fascinating husband. He insisted, standing over her with one toe pointed outward in the first movement of the dance, his hand held for her to take in a courtly attitude.

'Viens donc, Julie! Dansons un peu!'

Shedding shamefaced, pinched, and snuffling grins to right and left as she allowed herself to be drawn into this event, she rose. They danced a sort of minuet for me, advancing and retreating, curtseying and posturing, shuffling rapidly their feet. Julie did her part, it seemed, with understanding. With the same smile, at the same pitch, he resumed his seat in front of me.

'He composes verses also, to sing,' Julie then remarked.

'Songs for gavotte-airs, to be sung—?'

'Why, yes. Ask him!'

I asked him.

'Why, yes,' he said. 'In the past I have written many verses.'

Then, with his settled grin, he intoned and buzzed them through his scarcely parted teeth, whose tawny rows, he manipulating their stops with his tongue, resembled some exotic musical instrument.

Brotcotnaz is at once a fisherman, débitant or saloon-keeper, and 'cultivator.' In spite of this trinity of activities, he is poor. To build their present home he dissipated what was then left of Julie's fortune, so I was told by the postman one evening on the cliff. When at length it stood complete, beneath the little red bluff hewn out for its reception, brightly whitewashed, with a bald slate roof, and steps leading up to the door, from the steep and rugged space in front of it, he celebrated its completion with an expressive house-warming. Now he has the third share in a fishing boat, and what trade comes his way as a saloon-keeper, but it is very little.

His comrades will tell you that he is a 'charmant garçon, mais jaloux.' They call him 'traître.' He has been married twice. Referring to this, gossip tells you he gave his first wife a hard life. If this is true, and by analogy, he may have killed her. In spite of this record, poor Julie 'would have him.' Three times he has inherited money which was quickly spent. Such is his bare history and the character people give him.

The morning after a beating – Julie lying seriously battered upon their bed, or sitting rocking herself quietly in the débit, her head a turban of bandages, he noiselessly attends to her wants, enquires how she feels, and applies remedies. It is like a surgeon and a patient, an operation having just been successfully performed. He will walk fifteen miles to the nearest large town and back to get the necessary medicines. He is grave, and receives pleasantly your commiserations on her behalf, if you offer them. He has a delicate wife, that is the idea: she suffers from a chronic complaint. He addresses her on all occasions with a compassionate gentleness. There is, however, something in the bearing of both that suggests restraint. They are resigned, but none the less they remember the cross they have to bear. Julie will refer to his intemperance, casually, sometimes. She told me on one occasion, that, when first married, they had had a jay. This bird knew when Brotcotnaz was drunk. When he came in from a wake or 'Pardon,' and sat down at the débit table, the jay would hop out of its box, cross the table, and peck at his hands and fly in his face.

The secret of this smiling giant, a year or two younger, I daresay, than his wife, was probably that he intended to kill her. She had no more money. With his reputation as a wife-beater, he could do this without being molested. When he went to a 'Pardon,' she on her side knew he would try to kill her when he came back. That seemed to be the situation. If one night he did succeed in killing her, he would sincerely mourn her. At the fiançailles with his new bride he would see this one on the chair before him, his Julie, and, still radiating tolerance and health, would shed a melancholy smiling tear.

'You remember, Nicholas, those people that called on Thursday?' she now said.

He frowned gently to recall them.

'Ah, yes, I know – the Parisians that wanted the room.'

'They have been here again this afternoon.'

'Indeed.'

'I have agreed to take them. They want a little cooking. I've consented to do that. I said I had to speak to my husband about it. – They are coming back.'

He frowned more heavily, still smiling. He put his foot down with extreme softness:

'Julie, I have told you that I won't have that! It is useless for you to agree to do cooking. It is above your strength, my poor dear. You must tell them you can't do it.'

'But – they are returning. They may be here at any moment, now. I can do what they wish quite easily.'

With inexorable tenderness he continued to forbid it. Perhaps he did not want people in the house.

'Your health will not permit of your doing that, Julie.'

He never ceased to smile, but his brows remained knit. This was almost a dispute. They began talking in breton.

'Nicholas, I must go,' I said, getting up. He rose with me, following me up with the redoubled suavity of his swimming eyes.

'You must have a drink with me, Monsieur Kairor. Truly you must! Julie! Another glass for Monsieur Kairor.'

I drank it and left, promising to return. He came down the steps with me, his knee flexing with exaggerated suppleness at each step, placing his feet daintily and noiselessly on the dryest spaces on the wet stones. I watched him over my shoulder returning delicately up the steps, his massive back rigid, inclined forward, as though he were being steadily hauled up with a cord, only his feet working.

It was nearly three weeks later when I returned to Kermanec. It was in the morning. This time I came over in a tradesman's cart.

It took me to the foot of the rough ascent, at the top of which were Brotcotnaz's steps. There seemed to be a certain animation. Two people were talking at the door, and a neighbour, the proprietress of the successful débit, was ascending the steps. The worst had happened. Ça y est. He had killed her! Taking this for granted, I entered the débit, framing my *condoléances*. She would be upstairs on the bed. Should I go up? There were several people in the room. As I entered behind them, with a start of surprise I recognized Julie. Her arm was in a large sling. From beneath stained cloths, four enormously bloated and discoloured fingers protruded. These the neighbours inspected. Also one of her feet had a large bandage. She looked like a beggar at a church door: I could almost hear the familiar cry of the 'droit des pauvres!' She was speaking in breton, in her usual tone of 'miséricorde,' with her ghostly sanctimonious snigger. In spite of this, even if the circumstances had not made this obvious, the atmosphere was very different from that to which I had been accustomed.

At first I thought: She has killed Brotcotnaz, it must be that. But that hypothesis was contradicted by every other fact that I knew about them. It was possible that he had killed himself by accident. But, unnoticed, in the dark extremity of the débit, there he was! On catching sight of his dejected figure, thrust into the darkest shadow of his saloon, I received my second shock of surprise. I hesitated in perplexity. Would it be better to withdraw? I went up to Julie, but made no reference to her condition, beyond saying that I hoped she was well.

'As well as can be expected, my poor Monsieur Kairor!' she said in a sharp whine, her brown eyes bright, clinging and sad.

Recalling the events of my last visit and our conversation, in which I had tapped her bandages, I felt these staring fingers, thrust out for inspection, were a leaf taken out of my book. What new policy was this? I left her and went over to Brotcotnaz. He did not spring up: all he did was to smile weakly, saying:

'Tiens! Monsieur Kairor, vous voilà. – Sit down, Monsieur Kairor!'

I sat down. With his elbows on the table he continued to stare into space. Julie and her women visitors stood in the middle of the débit; in subdued voices they continued their discussion. It was in breton, I could not follow it easily.

This situation was not normal: yet the condition of Julie was the regular one. The intervention of the neighbours and the present dejection of Brotcotnaz was what was unaccountable. Otherwise, for the cause of the mischief there was no occasion to look further; a solution, sound, traditional, and in every way satisfying, was there before me in the person of Nicholas. But he whom I was always accustomed to see master of the situation was stunned and changed, like a man not yet recovered from some horrid experience. He, the recognized agent of Fate, was usually so above the mêlée. Now he looked another man, like somebody deprived of a coveted office, or from whom some privilege had been withheld. Had Fate acted without him? Such necessarily was the question that at this point took shape.

Meanwhile I no doubt encountered in turn a few of the perplexities, framing the same dark questions, that Brotcotnaz himself had done. He pulled himself together now and rose slowly.

'You will take something, Monsieur Kairor!' he said, habit operating, with a thin unction.

'Why, yes, I will have a glass of cider,' I said. 'What will you have, Nicholas?'

'Why, I will take the same, Monsieur Kairor,' he said. The break or give at the knee as he walked was there as usual, but mechanical, I felt. Brotcotnaz would revive, I hoped, after his drink. Julie was describing something: she kept bending down to the floor, and making a sweeping gesture with her free hand. Her guests made a chuckling sound in their throats like 'hoity-toity.'

Brotcotnaz returned with the drinks.

'A la vôtre, Monsieur Kairor!' He drank half his glass. Then he said:

'You have seen my wife's fingers?'

I admitted guardedly that I had noticed them.

'Higher up it is worse. The bone is broken. The doctor says that it is possible she will lose her arm. Her leg is also in a bad state.' He rolled his head sadly.

At last I looked at him with relief. He was regaining his old composure. I saw at once that a very significant thing had happened for him, if she lost her arm, and possibly her leg. He could scarcely proceed to the destruction of the trunk only. It was not difficult at least to appreciate the sort of problem that might present itself.

'Her erysipelas is bad this time, there is no use denying it,' I said.

A look of confusion came into his face. He hesitated a moment. His ill-working brain had to be adjusted to a past time, when what now possessed him was not known. He disposed himself in silence, then started in an astonished voice, leaning over the table:

'It isn't the erysipelas, Monsieur Kairor! Haven't you heard?'

'No, I have heard nothing. In fact, I have only just arrived.'

Now I was going to hear some great news from this natural casuist: or was I not? It was *not* erysipelas.

Julie had caught the word 'erysipelas' whispered by her husband. She leered round at me, standing on one leg, and tossed me a desperate snigger of secretive triumph, very well under control and as hard as nails.

Brotcotnaz explained.

The baker had asked her, on driving up the day before, to put a stone under the wheel of his cart, to prevent it from moving. She had bent down to do so, pushing the stone into position, but suddenly the horse backed: the wheel went over her hand. That was not all. At this she slipped on the stony path, blood pouring from her fingers, and went partly under the cart. Bystanders shouted, the horse started forward, and the cart went over her arm and foot in the reverse direction.

He told me these facts with astonishment – the sensation felt by him when he had heard them for the first time. He was glad to tell me. There was a misunderstanding, or half misunderstanding, on the part of his wife and all the others in this matter. He next told me how he had first heard the news.

At the time this accident had occurred he had been at sea. On landing he was met by several neighbours.

'Your wife is injured! She has been seriously injured!'

'What's that? My wife injured? My wife seriously injured!' – Indeed I understood him! I began to feel as he did. 'Seriously' was the word stressed naïvely by him. He repeated these words, and imitated his expression. He reproduced for me the dismay and astonishment, and the shade of overpowering suspicion, that his voice must originally have registered.

It was now that I saw him encountering all the notions that had come into my own mind a few minutes before, on first perceiving the injured woman, the visiting neighbours and his dejected form thrown into the shade by something.

'Your wife is seriously injured!' I stood there altogether upset – tout à fait bouleversé.

The familiar image of her battered form as seen on a *lendemain de Pardon* must have arisen in his mind. He is assailed with a sudden incapacity to think of injuries in his wife's case except as caused by a human hand. He is solicited by the reflection that he himself had not been there. There was, in short, the effect, but not the cause. Whatever his ultimate intention as regards Julie, he is a 'jaloux.' All his wild jealousy surges up. A cause, a rival cause, is incarnated in his excited brain, and goes in an overbearing manner to claim its effect. In a second a man is born. He does not credit him, but he gets a foothold just outside of reason. He is a rival! – another Brotcotnaz; all his imagination is sickened by this super-Brotcotnaz, as a woman who had been delivered of some hero, already of heroic dimensions, might naturally find herself. A moment of great weakness and lassitude seizes him. He remains powerless at the thought of the aggressive actions of this hero. His mind succumbs to torpor, it refuses to contemplate this figure.

It was at this moment that some one must have told him the actual cause of the injuries. The vacuum of his mind, out of which all the machinery of habit had been momentarily emptied, filled up again with its accustomed furniture. But after this moment of intense void the furniture did not quite resume its old positions, some of the pieces never returned, there remained a blankness and desolate novelty in the destiny of Brotcotnaz. That was still his state at present.

I then congratulated Julie upon her escape. Her eyes peered into mine with derision. What part did I play in this? She appeared to think that I too had been outwitted. I sauntered over to the counter and withdrew the bottle of eau-de-vie from its hiding-place.

'Shall I bring it over to you?' I called to Brotcotnaz. I took it over. Julie followed me for a moment with her mocking gaze.

'I will be the débitant!' I said to Brotcotnaz.

I poured him out a stiff glass.

'You live too near the sea,' I told him.

'Needs must,' he said, 'when one is a fisherman.'

'Ahès!' I sighed, trying to recall the famous line of the armorican song, that I was always meeting in the books that I had been reading. It began with this whistling sigh of the renegade king, whose daughter Ahès was.

'Why, yes,' Brotcotnaz sighed politely, supposing I had complimented the lot of the fisherman in my exclamation, doing the devil's tattoo on the table, as he crouched in front of me.

'Ahès, *brêman* Mary Morgan.' I had got it.

'I ask your pardon, Monsieur Kairor?'

'It is the lament of your legendary king for having been instrumental in poisoning the sea. You have never studied the lore of your country?'

'A little,' he smiled.

The neighbours were leaving. We three would now be alone. I looked at my watch. It was time to rejoin the cart that had brought me.

'A last drink, Madame Brotcotnaz!' I called.

She returned to the table and sat down, lowering herself to the chair, and sticking out her bandaged foot. She took the drink I gave her, and raised it almost with fire to her lips. After the removal of her arm, and possibly a foot, I realized that she would be more difficult to get on with than formerly. The bottle of eau-de-vie would remain no doubt in full view, to hand, on the counter, and Brotcotnaz would be unable to lay a finger on her: in all likelihood she meant that arm to come off.

I was not sorry for Nicholas; I regarded him as a changed man. Whatever the upshot of the accident as regards the threatened amputations, the disorder and emptiness that had declared itself in his mind would remain.

'To your speedy recovery, Madame Brotcotnaz,' I said.

We drank to that, and Brotcotnaz came to the door. Julie remained alone in the débit.

# Inferior Religions

## I

To introduce my puppets, and the Wild Body, the generic puppet of all, I must project a fanciful wandering figure to be the showman to whom the antics and solemn gambols of these wild children are to be a source of strange delight. In the first of these stories he makes his appearance. The fascinating imbecility of the creaking men machines, that some little restaurant or fishing-boat works, was the original subject of these studies, though in fact the nautical set never materialized. The boat's tackle and dirty little shell, or the hotel and its technique of hospitality, keeping the limbs of the men and women involved in a monotonous rhythm from morning till night, that was the occupational background, placed in Brittany or in Spanish Galicia.

A man is made drunk with his boat or restaurant as he is with a merry-go-round: only it is the staid, everyday drunkenness of the normal real, not easy always to detect. We can all see the ascendance a 'carousal' has on men, driving them into a set narrow intoxication. The wheel at Carisbrooke imposes a set of movements upon the donkey inside it, in drawing water from the well, that it is easy to grasp. But in the case of a hotel or fishing-boat, for instance, the complexity of the rhythmic scheme is so great that it passes as open and untrammelled life. This subtle and wider mechanism merges, for the spectator, in the general variety of nature. Yet we have in most lives the spectacle of a pattern as circumscribed and complete as a theorem of Euclid. So these are essays in a new human mathematic. But they are, each of them, simple shapes, little monuments of logic. I should like to compile a book of forty of these propositions, one deriving from and depending on the other. A few of the axioms for such a book are here laid down.

These intricately moving bobbins are all subject to a set of objects or to one in particular. Brotcotnaz is fascinated by one object, for instance; one at once another vitality. He bangs up against it wildly at regular intervals, blackens it, contemplates it, moves round it and dreams. He reverences it: it is his task to kill it. All such fascination is religious. The damp napkins of the inn-keeper are the altar-cloths of his rough illusion, as Julie's bruises are the markings upon an idol; with the peasant, Mammon dominating the background. Zoborov and Mademoiselle Péronnette struggle for a Pension de Famille, unequally. Zoborov is the 'polish' cuckoo of a stupid and ill-managed nest.

These studies of rather primitive people are studies in a savage worship and attraction. The innkeeper rolls between his tables ten million times in a realistic rhythm that is as intense and super-stitious as are the figures of a war-dance. He worships his soup, his damp napkins, the lump of procreative flesh probably associated with him in this task. Brotcotnaz circles round Julie with gestures a million times repeated. Zoborov camps against and encircles Mademoiselle Péronnette and her lover Carl. Bestre is the eternal watchdog, with an elaborate civilized ritual. Similarly the Cornac is engaged in a death struggle with his 'Public.' All religion has the mechanism of the celestial bodies, has a dance. When we wish to renew our idols, or break up the rhythm of our naïveté, the effort postulates a respect which is the summit of devoutness.

## II

I would present these puppets, then, as carefully selected specimens of religious fanaticism. With their attendant objects or fetishes they live and have a regular food and vitality. They are not creations, but puppets. You can be as exterior to them, and live their life as little, as the showman grasping from beneath and working about a Polichinelle. They are only shadows of energy, not living beings. Their mechanism is a logical structure and they are nothing but that.

Boswell's Johnson, Mr Veneering, Malvolio, Bouvard and Pécuchet, the 'commissaire' in *Crime and Punishment*, do not live; they are congealed and frozen into logic, and an exuberant hysterical truth. They transcend life and are complete cyphers, but they are monuments of dead imperfection. Their only significance is their egoism. So the great intuitive figures of creation live with the universal egoism of the poet. This 'Realism' is satire. Satire is the great Heaven of Ideas, where you meet the titans of red laughter; it is just below intuition, and life charged with black illusion.

### III

When we say 'types of humanity,' we mean violent individualities, and nothing stereotyped. But Quixote, Falstaff, and Pecksniff attract, in our memory, a vivid following. All difference is energy, and a category of humanity a relatively small group, and not the myriads suggested by a generalization.

A comic type is a failure of a considerable energy, an imitation and standardizing of self, suggesting the existence of a uniform humanity, – creating, that is, a little host as like as nine-pins; instead of one synthetic and various ego. It is the laziness that is the habit-world or system of a successful personality. It is often part of our own organism become a fetish. So Boswell's Johnson or Sir John Falstaff are minute and rich religions.

That Johnson was a sort of god to his biographer we readily see. But Falstaff as well is a sort of english god, like the rice-bellied gods of laughter of China. They are illusions hugged and lived in; little dead totems. Just as all gods are a repose for humanity, the big religions an immense refuge and rest, so are these little grotesque fetishes. One reason for this is that, for the spectator or partici-pator, it is a world within the world, full of order, even if violent.

All these are forms of static art, then. There is a great deal of divine olympian sleep in english humour, and its delightful dreams. The most gigantic spasm of laughter is sculptural, isolated, and essentially simple.

## IV

I will catalogue the attributes of Laughter.
1. Laughter is the Wild Body's song of triumph.
2. Laughter is the climax in the tragedy of seeing, hearing, and smelling self-consciously.
3. Laughter is the bark of delight of a gregarious animal at the proximity of its kind.
4. Laughter is an independent, tremendously important, and lurid emotion.
5. Laughter is the representative of tragedy, when tragedy is away.
6. Laughter is the emotion of tragic delight.
7. Laughter is the female of tragedy.
8. Laughter is the strong elastic fish, caught in Styx, springing and flapping about until it dies.
9. Laughter is the sudden handshake of mystic violence and the anarchist.
10. Laughter is the mind sneezing.
11. Laughter is the one obvious commotion that is not complex, or in expression dynamic.
12. Laughter does not progress. It is primitive, hard and unchangeable.

## V

The Wild Body, I have said, triumphs in its laughter. What is the Wild Body?

The Wild Body, as understood here, is that small, primitive, literally antediluvian vessel in which we set out on our adventures. Or regarded as a brain, it is rather a winged magic horse, that transports us hither and thither, sometimes rushing, as in the chinese cosmogonies, up and down the outer reaches of space. Laughter is the brain-body's snort of exultation. It expresses its wild sensation of power and speed; it is all that remains physical in the flash of thought, its friction: or it may be a defiance flung at the hurrying fates.

The Wild Body is this supreme survival that is us, the stark apparatus with its set of mysterious spasms; the most profound of which is laughter.

## VI

The chemistry of personality (subterranean in a sort of cemetery, whose decompositions are our lives) puffs up in frigid balls, soapy Snowmen, arctic carnival-masks, which we can photograph and fix.

Upwards from the surface of existence a lurid and dramatic scum oozes and accumulates into the characters we see. The real and tenacious poisons, and sharp forces of vitality, do not socially transpire. Within five yards of another man's eyes we are on a little crater, which, if it erupted, would split up as would a cocoa-tin of nitrogen. Some of these bombs are ill-made, or some erratic in their timing. But they are all potential little bombs. Capriciously, however, the froth-forms of these darkly-contrived machines twist and puff in the air, in our legitimate and liveried masquerade.

Were you the female of Bestre or Brotcotnaz and beneath the counterpane with him, you would be just below the surface of life, in touch with a tragic organism. The first indications of the proximity of the real soul would be apparent. You would be for hours beside a filmy crocodile, conscious of it like a bone in an X-ray, and for minutes in the midst of a tragic wallowing. The soul lives in a cadaverous activity; its dramatic corruption thumps us like a racing engine in the body of a car. The finest humour is the great play-shapes blown up or given off by the tragic corpse of life underneath the world of the camera. This futile, grotesque, and sometimes pretty spawn, is what in this book is snapshotted by the imagination.

Any master of humour is an essential artist; even Dickens is no exception. For it is the character of uselessness and impersonality which is found in laughter (the anarchist emotion concerned in the comic habit of mind) that makes a man an 'artist.' So when he begins living on his laughter, even in spite of himself a man becomes an artist. Laughter is that arch complexity that is really as simple as bread.

## VII

In this objective play-world, corresponding to our social consciousness, as opposed to our solitude, no final issue is decided. You may blow away a man-of-bubbles with a burgundian gust of laughter, but that is not a personality, it is an apparition of no importance. But so much correspondence it has with its original that, if the cadaveric travail beneath is vigorous and bitter, the dummy or mask will be of a more original grotesqueness. The opposing armies in the early days in Flanders stuck up dummy-men on poles for their enemies to pot at, in a spirit of ferocious banter. It is only a shell of that description that is engaged in the sphere of laughter. In our rather drab revel there is a certain category of spirit that is not quite inanimate and yet not very funny. It consists of those who take, at the Clarkson's situated at the opening of their lives, some conventional Pierrot costume. This is intended to assure them a minimum of strain, of course, and so is a capitulation. In order to evade life we must have recourse to those uniforms, but such a choice leaves nothing but the white and ethereal abstraction of the shadow of laughter.

So the King of Play is not a phantom corresponding to the sovereign force beneath the surface. The latter must always be reckoned on: it is the Skeleton at the Feast, potentially, with us. That soul or dominant corruption is so real that he cannot rise up and take part in man's festival as a Falstaff of unwieldy spume. If he comes at all it must be as he is, the skeleton or bogey of veritable life, stuck over with corruptions and vices. As such he could rely on a certain succès d'estime: nothing more.

## VIII

A scornful optimism, with its confident onslaughts on our snobbism, will not make material existence a peer for our energy. The gladiator is not a perpetual monument of triumphant health: Napoleon was harried with Elbas: moments of vision are blurred rapidly, and the poet sinks into the rhetoric of the will.

But life is invisible, and perfection is not in the waves or houses that the poet sees. To rationalize that appearance is not possible. Beauty is an icy douche of ease and happiness at something *suggesting* perfect conditions for an organism: it remains suggestion. A stormy landscape, and a pigment consisting of a lake of hard, yet florid waves; delight in each brilliant scoop or ragged burst, was John Constable's beauty. Leonardo's consisted in a red rain on the shadowed side of heads, and heads of massive female aesthetes. Uccello accumulated pale parallels, and delighted in cold architecture of distinct colour. Korin found in the symmetrical gushing of water, in waves like huge vegetable insects, traced and worked faintly, on a golden pâte, his business. Cézanne liked cumbrous, democratic slabs of life, slightly leaning, transfixed in vegetable intensity.

Beauty is an immense predilection, a perfect conviction of the desirability of a certain thing, whatever that thing may be. It is a universe for one organism. To a man with long and consumptive fingers, a sturdy hand may be heaven. We can aim at no universality of form, for what we see is not the reality. Henri Fabre was in every way a superior being to a Salon artist, and he knew of elegant grubs which he would prefer to the Salon painter's nymphs. – It is quite obvious though, to fulfil the conditions of successful art, that we should live in relatively small communities.

# The Meaning of the Wild Body

'From man, who is acknowledged to be intelligent, non-intelligent things such as hair and nails originate, and . . . on the other hand, from avowedly non-intelligent matter (such as cow-dung), scorpions and similar animals are produced. But . . . the real cause of the non-intelligent hair and nails is the human body, which is itself non-intelligent, and the non-intelligent dung. Even there there remains a difference . . . in so far as non-intelligent matter (the body) is the abode of an intelligent principle (the scorpion's soul) while other unintelligent matter (the dung) is not.'  *Vedânta-Sûtras.*
*II Adhyâya. I Pâda, 6.*

## 1. The Meaning of the Wild Body

First, to assume the dichotomy of mind and body is necessary here, without arguing it; for it is upon that essential separation that the theory of laughter here proposed is based. The essential us, that is the laugher, is as distinct from the Wild Body as in the Upanisadic account of the souls returned from the paradise of the Moon, which, entering into plants, are yet distinct from them. Or to take the symbolic vedic figure of the two birds, the one watching and passive, the other enjoying its activity, we similarly have to postulate *two* creatures, one that never enters into life, but that travels about in a vessel to whose destiny it is momentarily attached. That is, of course, the laughing observer, and the other is the Wild Body.

To begin to understand the totality of *the absurd*, at all, you have to assume much more than belongs to a social differentiation. There is nothing that is animal (and we as bodies are animals) that is not absurd. This sense of the absurdity, or, if you like, the madness of our life, is at the root of every true philosophy. William James delivers himself on this subject as follows:–

One need only shut oneself in a closet and begin to think of the fact of one's being there, of one's queer bodily shape in the darkness (a thing to make children scream at, as Stevenson says), of one's fantastic character and all, to have the wonder steal over the detail as much as over the general fact of being, and to see that it is only familiarity that blunts it. Not only that *anything* should be, but that *this* very thing should be, is mysterious. Philosophy stares, but brings no reasoned solution, for from nothing to being there is no logical bridge.

It is the chasm lying between being and non-being, over which it is impossible for logic to throw any bridge, that, in certain forms of laughter, we leap. We land plumb in the centre of Nothing. It is easy for us to see, if we are french, that the German is 'absurd,' or if german, that the French is 'ludicrous,' for we are *outside* in that case. But it was Schopenhauer (whom James quotes so aptly in front of the above passage), who also said: 'He who is proud of being "a German," "a Frenchman," "a Jew," can have very little else to be proud of.' (In this connection it may be recalled that his father named him 'Arthur,' because 'Arthur' was the same in all languages. Its possession would not attach him to any country.) So, again, if we have been at Oxford or Cambridge, it is easy to appreciate, from the standpoint acquired at a great university, the absurdity of many manners not purified or intellectualized by such a training. What it is far more difficult to appreciate, with any constancy, is that, whatever his relative social advantages or particular national virtues may be, every man is profoundly open to the same criticism or ridicule from any opponent who is only different enough. Again, it is comparatively easy to see that another man, as an animal, is absurd; but it is far more difficult to observe oneself in that hard and exquisite light. But no man has ever continued to live who has observed himself in that manner for longer than a flash. Such consciousness must be of the nature of a thunderbolt. Laughter is only summer-lightning. But it occasionally takes on the dangerous form of absolute revelation.

This fundamental self-observation, then, can never on the whole be absolute. We are not constructed to be *absolute observers*. Where it does not exist at all, men sink to the level of insects. That does not matter: the 'lord of the past and the future, he who is the same to-day and to-morrow' – that 'person of the size of a thumb that stands in the middle of the Self' – departs. So the 'Self' ceases, necessarily. The conditions of an insect communism are achieved. There would then no longer be any occasion, once that was completely established, to argue for or against such a dichotomy as we have assumed, for them it could no longer exist.

## 2. *The Root of the Comic*

The root of the Comic is to be sought in the sensations resulting from the observations of a *thing* behaving like a person. But from that point of view all men are necessarily comic: for they are all *things*, or physical bodies, behaving as *persons*. It is only when you come to deny that they are 'persons,' or that there is any 'mind' or 'person' there at all, that the world of appearance is accepted as quite natural, and not at all ridiculous. Then, with a denial of 'the person,' life becomes immediately both 'real' and very serious.

To bring vividly to our mind what we mean by 'absurd,' let us turn to the plant, and enquire how the plant could be absurd. Suppose you came upon an orchid or a cabbage reading Flaubert's *Salammbo*, or Plutarch's *Moralia*, you would be very much surprised. But if you found a man or a woman reading it, you would *not* be surprised.

Now in one sense you ought to be just as much surprised at finding a man occupied in this way as if you had found an orchid or a cabbage, or a tom-cat, to include the animal world. There is the same physical anomaly. It is just as absurd externally, that is what I mean. – The deepest root of the Comic is to be sought in this anomaly.

The movement or intelligent behaviour of matter, any autonomous movement of matter, is essentially comic. That is what we mean by comic or ludicrous. And we all, as human beings, answer to this description. We are all autonomously and intelligently moving matter. The reason we do not laugh when we observe a man reading a newspaper or trimming a lamp, or smoking a pipe, is because we suppose he 'has a mind,' as we call it, because we are accustomed to this strange sight, and because we do it ourselves. But because when you see a man walking down the street you know why he is doing that (for instance, because he is on his way to lunch, just as the stone rolling down the hillside, you say, is responding to the law of gravitation), that does not make him less ridiculous. But there is nothing essentially ridiculous about the stone. The man is ridiculous fundamentally, he is ridiculous *because he is a man*, instead of a thing.

If you saw (to give another example of intelligence or movement in the 'dead') a sack of potatoes suddenly get up and trundle off down the street (unless you were at once so sceptical as to think that it was some one who had got inside the sack), you would laugh. A couple of trees suddenly tearing themselves free from their roots, and beginning to waltz: a 'cello softly rubbing itself against a kettle-drum: a lamp-post unexpectedly lighting up of its own accord, and then immediately hopping away down to the next lamp-post, which it proceeded to attack: all these things would appear very 'ridiculous,' although your alarm, instead of whetting your humour, might overcome it. These are instances of miraculous absurdities, they do not happen; I have only enumerated them, to enlighten us as regards the things that do happen.

The other day in the underground, as the train was moving out of the station, I and those around me saw a fat but active man run along, and deftly project himself between the sliding doors, which he pushed to behind him. Then he stood leaning against them, as the carriage was full. There was nothing especially funny about his face or general appearance. Yet his running, neat, deliberate, but clumsy embarkation, *combined with the coolness of his eye*, had a ludicrous effect, to which several of us responded. His *eye* I decided was the key to the absurdity of the effect. It was its detachment that was responsible for this. It seemed to say, as he propelled his sack of potatoes – that is himself – along the platform, and as he successfully landed the sack in the carriage: – 'I've not much "power," I may just manage it: – yes *just*!' Then in response to our gazing eyes, 'Yes, that's me! That was not so bad, was it? When you run a line of potatoes like ME, you get the knack of them: but they take a bit of moving.'

It was the detachment, in any case, that gave the episode a comic quality, that his otherwise very usual appearance would not have possessed. I have sometimes seen the same look of whimsical detachment on the face of a taxi-driver when he has taken me somewhere, in a very slow and ineffective conveyance. *His taxi for him stood for his body*. He was quite aware of its shortcomings, but did not associate himself with them. He knew quite well what a taxi ought to be. He did not identify himself with his machine.

Many cases of the comic are caused by the reverse of this – by the *unawareness* of the object of our mirth: though awareness (as in the case of comic actors) is no hindrance to our enjoyment of the ludicrous. But the case described above, of the man catching the train, illustrates my point as to the root of the sensation of the comic. It is because the man's body was not him.

These few notes, coming at the end of my stories, may help to make the angle from which they are written a little clearer, in giving a general rough definition of what 'Comic' means for their author.

*Sigismund*
*You Broke My Dream*

# Sigismund

Sigismund's bulldog was called Pym. He believed implicitly in his pedigree. And every one understood that the names of famous dogs to be found on Pym's family tree constituted a genealogical crop which did great credit to him and his master. This lifted Pym for Sigismund into the favoured world of race. He staggered and snorted everywhere in the company of Sigismund, with a look that implied his intention to make the most of being a bulldog, and a contemptuous curl of his chop for the world in which that appeared to signify so much.

Now Pym was really rather peak-headed. Far from being 'well broken up,' his head was almost stopless. His nostrils were perpendicular, the lay back of the head unorthodox: he would have been unable to hold anything for more than twenty seconds, as his nose would have flattened against it as well as his muzzle, his breathing automatically corked up by his prey. His lips were pendent, but his flews were not: his tusks were near together, and like eyes too closely set, gave an air of meanness. The jaws as well were level: in short he was both 'downfaced' and 'froggy' to an unheard-of degree. As to his ears, sometimes he had the appearance of being button-eared, sometimes tulip-eared: he was defective in dewlap, his brisket was shallow, he had a pendulous belly and a thick waist.

As to the back, far from being a good 'cut-up,' he had a very bad 'cut-up' indeed. He had *no* 'cut-up.' He was 'swamp-backed' and 'ring-tailed.' He also possessed a disgusting power of lifting his tail up and waggling it about above the level of his disgraceful stern, anomalously high up on which it was placed. His pasterns were too long, his toes seemed glued together: his stifles were wedge-shaped, and turned in towards the body. His coat was wiry, of the most questionable black and tan.

He was certainly the ugliest, wickedest, most objectionable bulldog that ever trod the soil of Britain. In the street he conducted himself like the most scurvy hoodlam ever issued from a nameless kennel. But he was a *bulldog*. His forebears had done romantic things. They had fixed their teeth in the noses of bulls. Sigismund was very proud of him. He insisted that the blood of Rosa flowed in his veins. All Sigismund's friends thumped and fingered him, saying what a splendid dog he was. To see Sigismund going down the road with Pym, you would say, from the dashing shamble of his gait, that he was bound for the Old Conduit Fields, or the Westminster Pit.

This partnership continued very uneventfully for several years, to Sigismund's perfect satisfaction. Then a heavy cantrip, of the most feudal ingredients, was cast upon Sigismund. He became deeply enamoured of a deep-chested lady. He pursued her tirelessly with his rather trite addresses. She had the slightest stagger, reminiscent of Pym. She was massive and mute. And when Sigismund mechanically slapped her on the back one day, she had a hollow reverberation such as Pym's swollen body would emit. Her eyes flickered ever so little. Sigismund the next moment was overcome with confusion at what he had done: especially as her pedigree was like Pym's, and he had the deepest admiration for race. A minute or two later she coughed. And he could not for the life of him decide whether the cough was admonitory – possibly the death-knell of his suit – or whether it was the result of his premature caress.

The next day, grasping the stems of a bushel of new flowers inside a bladder of pink paper, he called. A note accompanied them:

DEAR MISS LIBYON-BOSSELWOOD, – There are three flowers in this bouquet which express, by their contrite odour, the sentiments of dismay which I experience in remembering the hapless slap which

I delivered upon your gorgeous back yesterday afternoon. Can you ever forgive me for this good-for-nothing action? – Your despondent admirer,

SIGISMUND.

But when they next met she did not refer to the note. As she rose to her thunderous stature to go over to the vase where the bushel of flowers he had brought was standing, and turned on him her enormous and outraged back, Sigismund started. For there, through a diaphanous négligé, he saw a blood-red hand upon her skin. His hand! And in a moment he realized that she had painted it to betray her sentiments, which otherwise would have remained, perhaps for ever, hidden. So he sprang up and grasped her hand, saying:

'Deborah!'

She fell into his arms to signify that she would willingly become his bride. In a precarious crouch he propped her for a moment, then they both subsided on to the floor, she with her eyes closed, rendered doubly heavy by all the emotion with which she was charged. Pym, true to type, 'the bulldog' at once, noticing this contretemps, and imagining that his master was being maltreated by this person whom he had disliked from the first, flew to the rescue. He fixed his teeth in her eighteenth-century bottom. She was removed, bleeding, in a titanic faint. Sigismund fled once more in dismay.

The next day he called unaccompanied by Pym. He was admitted to Deborah's chamber. She lay on her stomach. Her swollen bottom rose in the middle of the bed. But a flat disc of face lay sideways on the pillow, a reproachful eye slumbering where her ear would usually be.

He flung himself down on the elastic nap of the carpet and rolled about in an ecstasy of dismay. She just lisped hoarsely: 'Sigismund!' and all was well between them.

But she stipulated that Pym should be eliminated from their nuptial arrangements. So he sold Pym and wedded Deborah.

\*

On returning from the church – husband, at length, of the Honourable Deborah Libyon-Bosselwood – Sigismund's first action was to rub a little sandal-wood oil into both her palms. As she had stood beside him at the altar, her heavy hand in his, he had wondered what lay concealed in this prize-packet he was grasping. As the gold ring ploughed into the tawny fat of her finger, descending with difficulty toward the Mount of the Sun, he asked himself if this painful adjustment contained an augury. Appropriately for the golden mount, however, the full-bellied ring, of very unusual circumference, settled down on this characteristic Bosselwood paw as though determined to preside favourably over that portion of the hand.

Having oiled her palms, much to her surprise, he flew with Deborah to a steaming basin, drew out a sheet of dental wax, and planted her hand firmly on it. But, alas, the Libyon hairiness had invaded even the usually bald area of the inside of the hand. And when Sigismund tried to pull her hand off the wax, Deborah screamed. She had not at all understood or relished his proceedings up to this point. And now that, adhering by these few superfluous hairs to the inadequately heated wax, she felt convinced of the malevolence of his designs, she gave him such a harsh buffet with her free hand that he fell at full length at her feet, a sound shaken out of him that was half surprise and half apology. He soon recovered, rushed to fetch a pair of scissors, and snipped her hand free of the wax cast. His bride scowled at him, but the next moment bit his ear and attempted to nestle, to show that he was forgiven.

'Deborah! Will you ever *really* forgive me?' He gasped in despair, covering her injured hand with kisses and a little blood, the result of her impulsive blow. The great Bosselwood motto 'Never Forgive' made him shake in every limb as he thought of it. How *uncanny* to be united to such a formidable offshoot of such an implacable race!

'Say you *can* forgive!'

But she only murmured in sulphurous Latin the words 'Nunquam ignoscete.'

For she read his heart and remembered the motto (with some

difficulty). She always read his heart, but could not always remember the heraldic and other data required properly to prostrate him. On these occasions, she would confine herself to smiling enigmatically. This redoubled his terror. She in due course observed this, too. After that she did nothing but grin at him the whole time.

But now came the moment that must be considered as the virtual consummation of Sigismund's vows. The ordinary brutal proclivities of man were absent in the case of Sigismund. The monstrous charms of the by-now lisping and blushing Deborah he was not entirely unaffected by: but the innermost crypt of this cathedral of a body Sigismund sought in a quite public place. The imminence of her brown breasts was hidden to him. They were almost as remote as the furniture of the Milky Way. Enormous mounts, he saw them as (but of less significance than) those diminutive ones of Saturn or the Sun at the base of her fingers. The real secrets of this highly-pedigreed body lay at the extremities of her limbs. The Mount of Venus, for him, was to be sought on the base of the thumb, and nowhere else. The certain interest he felt for her person, heavy with the very substance of Race, that made it like a palpitating relic, was due really to the element of reference that lay in every form of which it was composed, to the clear indications of destiny that enlivened to such an incredible degree the leathery cutis of her palm. Her jawbone, the jutting of her thighs, the abstract tracts of her heavily-embossed back, meant so many mitigations or confirmations of the Via Lasciva or her very 'open' line of head. Surely the venustal pulp of her thumb, the shape of a leg of mutton, had a more erotic significance than any vulgarer desiderata of the bust or belly? The desmoid bed of her great lines of Race, each 'island' a poem in itself, adapted for the intellectual picnicking he preferred, was a more suitable area for the discreet appearance of such sex-aims as those of Sigismund.

So, still bleeding slightly from the feudal buffet he had lately encountered, he seized her hand, and slowly forced it round with the air of a brutal ravisher, until it lay palm uppermost. The pudeur and mystery of these primitive tracings sent a thrill down his spine.

It had been almost a point of honour with him not to ravish the secrets of her hand until now. 'Silent upon a peak in Darien' was nothing to the awe and enthusiasm with which he peeped over the ridge of her palm as it gradually revolved.

But now occurred one of the most substantial shocks of Sigismund's career. Deborah's palm was almost *without* lines of any sort. Where he had expected to find every foray of a feudal past marked in some way or another, every intrigue with its zig-zag, every romantic crime owning its little line, there was nothing but a dumbfounding, dead, distressing *blank*. Sigismund was staggered. The Palmer Arch, it is true, had its accompanying furrow, rather yellow (from which he could trace the action of Deborah's bile) but clear. The Mars line reinforced it. Great health: pints of blood: larders full of ox-like resistance to disease. It was the health sheet of a bullock, not the flamboyant history of a lady descended from armoured pirates.

All the mounts swelled up in a humdrum way. But from the Mount of the Sun to the first bracelet, and from the Mount of Venus to Mars Mental, it was, O alas, for his purposes, an empty hand! Her life had never been disturbed by the slightest emotional spasm: the spasms of her ancestors were seemingly obliterated from the recording skin. Nature had made an enigma of her hide! The life-line flowed on and on. He followed it broodingly to the wrist. It actually seemed to continue up the arm. Sigismund turned in dismay from this complacent bulletin of unchequered health.

He set to work, however, on the sparse indications that his noble bride was able to provide. He made the little insular convolutions of the line of heart spell simply 'Sigismund.' Kisses followed: coquettish and minute kisses attempted to land on each island in turn. Deborah glared in surly amusement.

A sinister stump where the head-line should have been disturbed him. It had a frayed ending. (More uneasiness.) Although in quantity this hand possessed few marks, those that were there were calculated to electrify any cheiromancer. It was a penny-shocker of a hand.

But most disquieting of all was a peculiar little island that mated a similar offensive little irregularity in his own hand. He had never seen it on the hand of any other being. And it was backed up by a faint but very horrible Star. This star furthermore was situated in the midst of Jupiter. But, worse still, a cross on another part of the hand completely unnerved him. He paced twice from one end of the room to the other. He was so abstracted that it was with a new anxiety and amazement that he found in a minute or two, that Deborah had disappeared.

He rushed all over the house. At last he came upon her in the dining-room, finishing a stiff whisky-and-soda. A rather cross squint was levelled at him across the whisky. Five minutes later she again vanished. Fresh alarmed pursuit. This time he discovered her in their bedroom, as naked as your hand (though he would never have used this expression, having an intense delicacy about everything relating to the hand), in bed, and trumpeting in a loud, dogmatic, and indecent way. The palliasse purred, and the bed creaked beneath her baronial weight. The eiderdown rose and fell with a servile gentleness. Her face was calm and forbidding. It was the dreamless, terrible sleep of the Hand he had just fled from. Yes. It was the Hand sleeping! He was united for better or for worse with this empty, sinisterly-starred, well-fed, snoring Hand.

Their honeymoon was uneventful. Sigismund went about with an ephemeris of the year of Deborah's birth, with Tables of Eclipses. He had the moon's radical elongation, and the twenty-two synods that represented his wife's life up to date. The mundane ingress of planets, their less effectual zodiacal ingress, had all been considered in their bearing on the destinies of Deborah and himself. But as on her hand, so in the heavens, the planets and Houses appeared to behave in a peculiarly non-committal, dull and vacant manner. The Spheres appeared to have slowed down their dance, and got in to some sort of clodhopping rustic meander, to celebrate the arrival of his wife upon the earth. But still the sinister star placed where her forefinger plunged into the palm perplexed him.

*

Back in London, he took her about as he had formerly taken Pym. He explained her pedigree. He pointed to her nose, which was heavy and flat, and told his friends that underneath was the pure Roman curve of the Bosselwoods. Also he detected a blue glint in her eye. That was the blue of the Viking! The Bosselwoods, it was gathered, were huge, snake-headed, bull-horned, armour-plated norse buccaneers. She would give him a terrifying leer when this transpired. It was her only histrionic effort. Her feet, on the other hand, were purely Libyon. If his friend could only see thier jolly little well-oiled knuckles! A world of race slumbered in her footwear.

'Race is so poetic, don't you agree?' he would say.

All agreed with Signismund that race was the most romantic thing imaginable, and that it lent a new interest not only to the human skeleton, but also to the smallest piece of fat or gristle. There were three friends especially of Sigismund's who felt things very much as he did. The four of them would sit around Deborah and gaze at her as connoisseurs in race. They all agreed that they had never met with quite so much race in anybody – so much of it, so exquisitely proportioned, or carried about with so much modesty.

'Deborah is amazing!' Sigismund would lisp. 'Her blood is the bluest in the land. But it might be green, she is so natural.'

'She is natural!' Fireacres said, with the emphasis proper to his years.

'Her language is sometimes – he! he! – as blue, I promise you, as her blood!'

They all shuffled and a break of merriment went on cannoning for about a minute. It ended in a sharp crack crack from Gribble-Smith. She scowled at them with a look of heavy mischief. She felt like a red, or perhaps blue, ball, among several very restless white ones. She liked laughter about as little as a Blackfoot brave of romantic fiction. Her tongue appeared to be dallying, for a moment, with the most mediæval malediction. They hushed themselves rapidly and looked frightened.

'You should have heard her to-day. A taxi-driver – he! he! – you should have seen the fellow stare! He wilted. He seemed to forget that he had ever known how to say "Dash it!"'

Deborah plucked at her chin, and spat out the seeds of her last plate of jam.

'How extremes meet!' said a newcomer.

A great insolence was noticeable in this man's carriage. He swung himself about like a famous espada. But when he tossed his locks off his brow, you saw that his bull-ring must be an intellectual one, where he would no doubt dispose of the most savage ideas. He was followed about by the eyes of the little group. Sigismund whispered to Deborah, 'He's a Mars Mental man.' An uninitiated person would probably, after being plunged for a little in this atmosphere, have thought of the Mars Mental man as possessed of phenomenally large muscular mental mounts, whatever they might be. The slender elevation on the side of his palm opposite to the thumb affected these simple people in the same way as athletic potentialities affect the schoolboy. In fingering his hand, as they sometimes did, it was with visible awe, and an eye fixed on the negative mount in question, as though they expected it to develop an eruption.

Deborah scratched her off leg. All were ravished. The Bosselwoods had no doubt always been great Scratchers: 'mighty scratchers before the Lord' Sigismund's mind proceeded.

Deborah bent her intelligence painfully for a moment on the riddle of this company. Could a stranger have glanced into her mind, the scene would have struck him as at once arid and comic. Sigismund's friends would have appeared as a group of monoliths in a frigid moonlight, or clowns tumbling in sacks in an empty and dark circus. Her mind would be seen to construct only rudimentary and quasi-human shapes: but details of a photographic precision arbitrarily occurring: bits of faces, shoes, moustaches and arms, large hands, palm outward, scarred with red lines of life, head and heart, all upside down. Stamped on one of these quasi-human shapes the stranger would have read 'Socialist' in red block letters. This was:

'Tom Fireacres. Awfully good family you know. Fire-acres.

Pronounced Furrakers. Jolly old bird. He is a queer fellow. A Socialist—' He would shake his head of rather long political hair from time to time over his young friend's aristocratic excess. But there was a light of kindly mansuetude that never left his eye.

The next of these dismal shapes would be a suit of clothes, not unlike Deborah's brother's: but a palpably insignificant social thing, something inside it, like its spirit jerking about, and very afraid of her. The form its fear seemed to take was that of an incessant barking, just like a dog, with the same misunderstanding of human nature. For it seemed to bark because it thought she liked it. This was: –

'Reddie Gribble-Smith. Been in the Army – Senior Captain. Awful nice feller.' This particular cliché propelled itself through life by means of a sort of Army-laugh.

One of these shapes was rather disreputable. To our hypothetic observer it would have looked like abstract Woman, Sex and its proper Tongue, in a Rowlandson print. The reason for this would be that when she looked at Jones – 'Jones: Geoffrey Jones. Charming fellow. He was up at Oxford with me. Very psychic. He's got a lot in him' – she always saw in his place a woman on whose toe she had once stepped in Sloane Square. Abuse had followed. The voice had been like an advertisement. Sounds came up from its sex machinery that were at once réclame and aggression. She felt she had trodden on the machinery of sex, and it had shouted in some customary 'walk-up!' voice, 'Clumsy cat! Hulking bitch! Sauce!' Whatever Jones said reached her, through this medium, as abuse. She did nothing: but she threw knives at him sometimes with her eyes.

Sigismund appeared to know dense masses of such men. As far as she could she avoided encounters. But there seemed no escape. So they all lived together in a sort of middle-class dream. Therein she played some rôle of onerous enchantment, on account of her beautiful extraction. They smoked bad tobacco, used funny words, their discourse was of their destiny, that none of them could have any but the slenderest reasons for wishing to examine. They very often appeared angry, and habitually used a chevaleresque jargon: ill-bred, under-bred, well-bred; fellow, cad, boor, churl, gentleman; good form, bad form, were words that came out of them on hot little breaths of disdain, reprobation, or respect. Had she heard some absent figure referred to as a 'swine-herd,' a 'varlet,' or 'villein,' she would not have felt surprised in any way. It would have seemed quite natural. You would have to go to Cervantes and his self-invested knight for anything resembling the infatuation of Sigismund and his usual companions.

In more bilious moments Deborah framed the difficult question in the stately mill of her mind, taking a week to grind out one such statement: *What is all this game about, and what are these people that play it?* Deborah could not decide. She abandoned these questions as they dropped, one by one.

Her noble attributes assumed in her mind fantastic proportions. Everything about herself, her family, her name, became unreal. One day she pinched Lord Victor Libyon-Bosselwood to see if he was a figment of Sigismund's brain or a reality. She caused him, by this unprovoked action, so much pain and surprise, that he shouted loudly. Sigismund was in ecstasy. Obviously the war-cry of the Bosselwoods, the old piratic yell! But Sigismund could not leave it at that. Possibly Lord Victor was the last Bosselwood who would ever utter that particular sound. He hesitated for some time. Then one day when Lord Victor was deeply unconscious of his peril, Sigismund led him up to the bell-shaped funnel of a gramophone recorder. He approached it jauntily, flower in buttonhole, haw-hawing as he went. As his face was a few inches off the recording mouth, Sigismund ran a large pin into his eminent relative's leg. The mask *à la* Spy vanished in a flash. And sure enough from a past, but a past much further back than that of the successful pirate, another man darted like a djinn into Lord Victor's body. This wraith contracted the rather flaccid skin of Lord Victor's face, distended its nostrils, stuck a demoniacal glint in each of Lord Victor's eyes, and finally curled the skin quickly back from his teeth, and opened his mouth to its fullest extent. Not the romantic battle-cry of the operatic pirate, but a hyena-like yelp, smote the expectant ears of the Boswell-like figure behind him: and the machine had recorded it for all time. But the next moment first the machine and then Sigismund crashed to the floor, as it took about thirty seconds for the pain to ebb and the djinn to take his departure. This period was spent by the ferocious nobleman in kicking the gramophone-box about the floor, then turning upon the ingenious Sigismund, whom he kicked viciously about the head and body. Even when no longer possessed of this dark spirit that had entered along with Sigismund's pin, he still continued to address our hero in a disparaging way.

'Necromancing nincompoop: what does that signify – to run a pin into a man's leg, and then stand grinning at him like a Cheshire cat? Half-witted, flat-faced, palm-tickling imbecile, you will get yourself locked up if you go round sticking pins into people's legs, and telling them to beware of gravel, that they have spatulate hands, and will be robbed by blonde ladies!'

The doors of Lord Victor's dwelling were in future guarded against Sigismund. He found it difficult to satisfy Deborah when she heard of his doings.

They spent a month at Bosselwood Chase.

The first book that Sigismund picked up in the library enthralled him. It seemed to betray such an intelligent interest in Race. He read, for instance, aloud to Deborah the following passage:

These luckily-born people have a delicious curve of the neck, not found in other kinds of men, produced by their habit of always gazing *back* to the spot from which they started. Indeed they are trained to fix their eyes on the Past. It is untrue, even, to say that they are unprogressive: for they desire to progress backwards more acutely than people mostly desire to progress forwards. And when you say that they hold effort in abhorrence, more inclined to take things easily, that also is not true: for it requires just as much effort to go in one direction as in the other.

The thoroughfares of life are sprinkled with these backward gazing heads, and bodies like twisted tendrils. It is the curve of grace, and challenges nobly the uncouth uprightness of efficiency.

That class of men that in recent years coined the word 'Futurist' to describe their kind, tried to look forward, instead. This is absurd. Firstly, it is not practical: and, secondly, it is not beautiful. This heresy met with bitter opposition, curiously enough, from those possessing the tendril-sweep. Unnecessary bitterness! For there are so many more people looking *back*, than there are looking forward, and in any case there is something so vulgar in looking in front of you, the way your head grows, that of course they never had much success. Here and there they have caused a little trouble. But the people have such right feelings *fundamentally* on these subjects. They realize how very uncomfortable it must be to hold yourself straight up like a poker. Through so many ages they have developed the habit of not looking where they are going. So it is all right. It is only those whom the attitude of grace has rendered a little feeble who are at all concerned at the antics of the devotee of this other method of progressing.

The training of these fortunate people – ancient houses, receding lines of pictures, trophies, books, careful crystallization of memories and forms, quiet parks, large and massive dwellings – all is calculated to make life grow backward instead of forward, naturally, from birth. This is just as pleasant, and in some ways easier. The dead are much nicer companions, because they have learnt not to expect too much of existence, and have a lot of nice habits that only demise makes possible. Far less cunning, only to take one instance, is required to be dead than to live. They respect no one, again, for they know, what is universally recognized, that no one is truly great and good until he is dead: and about the dead, of course, they have no illusions. In spite of this they are not arrogant, as you might expect.

'I think that is divinely well put, don't you agree, darling?' asked Sigismund closing the book. Deborah looked straight at him with genuine hatred: with the look of a dog offered food about which he feels there is some catch.

Some months later, settled in the midst of a very great establishment, Sigismund's fancy found a new avenue of satisfaction. He resolved to make a collection of pictures. His newly-awakened sensibility where pictures were concerned was the servant of his ruling passion, and admirably single-minded. His collection must be such as a nobleman would wish to possess. And again in this fresh activity his instinct was wonderfully right.

But Deborah grew blacker day by day. The dumb animal from the sacred Past felt by now that there was something exceedingly queer about her husband. The fabulous sums of money that Sigismund got through in the prosecution of his new fad awoke at last her predatory instincts. Solid bullion and bank balances was what she had wedded: not a crowd of fantastic and rather disturbing scenes. She secretly consulted with Lord Victor.

However, Sigismund proceeded to fill the house with pictures, engravings, drawings and pieces of sculpture. They all had some bearing on the Past. Many were historical pieces. They showed you Henry VIII., the king of the playing card, divorcing Catherine. He appeared, in the picture, to be trying to blow her away. They disclosed the barons after their celebrated operation at Runnymede, thundering off with the Charter: or William the Conqueror tripping up as he landed. There were pictures celebrating Harry Page's doings, 'Arripay': episodes on the Spanish main. There was an early lord earning his book-rights with an excellent ferocity: and a picture of a lonely geneat on his way to the manor with his lenten tribute of one lamb.

A rather special line depicted a runaway labourer being branded upon the forehead with a hot iron, at the time of the Labour Statutes of the fourteenth century: and sailors being bastinadoed after unusually violent mutinies. Stock and thumbscrew scenes. There was a picture of a Kentish churchyard, John Ball preaching to a rough crowd. As Sigismund gazed at this terrible picture, he experienced perhaps his richest thrill.

> When Adam delved and Eve span
> Who was then the gentleman?

He could see these unhallowed words coming out of the monk's lips and the crowd capering to them.

He had the six English regiments at Minden, mechanical red and accoutred waves, disposing of the French cavalry: and Hawke in

Quiberon Bay, pointing with a grand remote pugnacity to the French flagship: the old ceremonious ships, caught in a rather stormy pathos of the painter's, who had half attempted, by his colouring and arrangement, to find the formula for an event very remote in time from the day of the artist depicting it.

Charles II. dying – ('do not let poor Nelly starve') – Sigismund's model of how to die: 'forgive me, Deborah, for protracting this insignificant scene.' He was not sure about 'insignificant' and sometimes substituted 'tedious.' The word 'unconscionable,' he felt, was the prerogative of dying princes.

The masked executioner holding up the head of Charles I., whose face, in the picture, although severed from the body, still wore a look of great dignity and indifference to the little trick that had been played upon it by the London Magnificos. ('Eikon Basilike' drew as many tears from Sigismund's susceptible lids as it did from many honest burgesses at the time of its publication.)

Mary Queen of Scots over and over again: Fotheringay: many perfect deaths: the Duke of Cumberland holding the candle for the surgeon amputating his leg.

Gildas, Kemble's 'Saxons in England,' the life of Wilfrid, by Eddi, were three of his favourite books. And pictures dealing with this period he concentrated in a room, which he called the 'Saxon' room. In these pieces were seen:

The Crowning of Cedric.

Guthlac of Crowland vomiting at the sight of a bear.

The Marriage of Ethelbert with Bertha, daughter of King Charibert.

The Merchants telling Gregory that the angelic slaves came from 'Deira.'

Constantine on the chalk cliffs, Minster below, knees jutting out, for the first time, in a bluff english breeze; and Ethelbert, polite, elevated, but postponing his conversion with regal procrastination, or possibly leisureliness.

Eumer's dagger reaching Edwine through Lilla's body.

Coifi, the priest, at Godmanham, making his unexpected attack on an obsolete temple.

Aidan with a bag of hairy converts in the wilds of Bernicia.

Penda looking at the snowy fist blessed by Aidan after he had defeated the Northumbrians.

Alfred singing psalms and turning cakes, and Caedmon writing verses in his stable.

These were only a few of the many scenes that Sigismund roamed amongst: standing in front of them (when he could prevail on her to come with him) with his arm round Deborah's waist.

The pictures that Deborah hated most were those most economically noxious. These were pictures by masters contemporary with the Past. Van Dyck was his great favourite, at once a knight, a Belgian, and a painter. He reflected with uncertainty, 'a foreign title, obviously!' Contemporary painters who were at the same time knights, or even lords, he thought less of, it may be mentioned in passing: though he never grudged them, on account of their good fortune, the extra money he had to pay for their pictures.

His instinct manifested itself more subtly, though, in his choice of modern works. Burne-Jones was perhaps his favourite artist not belonging, except in spirit, to the wonderful Past. He recognized the tendril or twist he had read about in the book found at Bosselwood. Also the unquestionable proclivity to occupy himself with very famous knights and queens struck Sigismund as a thing very much in his favour. But our hero was an incomparable touchstone. His psychic qualities had their part in this. You could have taken him up to a work of art, watched his behaviour, and placed the most entire confidence in the infallibility of his taste in deciding as to the really noble qualities, or the reverse, of the artist. The Man in the Savage State propensity always met with a response. And you would not be surprised, if going further along the gallery with Sigismund, you came upon a work by the same painter of a very tender description, showing you some lady conceived on a plane of rhetorical spirituality. The Animal and the Noble, you would know, are not so far apart: and the savage or sentimental and the impulses to high-falute very contiguous.

*

Suffocated by this avalanche of pictorial art, Deborah had been constantly sending up S.O.S.'s, and Lord Victor had hurried to her assistance, unknown to Sigismund. This very 'natural' female splinter from a remote eruption grew more violent every day. The more animal she grew the better pleased was Sigismund. One day when as usual he strolled round his galleries, he was only able to examine his acquisitions with one eye, the other having been 'poached' overnight by his wife.

Then one day the end came with a truly savage unexpectedness.

Sigismund lay along the wall, nails in his mouth, on a pair of library steps. He was filling up the last space in his room of Prints with an engraving showing Ben White running his Bulldog Tumbler and Lady Sandwich's Bess at the head of Bill Gibbons' Bull. He was startled a little at the sound of a distant hurly-burly, and a bellow that something told him must be Deborah. Shrieks then rose, it seemed of dismay. Then a very deep silence ensued.

Sigismund scratched his head, and blinked discontentedly. But as the silence remained so dead as to be in the full technical sense a dead silence, he stepped down to the floor, and went out into the vast passages and saloons of his establishment, looking for the cause of this mortuary hush.

Deborah was nowhere to be found. But a group of servants at the foot of the main staircase were gathered round her prostrate maid. He was informed that this young lady was dead, having been flung from the top of the stairs with great force by his wife. A doctor had been telephoned for: the police were to be notified.

Sigismund was enraptured. He dissimulated his feelings as best he could. There was indeed a Bosselwood for you! ('The police' meant nothing to him. He never read Oppenheim.) He stood with a sweet absorption gazing at the inanimate form of the maid. He was brought to a consciousness of his surroundings by a tap on his shoulder. A strange man, two strange men, had in some way insinuated themselves amongst his retainers. The first man whispered in his ear: he was evidently under the impression that Sigismund was the author of this tragedy. He modestly disclaimed all connexion with it. But the man smiled, and he could not be sure, but he thought *winked* at him.

What was this fellow murmuring? If he had annihilated his entire domestic staff, he seemed to be saying, with a chuckle, it would have been all the same! Privilege, something about privilege: 'last little fling,' ha! ha! 'Fling' referred, he supposed, to the act of 'flinging' the maid. He held strange views, this newcomer! He was drawing Sigismund aside. He wanted to have a word with him apart. He was rather a nice sort of man, for he seemed to take quite a different sort of view of the accident from the servants. Where was he going? He wanted to show Sigismund something outside. Sell him a car? At a moment like this? No, he could not buy any more cars: and he must see Deborah at once. What was this strange fellow doing? He had actually pushed him inside the car.

Lord Victor had plotted with Deborah for some weeks past. But he had not counted on the Bosselwood fierceness manifesting itself almost simultaneously with the Libyon cunning. A few minutes after Sigismund had been driven off to an asylum, Deborah was also removed to a jail. After a trial that Sigismund would have keenly enjoyed (many a feudal flower in the gallery; the court redolent of the Past, and thundering to the great name of Libyon-Bosselwood), she also found her way to an asylum.

On thinking matters over in his new but very comfortable quarters, Sigismund concluded that that was what the two islands meant: and that that was also the signification of the star upon Jupiter.

# You Broke My Dream

## Or an Experiment with Time

Do not burst, or let us burst, into Will Blood's room! (I will tell you why afterwards.) Having flashed our eyes round the passages with which this sanctuary is surrounded, lurched about in our clumsy endeavours, as unskilled ghosts, not to get into the one door that interests us, we do at last blunder in (or are we blown in; or are we perhaps sucked in?) and there we stand at Will Blood's bedside.

You are surprised, I hope, at the elegant eton-cropped purity of the young painter's head (he has been a young painter now for many years, so his head is a young painter's head). It lies serenely upon the dirty pillow, a halo of darkish grey, where the hair-oil has stained the linen, enhancing its pink pallor. Its little hook-nose purrs, its mouth emits regularly the past participle of the French irregular verb 'pouvoir,' as though training for an exam. The puckered lids give the eye-sockets a look of dutiful mirth.

However, his lips twitch, his eyelids strain like feeble butterflies stuck together in some flowery contretemps, then deftly part. The play begins. Will's dream bursts, and out pops Will; a bright enough little churlish flower to win a new encomium every morning from his great Creator! But the truth is, that he has been a slight disappointment to his Creator, on account of his love for Art, and general Will-fulness. Therefore this great Gardener frowns always as he passes the bed where Will modestly blows. Will has to depend on stray sensitive young ladies. But they are usually not very moved by him. The fact is that he does not smell very nice. Quite satisfactory as regards shape, indeed a roguish little bobbing bud of a boy, his smell is not that of a thing of beauty, but is more appropriate to a vegetable. This causes a perpetual deception in the path, the thorny path, in which Will blows.

The Creator has given him this smell as a sign of his displeasure, because of his fondness for Art, and his Will-fulness! But that is a figure.

As his eyes open, the pupils rolling down into the waking position, Will violently closes them again, tightly holding them shut. For a few minutes he lies quite still, then cautiously slips his hand beneath the pillow, searches a moment, draws out a small note-book and pencil. Now he circumspectly opens his eyes, and, propped upon his elbow, turning over several leaves, he begins writing in his notebook.

'A dark wood,' he writes – 'I am lying in the shadow of an oak. I want to get up. I find I cannot. I attempt to find out why. – Children are playing in the meadow in front of me. One is tall and one short. One is full of sex. The other has less sex. Both girls. They are picking dandelions – pissenlits. – I find I can get on my hands and knees. I begin crawling into the wood. This makes me feel like an animal. I turn out to be an anteater. I attempt to make water. This owing to lack of practice is unsuccessful. I wake up.'

Poised above the notebook, he strains. Then at top speed he dashes down: '*A man with a hump.*'

He snaps-to the notebook and tosses it on to a chair at his bedside. Sliding two sensitive pink little feet out of the clothes, they hang stockstill above the carpet for a moment, then swoop daintily, and he is up. Pertly and lightheartedly he moves in dainty semi-nudity hither and thither. With a rustle, no more, he dresses extempore. He is soon ready, the little black-curled, red-bearded bird of talent, in his neat black suit, his blue eyes drawing him constantly to the mirror, and rolling roguishly about like kittens there. Oh, how he wondered what to do with them! A blue eye! Why should his lucky craftsman's eye be blue? All his visions of things accouched on a blue bed! The red road he knows through his blue eye! Who had had the job of pigmenting that little window? Some grandmother, at the back of yesterday, who brought her red cavalier to bed through her azure casement. No doubt that was it, or it was the result of some confusion in a ghetto, something sturdy and swarthy ravished by something pink and alert. A pity that Mr Dunne's time-tracts are so circumscribed, thinks he, or I'd find out for myself!

But where was his waist-strap?

> *'Goot heavens, Archivelt,*
> *Vere is your Knicker-belt?' –*
> *'I haf no Knicker-belt,'*
> *The little Archie said.*

These famous lines passed off the unacceptable hitch: else he might certainly have displayed temper; for he was shrewish when thwarted by things, as who will not be at times. But, once assembled, they fitted him to perfection.

He crossed his fat short legs and made his tie. Out to the A.B.C. for the first snack of the day. The top of the morning to the Norma Talmadge of the new Buszard's counter. He felt as lively on his springy legs as a squirrel. Now for the A.B.C.

A.B.C. The alphabet of a new day! A child was Will. Tootytatoot, for the axe-edged morning, the break of day! Was it an amateur universe after all, as so many believed? Oh, I say! is it an amateur world? It muddled along and made itself, did it, from day to day? At night it slept. He at least believed that was it. Believing *that*, you could not go far wrong. Every morning he comes up as fresh as paint: it is evidently *creative*, is all-things. Oh, it is decidedly a novel, a great creative, rough-and-ready affair: about that there can be no mistake. He throws his hat up in dirty Kentish Town air, as he dances forward. 'Give me the daybreak!' his quick actions say as plain as words. Any one could see he was just up. It is ten o'clock. 'Isn't this the time for rogues,' says he, 'not the night, but the day?' – He feels roguish and fine, and is all for painting the first hours red, in his little way. And also he must remember Mr Dunne.

The A.B.C. is cold. It has been sluiced by the chars, it faces north, its tiles marble and china repel the heat. It is an agreeable chill. He faces north, pauses and flings himself south and downwards on to the black leather seat at the bottom of the smoking-room. For some minutes he rides the springs, gentle as a bird on the wave, the most buoyant customer ever seen there. – A few black-sacks round the fire, like seamews on a Cornish Sabbath surveying their chapel of rock. Slovenly forces moved black skirts like wings. He is a force, but of course he needs his A.B.C.

But who will bring Will his burning eggs and hot brown tea? Who will bring the leaden fruit, the boiling bullet from the in-offensive serpentine backside of the farmyard fowl? Why, Gladys, the dreary waitress, in her bored jazz.

'I – hi! Gladys, what bonny thought for my name day?'

'What is your name?'

'Will, you know.'

Oh, what a peppery proud girl she is, with her cornucopia of hair the colour of a new penny. He observes it as a molten shell, balanced on the top of the black trunk. He models her with his blue eye into a bomb-like shape at once, associating with this a disk – a marble table – and a few other objects in the neighbourhood.

'Will!' What's in a name? Little for the heart of the mechanical slattern who bears the burning fruit of the fowl where it can be eaten by sweet Will Blood.

Will's a sprucer, thinks May, and tells Gladys so, as they sit side by side, like offended toys, at the foot of the stairs.

'I don't think he's right,' says Gladys. A combative undulation traverses her with dignity from toe to head. Her legs lie rather differently after its passage. She pushes down the shortened apron, upon her black silk sticks.

'He's balmy.' May cocks her eye Willwards, and lowers her voice. 'Yesterday he came to my table. 'Ere! What do you think he had the sauce to ask me?'

They eye each other with drifting baby-gazes.

'He asked me to go to his studio-flat, and be his nude-model!'

'I should say so! Then you wake up!' Gladys tossed her chin and nose-tip. 'He hasn't half got a sauce! I know what *I* should have said.'

'Chance would be a fine thing, I said: and he said he'd – I couldn't keep a straight face – there was an old girl at the next table who heard what he said. She didn't half give me a look—!' A few faint contortions ruffled May tenderly. She sheltered her mouth for a moment with her hand. 'He said he'd give me a strawberry leaf if I was a shy girl! He said all artists kept a stock, all different sizes.' May falls into faint convulsions.

'Soppy-fool! I told you he's not right. I'd soon tell him off if he came any of it with me. I do hate artists. They're all rotters. Young Minnie works with an artist now – you know, Minnie Edmunds.'

'*He's* not an artist. He's sprucing. He's a student. Ernie says he's in the hospital.'

'In the hospital? Noaa! That's not right. Was that Ernie told you that? He must have meant he was a patient.'

Will has the two waitresses in his bright-eye-closet, where he makes them up into a new pattern. He sees them twittering their cowardly scandal, he flattens their cheeks meanwhile, matches their noses, cuts out their dresses into unexpected shapes at every living moment.

The attention of May and Gladys drifts to the extremity of the shop farthest from Will. May's head slowly turns back, vacillates a little, veers a few points either way, then swings back sharply on to Will. Gladys is nudged by May.

'Look at him counting his mouldy coppers!'

Will arranges two columns on the marble table, silver and copper.

'Solidi: Ten. Denarii: Eleven. Must go to the Belge for lunch: supply myself with the pounds – the pence will look after themselves.'

He signs to May, who nudges Gladys. Gladys looks at May.

'He wants you.'

The great copper-red queen of the A.B.C. approaches with majestic reluctance.

'Goot heavens, Archivelt,

Fere ist your Knicker-pelt!'

(She says, in her mind, to May: 'He said something about my knickers, in poetry. I gave him such a look.')

Standing at the side of the table, she traces perfunctory figures on her ticket-block. She redraws them blacker.

'I say, Miss. One of those eggs you brought me smelt high.'

('He said: one of the eggs was high. I said I would have got him another if he'd said.')

'It was blue.'

('Blue, he said it was.')

'We don't often have the customers complain of the eggs,' she observed.

'That was a red egg. Red eggs are always a bit off.'

('He said his egg was red. All red eggs is a bit off, he said. He's crackers.')

'I like them a little *faisandé*.'

('He said something in latin, he gave me a funny look. If he gave me much of his old buck—!')

'All people should be a little *faisandé*, I think, don't you: so why not eggs?'

'I don't see the conjunction.'

'Not between eggs and people? She sees no connection between eggs and people! Oh, lucky girl, oh, how I envy you! where ignorance is bliss!'

*Ignorant!* Blood rushes to the face of the proud and peppery girl.

'I should be sorry to be as ignorant as some people! Do you want another egg?'

'Oh, don't be angry Mabel. I admire your style of beauty.' He drops a bashful eye into his tea-cup, computing the percentage of vegetable dregs in what remains. 'I can imagine you quite easily in a beautiful oriental bath, surrounded by slaves. You step in. I am your eunuch.'

'Fancy goes a long way, as Nancy said when she kissed the cow.'

'I could easily be your eunuch. I don't understand your last remark. What cow?'

A bright and sudden light flashes in Will's eye. He leaps up. The blood has left the cheek of Gladys, and she steps back with apprehension.

'*Cow!* You've broken my dream? What colour was it?'

With a gesture with her fingers as though to bore into her temple, the haughty waitress returns to her chair by the side of May. Will follows eagerly. Standing over May and Gladys he exclaims:

'You broke my dream! What sort of cow was it?'

Gladys half looks disdainfully at May.

'He's not right.'

Will touches a variety of brakes; he has rushed into an impasse. He turns slowly round. That dream-double has been flustered, she who holds the secret of life and death. 'Gently does it!' thinks he and hoods his eyes. 'How horribly he squints!' thinks Gladys. Slowly up on to the surface steals a dark sugary grin. He leans against a table, nonchalant, crosses one shoe stealthily over the other shoe.

'I know it must sound funny to you, Miss Marsh.' (May smiles, and Gladys pricks up her languid ears. Miss Marsh! the sauce!) 'But you did say something about *kissing a cow*, didn't you, just now? It's this way. I dreamt last night *I kissed a cow*. I know it *is* a funny thing to dream. But that's why I sort of want to know, being of an enquiring turn. The cow I kissed last night is my first cow. That's important. Don't run away with the idea, Miss Marsh, that *every* night—!'

'Oh no'oo!' Lofty withering lady.

'That's right, don't run away.'

May laughs and peers at Gladys. 'Oh, how I hate that man!' thinks Gladys, for he has put her in the wrong with all these cows.

'Of course I made a note of it when I woke up.'

Oh, what a hateful man! and that cat May. What's the girl looking at me for, I should like to know?

'You broke my dream!'

'Oh! fancy that!'

A customer calls and May jumps up: away she hurries, for what, she wonders, has that Gladys been saying about kissing a cow?

Gladys looks after May. She has been put in the wrong. Why does he stop there? Why doesn't he go, I should like to know? he's got his bill.

She won't say, thinks little Will, that she said 'kissed a cow.' I've torn it. I shouldn't have seemed so anxious. Now I've put her back up. Something else must be found. Let's see. He looks round inside his mind. Ah, ha, the very thing! for he catches sight of a red egg, blue inside, and at the same time a faint familiar smell glides into his nostril. He coughs.

'Did you charge me with that egg?'

Gladys immediately alters: her colour jumps up, her eyes fill with dignity. She is back in her classy shell instanter.

'Yes. But if you like I'll deduct it, as you say it was bad.'

'No, please don't: it's quite all right, Miss Marsh.'

'Not at all. If you're not satisfied, I'll deduct it.'

With great dignity she rises and holds out her hand for the check.

'No, I really couldn't let you do that. I meant I hoped that you *had* charged me. That's what I meant.'

'Yes, I did. But I'll deduct it,' she drawls. Every minute she is farther off. He looks at her with his sheep's grin of foolish offence: she bridles and gazes away. He is baffled. What next?

May returns: she settles herself stealthily.

'Won't you tell me before I go about the cow?' Gladys does not mind, she *did* say 'kiss the cow.' She looks away from May, very bored.

'It's an old country saying. My mother uses it. Haven't you ever heard it?'

'So you *did* say "kiss the cow"?' he shouts, standing on tip-toe.

Gladys' best proud manner is not proof against his shout quite. She will not relax towards May, but she cannot keep her eyes from casting a quick glance. That cat May's laugh, I do think it's soppy! 'No, I said "kissed the cow."'

May acts a spasm of pent-up mirth, the potty cat: 'kissed the cow! kissed the cow!' she rocks herself from side to side, droning to herself, she dies of laughing; she is dead.

'That's what I wanted to know. – Well, I must pony up with your firm, now. That's another old expression! Tralala!'

'Is it really!' A lady's simple bored reply, the last shot.

May has developed hysteria. Gladys rises in offended silence and goes over to the table. Will has left. But Will darts swiftly to the desk. An amiable oblique jewish face that has only one flat side at a time, or else is an animated projecting edge, receives with flattering vampish slowness his ticket on which the half-crown lies, and bakes him slowly with a cinema smile. 'A nice morning, isn't it? *Thank you*,' softly sliding three coppers and a shilling towards him.

He thanks the innocent bird in her cage at the receipt of custom, and darts erect through the door, out on to the shining pavement, where he skids through the dazzling light to the nearby P.O. Buying a postcard, he goes to the writing-desk and fills in the morning bulletin:

> Last night I dreamt that in crossing a tiny meadow I met two dappled cows. As I passed the second of the two I took its muzzle in my hands, and before it could say *knife*, I had kissed it between the horns. Going as usual this morning to the A.B.C. for my breakfast, I happened to engage in conversation there with a waitress, known as Miss Gladys Marsh. (I can obtain her address if you require it.) Being quite full of blarney, since it was so early in the day, I remarked to this high-spirited girl that I could see in my mind's eye her graceful perfumed form in a turkish setting descending into a beautiful bath. I represented myself as a eunuch (not to alarm her) participating in this spectacle at a discreet distance. At this she remarked:
>
> 'Fancy goes a long way, as Nancy said *when she kissed the cow*!'
>
> For the accuracy of this statement I am prepared to vouch. Time is vindicated! I offer you my warmest congratulations. It is certain that in our dreams the future is available for the least of us. Time *is* the reality. It is as fixed as fixed. Past, Present and Future is a territory over which what we call *I* crawls, and in its dreams it goes backwards and forwards at will. Again, my congratulations! Hip! Hip! – Further Bulletin to-morrow.
>
> *Signed*, WILLIAM BLOOD.

This he addressed to
R. DUNNE, ESQ.

PENGUIN BOOKS

# The Wild Body

Percy Wyndham Lewis, painter, novelist and essayist, was born of English and American parentage at Amherst, Nova Scotia in 1882. He came to England in his early childhood and was educated at several schools, the last of which was Rugby. He then studied at the Slade School of Art, where he won a scholarship, and afterwards spent some years travelling in Europe, with a period of bohemian living in Paris. By 1914 he had emerged as the leader of the 'Vorticist' group, of which some of the main figures were T. S. Eliot, Epstein and Gaudier-Brzeska, and with Ezra Pound he founded the periodical *Blast* (two issues, 1914–15), which Lewis edited.

Wyndham Lewis always regarded himself as an artist first, a writer second, and was one of the most advanced English painters of his time, influencing both his contemporaries and other young artists after the Second World War. Lewis's satirical and polemical writing was largely directed against the cultural and literary movements of the 1920s – as represented by D. H. Lawrence, James Joyce and the Bloomsbury Group. His first novel, *Tarr* (1918), drew on his life in Paris. It was followed by *The Childermass* (1928), the first part of his great trilogy *The Human Age*; the two subsequent parts, *Monstre Gai* and *Malign Fiesta*, appeared in 1955. In 1930 he published his great satirical novel *The Apes of God*, a gargantuan demolition of the cultural life of the 1920s, of which T. S. Eliot said, 'It is so immense I have no words for it.' His other works include *The Lion and the Fox* (1927), *Time and Western Man* (1927), *Men Without Art* (1934) and two volumes of auto-biography, *Blasting and Bombardiering* (1937) and *Rude Assignment* (1950). In 1949 he began to lose his sight and he became totally blind in 1953. Wyndham Lewis died in 1957.

Paul O'Keeffe is the author of *Some Sort of Genius: A Life of Wyndham Lewis*. His new biography *Gaudier-Brzeska: An Absolute Case of Genius* is published by Penguin. He is currently writing a life of the nineteenth-century painter and diarist Benjamin Robert Haydon.